A BLIND EYE

BOOKS BY JOHN HENDERSON

Anchor Man

The Musgrave Solution

Murder Scams & Gravy Trains

The Taipan Club

BLIND EYE

SIMON WEBSTER'S FIRST FIASCO

JOHN HENDERSON

A Blind Eye

Copyright © 2012 John Henderson

ISBN 978-0-6465769-6-1

Publisher: J. Henderson, Australia

ACKNOWLEDGMENTS

To my wife Jill whose support and encouragement, in light of her own successes as a novelist, has been the inspiration to start the Webster series. And to Fergus who purred throughout the writing.

CHAPTER 1

'Can you see anything?' Sergeant Rose asked as Constable Webster peered in through the front window of the Tattersall Castle Hotel located at the Circular Quay end of George Street.

'No, not a thing. But then the report did say the vehicle was parked around the back of the pub, not at the front door here in George Street.' Even with the cold night air, Constable Webster noticed the sergeant's face was bathed in sweat, a condition Webster would later learn was a natural affliction suffered by Sergeant Rose.

'You stay here and I'll go around the back to Kendall Lane and see if I can see anything there. I'll be back in five minutes,' said the sergeant.

It was quarter past two in the morning, the earlier Friday night crowd having dispersed from the many pubs located around The Rocks precinct. A phone call had been received at The Rocks Police Station reporting a vehicle had driven along Kendall Lane and had stopped at the rear of the Tattersall Castle Hotel, a regular drinking spot for many Friday night revelers.

While there had been other officers available to respond to the call, Sergeant Rose had decided this was an opportune time, and not a too difficult case, to demonstrate his extensive policing experience to the new boy on the block, Probationary Constable Simon Webster.

Webster was, to say the least, a rookie having graduated from the Redfern Police Depot's September class of '66 only ten days earlier. He had been out on a few beats accompanied by a senior officer which would be the normal routine until he had gained sufficient experience to be let loose on the poor unsuspecting public with another officer of similar rank. Constable Webster was well aware of Sergeant Rose's reputation, a man considered throughout the station as a very tough policeman, quite in contrast to that suggested by his corpulent frame and portly pot belly.

True to his word, Sergeant Rose returned to the front of the pub where Webster was waiting. 'Yes, there's a vehicle there all right, a black VW Kombi. A back door to the pub has been forced and I thought I saw a torch light, so whoever it is is probably still inside, after some grog, no doubt.' While Webster knew very little of Sergeant Rose, apart from his tough reputation, the thought crossed his mind that, just possibly, the sergeant had a long way to go to reach the super sleuth standards of the Sherlock Holmes, Hercule Poirot ilk. After all, Webster reasoned, why else would someone break into a pub at such an unearthly hour if not to steal the alcohol.

'So what do we do now, sarge? The Station's only two minutes away. I could go and get some help,' Constable Webster suggested.

'Hell no, boy. It's probably some young lout trying to get his hands on some vodka. We'd look bloody silly calling for help only to find it's some pimply faced teenager. No, we can handle this. The longer you're on the job, the more you develop an intuition, and always follow your intuition, or gut feeling. Understand me, boy?' Constable Webster had no idea why the sergeant kept referring to as "boy", but couldn't help feeling the title was somewhat the sergeant had dredged up from watching too many Foghorn Leghorn cartoons with Webster being The Barnyard Dawg.

'Yes, sergeant. Okay then, what do we do?'

'This will only take a couple of minutes. The front door appears to be well and truly secured so we'll both go around to the back door. You wait in the lane and I'll go in and haul the little bugger out. If on the off-chance I need you, which I won't, I'll call for you, so you just stay with the Kombi.'

The two policemen made their way along George Street, turned left into Mill Lane then left again into Kendall Lane. The one street light, located on the western side of the lane approximately twenty yards from the Kombi, provided a faint and stingy glow that quickly surrendered to the overwhelming darkness of the lane. Sergeant Rose put his index finger to his lips in the universal sign of "shush". Slowly he eased the door to the pub open and slipped inside. Webster, left to his own devices, withdrew a torch from his utility belt and gazed through the back window of the van. It was clear that whoever was doing the stealing had almost completed the task as he could count five or six boxes of various spirits, including whisky, rum and vodka, packed into the Kombi. He tried the sliding door and, to his surprise, found the door unlocked, probably to allow the robber easier access to the van while holding a case of grog, he decided.

Webster turned his attention to a rear window of the pub and could see a faint light moving around and assumed it to be Sergeant Rose. The constable was taken aback somewhat by the very nature of the situation, the whole episode becoming surreal. While there were probably a million other places he would rather be, not the least being tucked up in bed with his lovely wife, Georgie, here he was in Sydney, the largest city in Australia, in the middle of the night, waiting to nab a felon currently in the process of carrying out an indictable offence. No way could any amount of training at the Police Depot prepare a police recruit for such a scenario, he reflected.

Having nothing to do until Sergeant Rose had the culprit safely under arrest, Webster took stock of the laneway in which the Kombi was parked. The lane was no more than fifteen feet wide and bounded by old two storey buildings along its length. The buildings, once occupied as dwellings or living quarters during the early days of the settlement of Sydney Town, were now occupied for commercial purposes and, in view of the early hour, provided no additional lighting to the meager street lighting. Opposite the Kombi was a rusted wrought iron gate, about five feet high, which gave access to a small block of land overgrown with weeds where a building appeared to have been demolished many years before. It was this disused plot that provided Webster with, what he considered, a brilliant idea and an opportunity to display his initiative, an aptitude strongly encouraged by the instructors at the Police College. Seeing Sergeant Rose was preoccupied in dealing with the robber, Webster decided to ensure the thief would not get away with his ill-gotten booty should things not turn out exactly as the sergeant plainly expected.

After putting his plan into place, Webster's attention returned to the pub. It had been about fifteen minutes since Sergeant Rose had entered, surely enough time for a tough policeman to apprehend, how did the sergeant describe the scoundrel?– a pimply face teenage lout – in the process of committing a simple case of robbery.

'Webster, are you out there?' came the thunderous roar of Rose's voice from deep within the darkness of the pub.

'Right here, sergeant. Where are you?' replied Webster, a little surprised the sergeant hadn't been a little more circumspect with his enquiry.

'Just come through the back door, down the hallway and turn left into the main bar. Go straight ahead across the bar and you will see a door leading to the Ladies' Saloon. I'm in there.'

'On my way, boss.' Webster did as directed and found the Ladies' Saloon with a light shining brightly under the closed door. He was unsure whether to be polite and knock, or just barge in. Pausing to consider the problem, Webster came to the conclusion that, in view of the sergeant's indiscrete instructions, everyone on the premises would be aware of what was going on. Having decided there was little room for etiquette, Constable Webster quickly threw open the door and plunged into the room.

And then he saw the three men, and not one of them his sergeant. The first thing Webster noticed about the men was that two were armed; one with an ugly looking snub-nosed pistol, the other with what appeared to be a pickaxe handle. The third gentleman, who was casually leaning with his back against a small pool table and smoking a cigarette, was wearing a dark grey fedora, the brim pulled down low over his forehead, shadowing his facial features. Webster couldn't suppress the thought that he had just run into Bogey in some cheap gin joint somewhere in Morocco.

It took Webster several seconds before he noticed his mentor, Sergeant Rose, secured with his own handcuffs to a four foot high statue of the Roman goddess Minerva standing on a pedestal, wearing her coat of mail and carrying a spear. He reflected back to his school days and the Latin he had persevered with; 'ecce homo', he muttered to himself. Webster smiled and shook his head. He was sure the sergeant didn't have a clue as to whom he was handcuffed, but Webster thought it quite appropriate that of all the classical gods, Rose had chosen the Goddess of Wisdom as his custodian.

'Okay, copper. You obviously see some humour in the situation. What's so bloody funny?' demanded the henchman carrying the pick handle. Before Webster could answer, Sergeant Rose made a desperate plea to his colleague.

'For Christ sake, boy, don't antagonise them. They're in control of the situation and they could very well kill both of us, so just shut up and do whatever they want, and that's an order.'

'Yes, of course sarge.' Constable Webster had already made his own assessment of the situation and had come to the conclusion that it was quite likely none of the robbers were capable of committing murder. He realised, of course, he could be wrong, his assessment made purely on "gut feeling". Webster had attended lectures on criminal profiling and psychology while at the Police Depot. Clearly, such aspects of police training must have been introduced well after the graduation of Sergeant Rose who was, according to Webster's estimation, of the old school where a good punch-up in a dark alley ensured a win to any argument. But then again, Webster had read in one of Asimov's books that violence was the last refuge of the incompetent.

The cigarette man flicked some ash onto the carpet, pushed his hat back on his head with a well practiced nonchalance, and looked at his two colleagues. He was unmistakably the brains of the gang, the other two henchmen providing the necessary brawn. Whereas the cigarette man was easily identifiable by his manner and charisma as the leader of the group, the two henchmen were just as easily identifiable by their physical size and the noticeable feeling that both looked upon the cigarette man with great reverence. Irrespective of the façade they presented, Constable Webster couldn't help but feel a touch of sympathy for the gangland trio. He had a vague suspicion that none of the three had a clue as to what they were doing, nor any idea of just how to do it even if they did.

'You know, boys', the cigarette man said to the two henchmen as if he was a teacher addressing his pupils, 'I have an idea these two coppers will never see eye to eye. Young cops these days are encouraged to think for themselves and to use their brains, not like back in the good old days when people were respectful of the police and even feared some of the techniques they often used.' Constable Webster smirked. The cigarette man would have been aged somewhere in his mid twenties and Webster believed there was little chance of him being born in "the good old days", let alone having experienced them. Clearly the cigarette man had come to the same conclusion as Webster when it came to assessing the sergeant's policing methodology.

'Gee, Mr Mitchell, you know all about being a gangster. Jacko and I were really lucky you picked us to become your partners. We didn't know how to rob a pub and here we are with you teaching us,' the six foot two henchman armed with the ugly snub nosed pistol said with pride and admiration for his boss.

'Benny, Benny, Benny. How many times have I told you? No names during a job,' responded Mr Mitchell, clasping a hand over his eyes and shaking his head in disbelief.

'Sorry, boss. I won't say another word,' replied Benny ashamedly. Mr Mitchell looked at Constable Webster and shrugged.

'Honestly, mate. You just can't find good help anymore these days. It's this bloody Vietnam War. All the blokes are being conscripted and sent off overseas. There just isn't the quality of blokes around, not ones wanting a career in crime, that is,' said Mr Mitchell, a hint of exasperation in his voice.

'Well, let's get on with it,' said Jacko, tapping the palm of his left hand with the pick handle. Constable Webster had a mental picture of what he thought the lumberjack Paul Bunyan might have look like, and Jacko seemed to fit the bill admirably. He was a giant of a man dressed in a red flannel checked shirt and a dark blue bib and brace, not the attire generally worn in downtown George Street. 'We're in a bit of mess now we have two coppers to deal with. I'm for doin' 'em in, shovin' their bodies in the van along with the booze and getting the hell out of here as quickly as possible.'

Sergeant Rose couldn't believe what he was hearing. 'Hey, you can't kill me; I'm a sergeant of police, married with a wife and family. I'm not in your way here so if you must kill someone, kill the constable over there,' he said nodding to his colleague.

'Oh, thanks sarge, but as you said, they're in control and they've put forward a proposal to do us in. Now, I don't know about you, but Georgie would be awfully pissed off if I didn't come home tonight, and I expect your wife would be too.' Georgie was Webster's wife of a few months. They had finally met on the Manly ferry "South Steyne" after spending an utterly useless twelve months commuting, sitting opposite each other on the ferry, with nothing more than a nod of recognition. It had taken Simon Webster almost a year to pluck up the courage for the next step with an introduction which just happened to turn out to their mutual benefit.

Mr Mitchell, deep in thought, looked at Jacko and raised his eyebrows. 'Okay Jacko, seems like a good idea; but do you want to do the doing in?'

'No, not me. Not on your life. You're the boss so it's up to you, unless of course, Benny wants to shoot that little pee-shooter of his.'

Benny looked at Jacko with horror. 'Ah, come on mate. I've

never fired a gun in my life, and besides, the gun's not real, just a replica.'

Mr Mitchell rolled his eyes to the heavens, sighed in resignation and mumbled something incoherently. He dropped the cigarette he was smoking onto the carpet and squashed it with the toe of his shoe before turning to his two associates. 'There'll be no "doin' in". If we did kill the cops, they'd never stop looking for us and we'd end up dead meat ourselves.'

'Look, Mr Mitchell.' It was Constable Webster's turn to take the floor. 'Why don't you just leave things as they are and write tonight off as a bad example of how not to rob a pub? You have a few cartons of grog in the van, so why not just call it quits and go disappear into the ether?'

'Hey, where's this place ether, 'cause if it ain't in Sydney, I'm not goin'?' asserted Benny.

'God help me, just where did I find this yo-yo, in a cabbage patch?' said a thoroughly exasperated Mr Mitchell. 'Look, come on, boys. We'll have to get rid of the van pretty quickly as it's getting late, and no doubt it will have been reported stolen by now.'

'No, boss, I don't think we have to worry about that.' It was Benny, notwithstanding his pledge of silence, who interrupted the boss's thoughts. Mr Mitchell suddenly experienced a sense of foreboding as he anticipated Benny's next revelation was not going to be good news.

'What is it now, Benny? All I asked you to do was go pinch a van suitable to load some grog into. The van out the back is okay, so what's the problem?'

'It's Dad's.'

'What do you mean, it's Dad's?'

'Well, I knew he wouldn't be using it at this hour of the day and I knew where he kept the keys. I just thought it would be a lot easier to pinch it for a while, and then give it back later.'

'Christ all bloody mighty. Just which one of the seven dwarfs are you, you idiot. Even if these two coppers hadn't turned up, you may as well have sent the police a letter telling them what we plan to do. Your dad's business details are painted all over the bloody thing.'

'Sorry boss. But I am learning.' Benny's comment was lost on Mr Mitchell who couldn't imagine just what Benny thought he was learning.

Mr Mitchell turned to Constable Webster. 'So, you're prepared to let us go, just like that?'

'No we're not,' roared the handcuffed Sergeant Rose, his face bathed in sweat. 'I'm the senior officer here and I make the decisions. If we don't take 'em in, Webster, your career's busted. Do I make myself clear?' the sergeant seethed.

Constable Webster, who harboured the opinion his sergeant was probably in no position to be giving orders, ignored the sergeant's comments and turned to Mr Mitchell. 'That's right. The three of you can just walk away and that'll be the end of it.'

Mr Mitchell shrugged and looked towards his associates. 'The constable's right lads. Let's call it quits and get the hell out of here. Come on, we've got enough grog in the van to make a few bob with a couple of bottles each for us. Oh yes, here's the keys to the cuffs. Your boss looks like he's about to have a coronary.' With that, Mr Mitchell tossed the keys onto the bar and strode from the saloon; the two henchmen following close behind slamming the door shut behind them.

'By Jesus, boy. Your career is well and truly stuffed now. It's quite clear to me, boy, you need a lot more experience. You're unable to handle yourself in a stressful situation and are totally incapable of assessing the operational requirements demanded. You should have used a bit of force on those clowns. Didn't they teach you anything about resorting to physical methods of persuasion against such criminals?'

Constable Webster was somewhat piqued by the outburst. 'Yes, they did, but they also taught us that discretion is the better part of valour,' he replied with a touch of annoyance. 'Anyway, I expect we haven't seen the last of Mr Mitchell.'

'Why? What do you mean?' queried the sergeant, impatiently. Just at that moment the two police officers heard heavy footsteps before the door was violently flung open with Mr Mitchell standing there, arms akimbo, his face contorted in anger.

'I've been robbed. Some bastard has stolen the booze from the van.'

'Well now, this is a turn up. Do you wish to lodge a formal complaint?' asked a bemused Constable Webster. 'Of course, I take it you will be able to establish legal ownership of the stolen property?'

'What do you mean, legal ownership? You know damn well me and the boys stole it from the pub here,' replied Mr Mitchell indignantly.

'Well, as you cannot produce receipts for the goods, I gather you are not the legal owner. In addition, it sounds very much like you've made a verbal confession of guilt to the stealing of the liquor. Is that correct?' Webster queried.

'It's a bit late now to deny we robbed the place. But I don't care about that. I just want our booze back.'

Constable Webster looked at his sergeant, still secured to the Goddess of Wisdom, and shrugged. 'I'm sorry Mr Mitchell, but we let you go the first time and now you're asking us to investigate a theft on your behalf. I beginning to think you're pushing your luck, don't you? Of course, in view of the circumstances and your recent confession of having robbed the pub, we could still arrest you. Isn't that correct, sergeant?'

'Of course it's correct, you moron,' replied the sergeant angrily. 'We should have done that as soon as we got here.'

Constable Webster refrained from the obvious response, his thoughts reflecting back on how the sergeant, in complete control of the situation, was going to drag the pimply faced youth from the pub, having caught the miscreant in the process of carrying out a criminal act. Irrespective of the reputation, Webster had the uncomfortable feeling Sergeant Rose was having difficulty keeping up with the night's events.

'Now, look here, that's not fair. We've gone to great lengths to organise this heist and the two knuckleheads outside expect something for their night's work,' said Mr Mitchell, his initial rage moderating to seething anger.

Constable Webster shrugged. 'Gee, I'd really like to help but it seems to me the booze isn't, or wasn't, yours to give away. But now that you've lost the booze you previously stated to have stolen, the best we can do is for you to give me ten quid and you can take a couple of bottles of Johnny Walker from the bar. I'll see that the owner of the pub gets the money. But I suppose that's all beside the point, in view of your verbal confession. I'm sorry, Mr Mitchell, but it looks like we'll have to take you in for stealing the booze in the first place.'

'Hey, hang on. What booze?' interrupted Mr Mitchell, as it finally dawned on him that he was definitely in a no-win situation. 'Have I got any booze on me, or have you seen me with any booze? There certainly isn't any in Benny's van outside. I know nothin' about any stolen booze. This mightn't have turned out the way I had planned, but here's a tenner for the scotch,' growled Mr Mitchell as he helped himself to two bottles of Johnny Walker Red Label from behind the bar. 'Don't bother, I'll see my way out,' he said and headed from the saloon, the two bottles tucked firmly under his arm.

'Just one thing before you go,' interrupted Webster. 'There's about twenty quids worth of damage to the back door. Give me the twenty and I'll make sure the pub's owner gets it for repairs.'

'You're joking?' replied Mr Mitchell incredulously.

'No, not at all. At the moment you could go for break and enter, or at least willful damage, to the hotel. Pay for the damage and we can get that side of things squared away with the hotel owner.'

'Holy hell. I knew this wasn't going to be my day,' replied Mr Mitchell as he withdrew a further two ten-pound notes from his wallet.

'Sit down, boy. I want to have a talk with you before I go back to the station and write up a couple of reports, one about the alleged theft of grog from this pub, and the other an administrative report on your conduct. Do you understand me, boy?' Constable Webster understood exactly and knew that Sergeant Rose's theft report would have a very slim chance of reflecting the true events of the night.

Constable Webster pulled out a chair from one of the saloon's tables and sat down, fully expectant of the impending bollocking. He waited, quite relaxed in view of the situation, and watched the sergeant pace back and forwards in front of the bar, his hands clasped behind his back. He finally stopped his pacing and stood in front of Constable Webster, glaring menacingly. 'Okay, boy, just how did you know Mr Mitchell would be back claiming he'd been robbed of his grog?'

'Simple, sarge. I stole it.'

'You stole it?' queried Sergeant Rose, unsure as to whether he had heard Webster's answer correctly.

'Well, sort of. While I was waiting outside for you to make the arrest, I unloaded the van and stacked the grog behind the fence to the vacant allotment.'

'And what the bloody hell did you do that for?' asked Sergeant Rose utterly perplexed.

'I'm sorry sarge,' said Constable Webster trying to be as contrite as possible, 'but I figured if things didn't turn out exactly as you planed, due to unforeseen circumstances, we should have a back-up plan. I've no doubt the grog's still there so I'll get it back inside the pub here while you're back at the station. I'll hang around until someone from the pub arrives and I'll explain what happened. In this way there was no theft, and Mr Mitchell has paid for the grog he took with him. He's also paid for the damages to the back door.'

'But they're criminals,' roared Sergeant Rose, the sweat dripping from his face, his uniform coat buttons straining to contain his heavy breathing.

'Well, as Mr Mitchell said, sarge, it looks like you and I see things differently. I doubt very much if the three of them could rob a piggy bank. No, sarge, I don't think they're criminals, and that's why it turned out as it did.'

'You were in no position to make such decisions and I'm the one to write the report,' sneered Sergeant Rose. 'I'm also the one to write the administrative report on your conduct, and I don't mind telling you, it will be unpleasant reading, for you, that is. You just haven't the balls for policing, boy. There are just some times when push comes to shove and tonight was one such time, and you failed dismally. It's a good thing for you I'm being promoted out of The Rocks station for greener pastures as I would really make life hell for you if I was to continue being your boss.' With that, Sergeant Rose picked up his cap and departed, muttering something to himself about the new breed and pansies.

CHAPTER 2

*T*he morning ritual of the Webster household was normally a routine affair predicated on the method of transport Simon was taking to get to the City. He and his sergeant, Noel Elliott, had agreed that it was more convenient to take one car to town when they chose not to use public transport, which was often in light of the painfully inadequate bus service. As the Websters lived at Collaroy, some twenty kilometers north of the City, and Noel and his wife, Susan, at Mona Vale, at least another ten kilometers further north again, they had decided the logical solution was to combine the assets and half the costs. However, on this particular day Simon chose to take the bus as Noel and Sue had organised a night in town and would not be returning to Mona Vale at the usual hour.

'Come on, Simon, you're a detective and you should know these things. I have this troublesome character I want to do away with, but I don't want it to look like a murder. Just how do I do it?' Simon knew Georgie was having problems on how to do away with someone, but the cutting of the car's brake cables or the surreptitious turning on of the gas stove, and crimes of a similar nature, had been done to death by Hollywood. And Georgie wanted something original.

Breakfast time was one of the rare opportunities Georgie had to talk to Simon about her crime fighting novels. Notwithstanding the fact that Georgie had been successful in having her first book published, Simon had the distinct impression her somewhat sheltered life had left her ill informed as to how brutally unprincipled and corrupt the criminal mind could be. Nevertheless, he did try to offer support for Georgie's literary aspirations, albeit somewhat cynically at times.

Simon folded the morning paper and placed it beside him on the kitchen table. 'Well, I suppose you could nudge him off the platform into the path of an oncoming train. That could prove fatal and difficult to prove, especially if it was during the peak hour rush.' Simon paused and absently stroked his chin, deep in thought. 'I suppose getting your character to stand in front of you at the same station and the same time might be a tad difficult to arrange.'

'Can't you be serious for just once in your life?' scolded Georgie as she pulled the toast from the toaster. 'What was it that killed those two over at Lane Cove a couple of years ago? The police never arrested anyone so it must have been well thought out.'

'If the truth be known,' replied Simon becoming a little impatient with the discussion, his thoughts more on the marmalade he was trying to extract from the jar, 'the police haven't a clue as to what killed them so we don't really know that it was murder. While we have the where and the when, the how and why are mysteries the investigators are still trying to nut out. Anyway, let's change the subject. How are you getting along with the sweet little old lady from next door? I haven't seen her for a while.'

'Well, lucky you,' responded Georgie, shaking her head and

screwing up her face in feigned sarcasm. 'She's been at me a few times since we had the pest man come and spray. She claims all the bugs and cockroaches we had here have migrated to her place and we're responsible for her sudden pest infestation. You know, that sweet little old lady, as you so kindly put it, is not so sweet and kindly. If the truth be known, she's a nasty, offensive and obnoxious old bitch with a huge chip on her shoulder. You don't have to put up with her but I'm home nearly all day and she's invariably got something to have a moan about. At the moment she's moaning about the number of spiders she's noticed, and she's a definite arachnophobe, to say the least. She really can't stand seeing a spider.'

The little old lady next door was Dorothy, her exact age unknown to the Websters although they placed her at being in her late fifties. The story went that she had been married, maybe still was, but apparently as soon as the kids had left home, so too did her husband who had run off with a much younger woman. Georgie and Simon had both come to the conclusion that Dorothy's poor husband must have lasted for as long as he could and then given up and walked out. Irrespective of the past history, Dorothy was bitter and hell-bent on making life as difficult as she could for everyone she came into contact.

Georgie poured Simon and herself another coffee and sat down. 'Anyway, how are you getting on with Rosey?' Simon had used Georgie as a whipping post, not so much when he had been transferred from The Rocks to Day Street some fifteen months previously, but on discovering he would be working directly to Chief Inspector Rose.

'I try and have as little to do with him as possible,' Simon responded. 'As soon as I submitted my report on illegal gambling, I put in an application for transfer to another station. I haven't heard anything back yet, although I wouldn't put it past Rosey to reject it just to be a sheer bastard. And you can bet your life he'll go to Fisher for support for his decision, irrespective of what that decision is.'

Fisher was Superintendent Fisher, an individual who wasn't, according to Simon's reckoning, all that kosher. Simon could not put his finger on the problem, he just had this gut feeling, a feeling enhanced by the fact he couldn't believe anyone could get on with Chief Inspector Rose as well as Superintendent Fisher did. 'Anyway, I'd better be going,' said Simon finishing off the last of his coffee.

'Okay, sweetie. But can you give my murderer some thought? It'll give you something to think about on the bus.' Simon bent down and planted a hasty kiss on Georgie before he picked up his briefcase, opened the door and headed down the road to catch the 190 bus to Wynyard.

CHAPTER 3

'Inspector Webster, if you're at work, get down to my office, now. Elliott, if he's not, tell him to get here as soon as he shows his face.' It was the voice of Chief Inspector Rose, booming out from behind the closed door of his office located on the third floor of the Day Street Police Station.

Cripes, let me got my coat off first, thought Webster having just entered the office he shared with his partner, Detective Sergeant Noel Elliott. Before saying a word to the Sergeant, Webster did an immediate about turn and walked briskly down the greeny coloured linoleum corridor, past the conference room and several other CIB offices located on the third floor, to the chief inspector's office. He knocked on the door and entered before receiving a response, the normal procedure following a summons for attendance.

The office was a somewhat drab affair although the chief inspector had tried to brighten it up to some extent by placing a worn-out rug in the middle of the linoleum floor. Upon the rug was a small pine coffee table with a glass ashtray, now full of cigarette butts, undoubtedly the source of the stale air that permeated the room. The chief's pine desk, positioned at the far end of the office, was somewhat less than extravagant but functional having three drawers on either side. There were three, four drawer metal filing cabinets against an internal office wall, while the external wall had two windows fitted with sheer curtains that looked like they hadn't been cleaned since their installation some twenty years earlier. The saving grace of a very ordinary office was that the windows provided something of a view, albeit limited, of the Darling Harbour docklands freight terminal, or what remained of the terminal, the facility in its death throes with a new cargo terminal being constructed at Botany.

'You wish to see me, sir?'

'Yes. Take a seat.' Inspector Webster sat on one of the two vinyl lounge chairs placed in front of Chief Rose's desk and looked at the chief inspector as he busily wrote something on a notepad. Ah, the old "I'm the boss, you can wait for me" trick, Webster thought. Rose is making me wait, just to reinforce his position, no doubt. Webster took the time to scrutinize the chief and came to the conclusion the man had not changed since those heady days at The Rocks. Chief Inspector Rose was still big, obese probably a better word to describe his physical appearance, in stark contrast to Webster who was built more like a whippet. Rose was wearing civvies, as was Webster, but where Webster was wearing a dark grey suit and tie and looked respectable, the chief had removed his coat, loosened his tie and unbuttoned the top button of his shirt. Even with these comfort enhancing measures, his face continued to drip beads of sweat onto his portly frame while his breathing, more of a gasp for air, probably reflected the effort it took him to push a pen.

There was nothing Inspector Webster liked about his boss and the passage of time had not altered his initial opinion of Chief Inspector Rose. Inspector Webster was well aware the loathing he had for the chief was reciprocated, but unfortunately for Webster, he was the inspector and Rose the chief inspector. Inspector Webster turned his attention to the window, too depressed to carry on with his scrutiny. Who cares if he's as useless as tits on a bull, Webster mused. He's a definite candidate for a heart attack anyway.

Chief Inspector Rose finally stopped his scribbling on the notepad, picked up a Police Department manila folder and frowned. 'Ah, yes, Webster. I've read the report on your investigation into illegal gambling. I've also discussed it with the superintendent. Both of us compliment you, it's well written.' Straight away the inspector knew something was amiss, not enough pretty pictures for Rose, Webster thought cynically. He knew Rose would have taken the report to Fisher, irrespective of its content, as Rose always seemed to need the superintendent's support for any decision most chief inspectors would normally make without reference to a higher authority.

Chief Inspector Rose closed the file. 'Unfortunately, both Superintendent Fisher and I believe your evidence does not fit with your conclusions. You seem to have drawn a very long bow to suit your own preconceived ideas. I'm sure if the problem of illegal gambling was as rampant as you seem to think, there would be much more compelling evidence to support your claims.' Inspector Webster stifled the urge to tell Rose exactly what he thought of him, knowing Chief Rose would almost certainly take disciplinary action, and enjoy doing so. However, the thought crossed his mind that Rose should get off his backside and get out into the real world, just to find out what life was all about. Webster knew illegal gambling existed in Sydney; he'd taken part in it to gather information. He couldn't imagine a city where illegal gambling didn't take place, to some extent, at least.

'So, it goes no further, no follow-up action?' asked Inspector Webster.

'No. Not at this stage,' replied Chief Inspector Rose, throwing the folder onto his desk. 'The decision has been made by Superintendent Fisher so we will leave it at that. Oh, before you leave. Your application for transfer has been rejected. Superintendent Fisher believes you need more investigative experience and your illegal gambling report tends to support his view. Apart from that, there are no vacancies available within your rank structure. Thank you, Inspector Webster. That is all.'

Detective Inspector Simon Webster closed the door to Chief Inspector Damien Rose's office behind him, placed his hands in his pockets and slowly, head down, meandered back along the corridor to his own office. He nudged the door to his office open with his foot, crossed the room to his desk and flopped down in an old battered swivel chair. He rested his chin on the palm of his left hand while the other drummed a rhythm on the desk.

The office had the ubiquitous linoleum floor and one central fluorescent light with a length of cord to operate the light hanging from the ceiling. Office furniture consisted of two office desks located at each end of the rectangular room, both desks having two drawers on each side, a standard reading lamp and a paper waste bin. There were three, four drawer filing cabinets, a hat stand located next to the door and, in one corner of the office, an easel and blackboard. The only window in the office overlooked an adjacent building's brick façade and was fitted with a pull-down blind that never seemed to function in the manner in which it was designed. All in all, the office could have been picked straight out of any Rank production B grade movie of the 1950s.

'Not one of the better ways to start the day.' It was more of a statement than a question that came from Detective Sergeant Noel Elliott, a young man aged in his late twenties, a pleasant face with the exception of a flattened nose that had been broken on numerous occasions, the legacy of his younger rugby days. Sergeant Elliott and Inspector Webster were at different ends of the spectrum when it came to physical appearances. Inspector Webster, a couple of years older than Noel, was tall, narrow at the waist and broad across the shoulders, and although he enjoyed the occasional beer, still managed to control his weight with no signs of excess fat. Like a good many people from the Manly Warringah area, he was well tanned with a receding blond hairline, probably bleached as a result of time spent in the surf. He was still an active member of the Collaroy Surf Club and a proud member of their renowned march-past team.

Simon had been born in Singleton where his father ran a barber shop in the centre of town. It had taken Simon some time to work out that his father was, apart from being the town's barber, also the town's SP bookie which explained the multitude of phone calls received, both at the barber shop and at his home. Simon had moved to Sydney, at the age of thirteen after completing primary school, where he lived with an aunt at Manly. His first job after completing high school at Manly Boys' High was with the Commercial Banking Company of Sydney. However, after a couple of years he had tired of banking and, following several unsuccessful attempts at other clerical positions, had finally came to the conclusion that a career in the Police Force may be the answer to what he was looking for.

Noel, on the other hand, was short and stocky, his height bordering on the minimum for entry into the Force. He had dark brown eyes and black hair, along with the physical appearance of what could be described parochially as a small brick outhouse. Noel was a Sydney boy, born and bred. His parents lived at Balgowlah which was convenient for Noel when he became a student of Balgowlah Boys' High School. Having passed his Leaving Certificate, Noel became a deck-hand on a Manly ferry while trying to decide on the career to pursue. Although he thoroughly enjoyed working on the ferries, Noel was aware he needed a job offering a career and it wasn't long before he decided that career might just be in the Police Force.

Noel had met Susan at a rugby union match while he was playing for Manly's second grade team against Eastwood at Manly Oval. Despite Susan being an avid Eastwood supporter, and having a pronounced height advantage over Noel, the two confirmed the love at first sight adage and had embarked on a lifelong partnership.

It was hard not to like Sergeant Elliott and the relationship between the two detectives had developed from the purely professional to be now well entrenched into their social lives. The Websters and the Elliotts got on very well and a close friendship had developed, notwithstanding the tacit acknowledgement of the disparity in ranks between the two detectives. Quite apart from Simon's and Noel's friendship, Georgie and Sue had developed a warm relationship and now spent much of their spare time at the beach or browsing through the modern shopping plazas that were now becoming the trend.

'Okay, what's he done this time?' Noel asked Simon.

'God help us, Noel,' said a dejected Inspector Webster. 'My application for transfer has been knocked back. Rose says it was Fisher's decision, but I bet it's just a case of sheer bastardry on Rose's part. You can bet Fisher had a look at it after Rose had already rejected it. Crikey, Noel, it's not as though I haven't been here long enough and I've got this nagging feeling Rosey would love to be rid of me.'

'I know you two don't get on. Does this go back to the days at The Rocks?' enquired Sergeant Elliott.

'Yes,' replied Webster. 'We were in a situation together when he was a sergeant and I was fresh out of the Depot. It's all so stupid, but Rose has always worked on the assumption violence will win you any argument and get you all the convictions you want. I didn't see it that way and I let him know, which was not a career enhancing move. And Rosey didn't appear half as tough as his reputation made out. If the truth be known, he made a bit of a gig of himself. I've never told anyone about it, so keep it under your hat. Trouble is, Rosey knows I have this knowledge and he's scared I'll use it someday.'

'And will you?'

'Who knows? Let's just say I have no plans to, at the moment. I can understand why he has a set against me as he has this fear I will reveal all. The thing I can't understand is his animosity towards you. I can't remember you having done anything to upset him, or have you?'

Sergeant Elliott shook his head. 'No, not a thing. Maybe his malice is fuelled by his belief you've already told me about The Rocks incident. Mind you, it seems Rosey and I have come to a mutual understanding; we both hate each other's guts.'

'Well, I somehow think you're not Robinson Crusoe on that score. Oh yes. I knew there was something else I meant to tell you,' said Inspector Webster taking a deep breath. 'They've gone and binned our report on illegal gambling. When I say "they", I mean Rosey and Fisher. Lack of evidence, apparently. Stuffed if I know how much more evidence they need, but the whole thing's been a complete bloody waste of time. With six months of investigating down the gurgler, you could say I'm one pissed off detective. Look, I'm sorry, Noel, I'm just fed up at the moment.'

'Hey, you've no reason to be sorry. The last thing you need do is to let Rosey know he's getting to you,' replied Noel as he folded a piece of paper into something resembling an aircraft.

'Noel, you know me better than anyone else at Day Street. Am I stupid, or am I missing something? I'm not a bad judge of character and I can't help thinking all is not as it should be with our illustrious Chief Inspector. The way I see it, Rosey has a two-way problem; he's a very unpleasant person, and he fails to set the example professionally. You'd think he would get one right, either obnoxious and a good cop, or a good bloke and a poor cop.'

'Well, don't think for one minute you're the first person to have come to that conclusion,' replied Noel, as he watched his delta wing aircraft fail dismally. 'He's not well liked here in Day Street as he never appears to do any investigating. Whenever there is a successful investigation, Rosey jumps in and takes all the credit without acknowledging the work of his subordinates who have done all the work. I've seen him start a few investigations but he always seems to get himself into such a hell of a mess he passes it on to someone else. The queer thing is, Fisher seems to regard Rosey as the greatest thing since sliced bread.'

'Strange isn't it?' mused Simon. 'I somehow think we joined the Force at a time of change between two philosophies of policing; the old way where the police would haul away the drunks, put 'em in jail or let 'em out on a two-bob bond. Even the public used to hold some police officers in reverence based solely on their reputation, like that bloke who played league footy for Newtown. It seems few people have any respect for authority these days. And now we have all these do-gooders running around saying people like Jack the Ripper just need a little love and understanding. Apart from that, the Force is getting more technical and sophisticated to the extent where brain power is replacing brawn power, at least it will when all the old coppers die out. Hell, sometimes I think I made a bad choice by joining the Force.'

Noel sat back in his chair and folded his arms. 'Look, boss, I came through the Depot after you and there are things they can't teach you, only stuff you can learn on the streets. One thing you've taught me is that there are illegal activities going on that you should ignore as they really mean bugger all in the overall scheme of things. Unfortunately, that philosophy is in total contrast to Rosey's way of thinking. Let's face it; we're not being employed as detectives and chasing the bad guys anymore as our duties seem to have been downgraded to traffic warden status.'

'Yes, we're fighting a losing battle, thanks to Rosey and Fisher. Want to change sides?'

'What, you mean join the bad guys?' asked Noel, as he screwed up a piece of paper for a shot into Simon's paper waste bin, and missed; nothing unusual. 'If this keeps up, who can tell? I know you're joking this time, but if you should ask me again, I think I would have to give the matter some serious thought. Come to think of it, it would be a chance to see what life's like on the other side; you know, jump ship and join the bad guys. It would be a change and we wouldn't have to put up with Rosey. By the way, talking of Rosey, boss, just where does he disappear to on a Wednesday afternoon? He never lets anyone know where he's going, he just goes.'

'Yeah, and we have to apply in triplicate to get time off for a coffee. There's a lot of speculation around Day Street as to what he gets up to; golf, a girl friend, a Swedish massage. Who knows? Who gives a stuff anyway?' grumbled a dejected Webster.

'Look, how about I bring Sue over next Saturday for a couple of beers?' Noel suggested. 'Georgie and Sue are going shopping on the Saturday morning at the Warringah Mall so they will probably want to relax with a glass or two of wine.'

'Great idea. All we have to do is survive until then,' replied Simon.

The conversation between the two detectives was rudely interrupted by Sergeant Elliott's phone which he answered with ponderous alacrity. A few moments later, Sergeant Elliott replaced the receiver and turned to Inspector Webster. 'Boss, is this for real? Rosey wants us to go to an antiVietnam demonstration. I thought that was Special Branch's domain?'

'It is, but with LBJ coming to town the Special Branch boys are beside themselves running around in ever diminishing circles. You've only to look at what we've been doing lately; a punch-up at The Rocks is hardly a case for the CIB, and yet we're told to get along and sort it out. For our workload to be downgraded at the same time our report is trashed just happens to be too much of a coincidence. I wouldn't mind betting there's something more to this than meets the eye.' Inspector Webster pushed his chair back from the table, folded his arms and gazed at the ceiling, deep in thought. After a few moments he turned to Noel and said, 'Just suppose there's a higher level of investigation going on and our poking around might compromise that investigation. Or, heaven forbid, there may even be some corruption in the Force.'

Inspector Webster acknowledged that there probably were instances of impropriety, indiscretion and possible corruption perpetrated by members of the Force. There was always enough talk of such activity, and you could expect some degree of corruption in any organization as large as the police force. But there seemed little in the way of action to either confirm or deny that such activity existed. All in all, as far as corruption and illegal goings on were concerned, Detective Inspector Webster hadn't come across it, - yet.

'Yes, that might be true. But do you think the hierarchy would let Rosey near an important investigation? Everyone, including the tea lady, know Rosey isn't the full quid, and even Fisher himself has his doubts, notwithstanding his blatant support for Rosey, which is odd to say the least,' replied Sergeant Elliott. 'There's something funny going on there, but whatever it is, I don't want to know. Strange, isn't it? It's not often you come across two people you are expected to work closely with and yet find both of them so difficult to get along with. Rosey isn't the brightest cop on the planet, and as for Fisher, there's something about him that makes my skin crawl.'

Inspector Webster shrugged, clasped his hands behind his head and stretched back in his chair. 'You know I should reprimand you for speaking out this way about your senior officers, but I won't because I totally agree with you on both counts. I feel really sorry for Fisher's wife, I think her name's Agnes. Fisher is nothing more than a sleaze, okay, a superintendent sleaze, but a sleaze all the same. He thinks he's God's gift to women and chases after anyone in a skirt. Apart from that, he gives me the impression he's nothing more than a "yes" man who endorses anything Rose puts up to him, sort of like Rosey drives Fisher instead of the other way around.'

'Ah, what the hell. Only the good die young. By the way, you haven't forgotten I won't be able to give you a lift home tonight? I'm meeting Sue for a coffee then off to a five o'clock session of Robin and the Seven Hoods at the Liberty- you know- Cranky Frankie and the Rat Pack stuff,' Sergeant Elliott said apologetically.

'And that's just who I'd like to see running rampant in the city right now, Robin bloody Hood with Rose on his trail. And no, I haven't forgotten. I've got to pick up some dry cleaning at

Wynyard and the bus trip will give me time to think about things.'

Actually Inspector Webster had a few thoughts running through his mind, not the least the acrimony that existed between Chief Inspector Rose and himself. Simon believed he had stood by his word given to Chief Inspector Rose, that he would not divulge the details of The Rocks incident, albeit a couple of years ago now. Simon was of the belief the meager details given to Sergeant Elliott did not constitute a breach of his word, but if Rose thought otherwise, so what. God, what a mess, thought Simon.

CHAPTER 4

*A*fter collecting his dry cleaning at Wynyard Station, Inspector Simon Webster made his way up the long escalator to York Street, crossed the road and joined the queue for the 184 bus to Collaroy. Fortunately he was near the front of the queue which meant he would get a seat by a window, thus avoiding the embarrassment of remaining seated by the aisle while some poor little old lady would no doubt have to stand. Simon, being a gentleman, would normally give up his seat to such commuters, but trying to juggle a brief case and the dry cleaning made standing impractical.

Having eventually seated and settled himself for the journey, Simon remembered the simple task Georgie had asked him to consider before leaving for work that morning. Georgie had proved successful in her literary pursuits and had had her first book published, the first step on the road to fame and fortune, soon to be spoken of in the same breath as Agatha Christie. Naturally, Georgie's novels were murder mysteries, Simon being her prime source of information on matters, such as methods of doing away with victims, crime scene stuff and pathology. Georgie had been employed as a secretary to a solic-itor in Phillip Street before deciding, at the ripe old age of thirty-one, she was a year or so older than Simon, to get a real job. After much thought and discussion with Simon, she had come to the decision to become a highly successful crime novel-ist, an occupation she could quite happily carry out from their comfortable Collaroy bungalow.

The bus made its first set-down at Warringah Road and it wasn't long before Inspector Webster alighted outside the Eleven Fifteen Coffee Shop opposite the Collaroy Surf Club. As it was six thirty and the middle of August, the lights of Pittwater Road shone brightly as he made his way past the Odeon Theatre to West Bank Lane. The small brick bungalow at number 24 had the verandah light shining and, as he approached the front door, he could hear the tap of the typewriter beating out the epic novel that would rock the literary world. 'Honey, I'm home,' called Simon.

'Thank heavens, I was running out of ideas,' said Georgie as she appeared from the spare bedroom that she had converted to a study. 'I've had a bugger of a day and I still haven't thought of a way to rid myself of this turbulent victim. Glass of wine?'

'No, I'll have a few, thank you, - and fill 'em up, none of this half glass stuff thanks.' Simon flopped into his favourite lounge chair and picked up the TV guide, slipping off each shoe with the other foot as he settled back comfortably into the chair. 'And what was your problem today, apart from not being able to come up with a simple murder? I did give your question some thought, but I honestly can't come up with a murder that looks so much like an accident that the forensic boffins wouldn't be able to tell.' The TV guide was discarded unread onto the coffee table.

'That's okay,' said Georgie as she handed Simon his glass and planted a kiss on the top of his head. Georgie was tall, slim

with dark short hair and an engaging smile. Simon often remi-
nisced of the days sitting opposite Georgie on the Manly ferry
and gazing forlornly, if not extremely rudely, into the dark
brown eyes that had absolutely captivated him, and how stupid
he had been for not taking the plunge and speaking to her
sooner.

'Dear old Dorothy had an incident this morning', Georgie
said as she settled herself on the sofa. 'She screamed so loudly I
even felt obliged to go and see what was wrong. Apparently she
thought, only thought mind you, that she saw a spider. Instead
of thanking me for making sure everything was okay, she
abused the hell out of me saying it was my fault the spider had
been in her house in the first place. Anyway, now you've heard
my bit of excitement, how was your day?'

'Another day like that and I'm on the Valium. Obviously I'm
missing the point somewhere but the whole thing seems
screwed up. Everyone, well, nearly everyone at the station,
thinks the Chief Inspector doesn't come up to scratch as a chief
inspector. At the same time the Superintendent, Fisher that is,
thinks Rose is the greatest detective since Cadfael joined the
monastery. There's something funny going on and I don't know
what it is.' Simon shrugged and gulped down the last of his wine
before getting up and making for the kitchen. He soon returned
with a bottle of moselle in his hand, pausing to top up the two
glasses before resuming his seat with a deep breath and a sigh.
'Personally, I find Rosey as repulsive as a ferret, but that's
casting aspersions on a ferret I suppose, and maybe ferrets
aren't repulsive; I've never met one.'

'Well, do something about it if it's that bad, and I don't mean
about meeting a ferret.' remarked Georgie. 'I think you're
finding the job a little different to what you expected, at least
over the last year or so.'

'And what do you have in mind? I've already applied for as

transfer and had it knocked back, and anyway, that may not solve the problem.'

'You should draw on your family history. I've no doubt some of your ancestors made the police look foolish at times,' replied Georgie, settling herself more comfortably into the sofa by drawing her legs up underneath herself. Georgie was referring to one of Simon's great great something or other grandfather, Samuel, who was sentenced to fourteen years transportation for the theft of ten shillings from a lady's bag at the Leeds market back in the 1830s. The sentence was harsh; his accomplice only received seven years transportation. But then again, Samuel had been known to the police and had appeared before the presiding judge on previous occasions.

'Ooh, now that would require a career change, wouldn't it? From constabulary to villainy,' said Simon with a look of scorn on his face. 'I know things are desperate, but not that desperate, yet. Anyway, what specifically did you have in mind?'

Georgie pursed her lips while giving the question some thought. 'Well, I suppose you could rob a bank. It appears quite simple from what I've seen on the telly, and from what you've told me, most bank robbers aren't overly endowed with brains. At least you're ahead on that aspect, and I would help you, of course.'

Good God, thought Simon and rolled his eyes to the heavens; Bonnie and Clyde alive and well. Let's go rob a bank, any bank, just to see if the good guys can catch and lock us up for ten years, all for the sake of highlighting the Chief Inspector's incompetence. Heaven knows, I love you Georgie, but you do get some wonderfully loopy ideas at times.

CHAPTER 5

The door to Chief Inspector Rose's office opened and a red face appeared. 'Webster, get down here, and bring your sergeant with you, now.' The voice roared down the corridor, easily heard by both Inspector Webster and Sergeant Elliott behind the closed door to their office. The manner in which the two detectives had been summoned was no different from previous invitations extended by the Chief. In general, they were made without thought given to the recipient's confidentiality, everyone in the station being privy to the Chief's boisterous demand for the detective's presence. The Chief's door slammed shut adding further credence to the perception that he was not a happy man.

Inspector Simon Webster shrugged and took a deep breath. 'Why do I get this sinking feeling I have my deckchair firmly placed aboard the Titanic? Come on, Noel, we better go and see what's up. I expect it's something earth shattering; can't find his bus pass or he needs a new typewriter ribbon,' he said dryly. With that, the two men donned their coats and walked down the corridor to their awaiting fate.

Inspector Webster knocked on the door and, before being able to get the door open, received a brash 'Come'. As the two men entered the Chief's office, Sergeant Elliott immediately noticed the seating arrangements. Usually, if Chief Inspector Rose was expecting the meeting to be protracted, he would place the required number of chairs in front of his desk. However, this time there was only one chair in front of his desk with two further chairs around the coffee table in the centre of the office.

'Don't bother to sit; this won't take long,' Chief Inspector Rose snarled from behind his desk. 'The hierarchy has decreed that we, meaning the CIB here at Day Street, are over our establishment strength. This has been bought about following a review of all CIB manning establishments, so don't feel that this is a sudden one-off case pertaining specifically to Day Street. The upshot is that I have to reduce our strength by two officers, and guess what?' the Chief asked, a look of arrogant pomposity etched across his face.

Sergeant Elliott looked at his partner who appeared to be troubled, his brow furrowed in a look of disappointment and regret. 'Oh gee, Chief, we'll be sorry to see you leave, and just when we were getting along so well together. But I have no doubt you and the other officer to leave will be moving to greener pastures,' said Inspector Webster, with cynical glibness.

'Well, I'm sorry to disappoint you boys, because it's not me that will be doing the leaving.' The arrogant look on Rose's face was replaced with a broad smile, a victory to Chief Inspector Rose over this petulant subordinate. 'Now listen here, Webster,' the Chief Inspector said patronizingly, 'I spoke to you before about your application for transfer and that both Superintendent Fisher and I believed you needed further investigative experience. Well, I'm happy to say an opportunity has now arisen for us to approve your transfer. We believe the transfer, that we have gone to great pains to arrange, will provide the investigative experience you obviously lack.' Inspector Webster had the distinct impression Chief Rose was enjoying himself and probably looked upon his subordinates as having come down in the last shower of rain. Evidently the 'arrangements' Rose had made were going to be far more detrimental to Webster than anything he could expect by remaining at Day Street.

'So my application for transfer is now a goer?' enquired Inspector Webster.

'Yes, it is. After going to great lengths to persuade the Super, I've been able to post you to the supernumery list where you will be required to fill in at stations needing temporary staff.' Webster had the urge to jump across the Chief's table and throttle the man. Every officer in the Force regarded the super-numery list as the forlorn hope before hell and was the career abyss from which no-one ever returned. The Chief Inspector continued, choosing to ignore the look of hostility on Webster's face. 'As for you Elliott, you will be staying here at Day Street but you will be going back into uniformed general duties. It seems the general duty boys are hard pressed with the increase in anti-Vietnam demonstrations here in the city and need all the help they can get.'

'And what about me?' enquired Inspector Webster. 'You haven't mentioned just exactly where I'll be supernumeried to.'

'God damn, I knew I had forgotten something,' replied the Chief theatrically. 'Inspector, you will need to get up a tad earlier. Detective Inspector Burroughs of the Metropolitan Region has gone on furlough, or will shortly, resulting in a vacancy within the CIB for the next six months, at least. You will fill in for him while he's away. That's assuming he does return from furlough, of course.'

'That's all very nice, Chief, but you still haven't said where

Detective Burroughs is going on furlough from,' reminded Webster who was now getting a little impatient with the proceedings.

'Ahh, yes, of course. You'll be working down at Cronulla. God, that's a long way from Collaroy but that's the best we can do.' Yeah, I bet, thought Webster as his deck chair started sliding down the slippery sloped deck. 'I suggest you both report to Sergeant Mathieson in the near future to get the administrative arrangements under way,' added Chief Rose as an afterthought measured to press home his rank and influence he wielded over the two detectives.

Sergeant Elliott and Inspector Webster said nothing until they reached their office and had the door shut firmly behind them. 'I wonder if we're the last in Day Street to know what's going on. I knew there were rumours of some changes going around, especially in light of the proposed specialist crime squads being formed, but this seems to be taking vindictiveness to extremes,' remarked Inspector Webster as he removed his jacket and tie before slouching onto his swivel chair.

'Well, it comes as a complete surprise to me as I knew nothing about it,' replied Sergeant Elliott. 'I think I got the better of the deal as at least I get to stay here at Day Street. It seems you won't be seeing much of Georgie in the future with all the travelling you'll have to do.' The Sergeant sank back in his chair, folded his arms and placed his feet up on his desk. 'Christ, Cronulla may as well be on the other side of the planet. You'll get to work quicker if you get the train to Collins Street and walk back.'

'Might be an idea. I know I'll have to listen to the Melbourne forecast to see what the weather's like. I think Cronulla closer to Melbourne than Sydney. I don't know, Noel, but I think it's a safe bet Fisher is in on the act. At least you have some idea of where Rosey's coming from, like, he is up front, most of the time. But Fisher is a different kettle of fish and it's a bit on the nose. Seems you never know just what he's thinking or what he's up to. Ah, what the hell,' declared Webster pushing his chair away from the table and jumping to his feet. 'Let's get out of here for a while and go drown our sorrows in a cup of coffee somewhere,' he said, already out the door, his coat slung over his shoulder.

The detectives walked up Bathurst Street and found a coffee shop on a windswept George Street. With spring only days away, the cold southerly did nothing to temper the frosty, indifferent enthusiasm of either Inspector Webster or Sergeant Elliott towards the world in general, more notably one Chief Inspector Damian Rose. They found a vacant table against a window, settled themselves and ordered a flat black and a cappuccino from a young waitress.

'What now, Simon?' asked Sergeant Elliott, his chin resting on the palm of his hand, his elbow on the table. Sergeant Elliott was keen to drop the rank structure and place the conversation back on the mutual friendship arrangement he knew Inspector Simon Webster preferred once out of the office.

Simon sighed and scratched the back of his head. 'Nothing much we can do. It seems like we were the bunnies right from the beginning. I have no doubt any other chief inspector would have handled the situation differently by at least discussing the matter with us first before coming to a decision. No, this was a fait accompli, and all attributed to Rosey with a touch of Fisher's influence, whatever that may have been.'

'Is there nothing we can do?' asked Noel.

'Well, Georgie suggested we have a crack at making Rosey look bad. That in itself would be pretty easy to do, in theory, but in reality could prove difficult, if not impossible, considering his buddy buddy relationship with Fisher.'

'Was Georgie a little more specific?'

'Yep. She suggested we rob a bloody bank,' replied Simon, a look of defeatism on his face.

'Sounds like a good idea to me,' replied Noel after a minute of silence broken only by the waitress delivering the two coffees. 'Our careers seem to have been torpedoed by the hierarchy for one reason or another, so stuff 'em; let's go and join the bad guys. After all, you've already suggested it yourself.'

'Come on, Noel. This is serious so stop joking. Our very future with the Force depends on how we handle this situation, and running off to join the baddies isn't the solution.'

'Why not?' responded Noel belligerently. 'I'll get my arse kicked from pillar to post by the boys in uniform. They'll know, and rightly too, that I've gone backwards. No-one goes from CIB back to general duties. It's always the other way around. And you. You know there's no life after being posted to the supernumery, so our careers are already shot to pieces.'

'Christ, you're serious,' said Simon with surprise.

'And why not? I think we could work out a fairly decent job if we pooled our resources. Bank jobs are usually committed by young blokes who race in, wave a gun around, and race out again with a bag of cash. Half the time they're caught within the first fifteen minutes of doing the job. I think we could do a lot better than that,' responded Noel, a touch of excitement and enthusiasm in his voice.

'Now hang on a second. You sound like you want to do a bank job for the money, not necessarily to show Rosey up for what he is which, to my mind, would be the whole object of the exercise,' said Simon, still not entirely convinced of the idea.

'Ah ha. So you haven't totally dismissed the thought?' replied Noel, a wry smile on his face.

'I haven't decided anything. Look, we're not rostered next Tuesday, so come over and we'll have a beer or two. Bring Sue along, although I know she'll think it's a great idea and side with Georgie,' said Simon as he drained the last of his coffee.

CHAPTER 6

$\mathcal{T}$he Thursday night traffic was unusually heavy as the EJ Holden slowly made its way through Spit Junction and headed for the bottleneck generally experienced at the Spit Bridge. 'For the life of me, I just don't understand those so-called urban planners. Here we have a bridge only seven years since opening, and it's already passed its use by date. We may as well have kept the old punt that was here before they built this bloody thing,' exclaimed an exasperated Noel Elliott as he squeezed the Holden in front of a double decker bus. 'Apart from the traffic situation, what the hell is going on at work? I know Chief Rose has it in for us, but surely he isn't vindictive enough to end our careers.'

'Yeah, I know,' replied Simon with a shrug of the shoulders. 'I can't get rid of the idea my report on illegal gambling in the Darlinghurst area may have been a little too close for someone's comfort. Look, I'm not suggesting the Chief is involved, or even could be involved, but I didn't get a chance to look up the associates or links to those I had already identified before the report was binned. After that little exercise in futility the Chief directed me to organise lollipop ladies for the Fort Street Girls' School.'

'You're kidding?' said Noel, shocked at the thought.

'Yes, I'm kidding, but I may as well have been for all the good I'm doing now,' replied Simon dejectedly. 'Look, I know there has always been some scuttlebutt regarding corruption, payoffs, bribery and such stuff within the Force, you'd have to be naive to think there isn't something going on somewhere. I have this gut feeling Rosey isn't kosher and Fisher is right up there with him. Just say, for argument sake, the Chief didn't expect us to uncover as much as we did on the illegal gambling, and if we had gone any further we may have trodden on someone's toes.'

'And you think those toes might belong to Fisher?' ventured Noel.

'Well, what do you think? Rose said he discussed the report with Fisher and the report was subsequently binned together with our careers.'

'At this stage I daren't hazard an opinion, but I can see where you're coming from,' replied Noel as he eased the car into the curb.

Simon Webster walked slowly up West Bank Lane from Pittwater Road, his mind mulling over the events of the day and the ramifications they would have on both his personal and professional life, if he now had a professional life left at all. It wasn't until he had nearly reached number 24 that he suddenly became aware of the flashing blue light of a police car parked directly outside number 26 West Bank Lane, dear old Dorothy's house. He decided against being snoopy and find out what was going on from the attending police officers as he was sure all would be revealed as soon as he entered his own front door.

'What's going on?' he enquired even before putting down his briefcase.

'Don't know exactly,' said Georgie as she continued to peer discretely at "the old bitch's," house through the small gap in the curtains. 'She came home from shopping sometime around four-thirty; I heard her car. Around five-thirty the ambulance arrived and then the police. She might have had an accident or something, although the police have been here for some time now. Must be serious.'

Georgie gave up on her clandestine observation of the house next door, closed the curtains and proceeded to the kitchen to pour the obligatory glasses of wine. 'You know, I think I've worked out how my victim is done away with. My Chief Inspector and his forensic boffins will never be able to prove murder even if they catch the suspect, which they won't because my baddie is too clever; one for Moriarty and the bad guys.'

'Glad to hear it,' said Simon, taking his glass and leaning back in his lounge chair. Detective Inspector Simon Webster had other things on his mind, not the least being how to tell Georgie he would be leaving for work an hour earlier and getting home an hour later, at best, and that his career, to all intents and purposes, was on the rocks. Perhaps I'll wait for Tuesday and tell the sad story with Noel here - he'll need to talk about his career options too, Simon reflected. For some unknown reason the thought of Moriarty getting the better of Holmes crossed his mind; one for the bad guys. Maybe.

~

Next morning Detective Inspector Simon Webster was reading the Daily Telegraph while having his morning cup of coffee. This was a daily ritual, off the bus at York Street, down the York Street escalators to Wynyard Station, train to Town Hall, and a cup of coffee at the coffee shop on the corner of Bathurst and George. He had read the sporting pages; Saint George heading for another Grand Final, probably against Balmain, the way the Tigers had put Manly away in the semi final. Inspector Webster sighed and turned the paper over and started on the mundane, boring front page.

The inspector brushed over the first three pages before deciding to see if the crossword was doable. No, that article wasn't of interest, maybe it was, he thought. He shuffled the pages back to page three.

"Woman Dies of Heart Attack in Backyard. An elderly lady was found dead in the back yard of her northern beach home ..." Inspector Webster continued to read the article. Oh hell, no, can't be. No, your imagination is running away with you. Forget it and go to work. While trying to rationalise his thoughts, Detective Inspector Webster had that uncomfortable feeling most brilliant detectives rely on, and that was "the gut feeling."

Sergeant Elliott had already been in the office for some twenty minutes by the time Inspector Webster finally entered. 'Hi boss, I'll clear out my stuff today and get myself organized downstairs if that's okay? Sergeant Mathieson says I'm to be on the beat by next Wednesday. I asked him about my rostered day off on Tuesday. There are no problems there so if it's okay with you, Sue and I will drop over for that ale?'

'No, look forward to it. I think we need to have a little chat anyway,' replied the Inspector.

Oops, what's going on here? was the first thought of Sergeant Elliott. The boss has never wanted a "little chat" with anyone.

'Have you read the Tele today, Noel?'

'No, haven't had a chance yet. Why, anything interesting?'

'Hope not, but just maybe. Here, page three.'

Sergeant Elliott read the article and raised an enquiring eyebrow to the Inspector. 'So?'

'Maybe nothing. Just got a funny feeling,' the inspector replied, a hint of apprehension on his face. 'Anyway, I'll drop down and see Sergeant Mathieson and get myself organised.'

Inspector Webster and Sergeant Mathieson got on pretty well, Sergeant Mathieson not ignorant of the position Inspector Webster had been placed while working for Chief Inspector Rose. 'Hey, look Inspector, I know the Chief wants to move you off as soon as possible, but I know Detective Inspector Burroughs doesn't go on leave for another month, and there is no need for a handover of existing investigations. Can I suggest you take a couple of weeks leave now just to settle yourself? In that way you can make the move without any degree of urgency. I can organize the administrative side so there'll be no problems with getting it approved. Just come and see us after you get back from leave, that should be sometime around the end of September. Okay?'

'Hey, what a wonderful idea, that would be great. I don't know how you'll get it done, but if you say you can, I'll leave it in your capable hands. And thanks,' said a relieved Inspector Webster.

By the time Inspector Webster arrived home that night, he had made the decision he would not ask Georgie about "The Woman's Death". He knew if Georgie had anything to say, she would eventually reveal what it was. Sure enough, it wasn't long before Georgie raised the subject only to confirm poor Dorothy had suffered a heart attack while taking in the washing and that poor Dorothy was no longer "that stupid bitch".

'Yes, her body was found by the meter man who had come to

read the electricity. He'd been running a bit late fortunately, otherwise she could have been left outside all night, though I s'pose if he had been running on time she mightn't be dead at all. Surprising, I never knew she had a dicky ticker.' Simon faltered as he suddenly became aware of another side of Georgie's personality as she displayed a somewhat indifferent attitude to the death of the poor lady who lived, had lived, next door.

'How's the book going, sweetie?' enquired Simon as nonchalantly as he could.

'Oh, real good. I came up with a wonderful way to murder my victim. You can read it if you want.'

'No thanks, I'll have a look later,' replied Simon, the detective in him quietly telling him he really didn't want to know how she did away with the victim. 'Noel and Sue are coming over for a drink on Tuesday afternoon. Nothing special. We have a few things to talk about. You be here then?'

'Of course. Where do you think I'd go on a Tuesday? No, that'll be nice.' The prospects of the afternoon being "nice" wasn't exactly how the Detective Inspector imagined the afternoon turning out, although he did think it may be different.

CHAPTER 7

*S*imon and Noel sat on the coloured canvas director's chairs Simon had placed, together with a small table, on the back lawn. Georgie appeared from the bungalow's back door with a bottle of moselle and two wine glasses, closely followed by Sue with a six pack of Fosters and two stubby holders. As Sue sat down next to Noel, Simon couldn't suppress the thought of how opposites attract. How could such a short, pugnacious looking bloke like Noel win a girl as good looking as Sue? Sue was a tall, blue eyed blond with shoulder length hair. She towered over Noel and gave the impression she could easily take him under her wing to protect him. Their marriage of six years had worked well, both devoted to each other and happy with their lot.

The small gathering was fortunate in that the forecast southerly change had stalled around Kiama, the weather at Collaroy showing the first signs of the approaching summer, the gentle nor' westerly touched with more than a hint of warmth for the first time in months. Having dispensed with the idle chatter of weekend footy results, the political situation, including Australia's involvement in Vietnam, and a rehash of the Shark Arm Murder some thirty-five years earlier but still unsolved, Simon thought it was time to get down to more pressing matters. The women had participated during the period of idle conversational chit chat, albeit minimally, both having used their women's intuition to conclude something was in the air.

'Before we go any further,' said Simon, pausing while he carefully placed his third empty can of Fosters to the growing pyramid of empty cans being constructed on the table, 'there's a few things both Noel and I wish to say. Well, at least I do.'

Simon reached for another tinny, pulled the ring pull cap and sat back into his chair. 'Georgie, it seems the Force now considers me as being what they call a supernumerary. A supernumerary is…'

'Simon, I know what a supernumerary is. You don't have to explain.'

'I'm sorry, I'll continue then. I'm being shifted from Day Street to fill a temporary vacant position at Cronulla and yes, I know it will probably be quicker to live at Toorak and get a bus back. And yes, we all know who's responsible for the dirking, but there's little I can do. The Superintendent loves Chief Inspector Rose and he undoubtedly follows Rose's recommendations. I don't believe for one minute Day Street is above the CIB established strength, it's just a ploy for Rose to be rid of me, and I have a pretty good idea why. But irrespective of his reasons, he wins. I don't deny I may not have cooperated with him as well as I may have been able, but he's not the easiest bloke to get on with. Anyway, who knows?' Simon said with resignation. 'Maybe a change will work out for the better. I don't know how much Noel has told and you, Sue, but maybe he has something to say.'

'Yes' said Noel. 'I'm going back into uniform, fortunately still at Day Street. I'll apply for a transfer to Manly CIB, but I doubt such an application will receive a favorable response. Like Simon, all I can do is to try and make the best of things. Sorry Sue.'

'Hell, what have you to be sorry for,' replied Sue, as she leaned across and gently rubbed the back of Noel's neck. 'I think you will be better off away from Rose. I'm just sorry that you and Simon won't be working together as you get on so well.'

Georgie frowned as she poured herself another wine. 'As I said earlier, it stinks. Rose needs a kick up the bum from someone at superintendent level at least. Maybe you two should change sides and play him for the twit he is,' she said, placing significant emphasis on the "should". 'Instead of Holmes and Watson, how about becoming Butch and Sundance? I bet you could drive Rosey nuts.'

'Yes, Simon's told me about robbing a bank. Good thought,' said Noel with a smile. 'I'm all for being a baddie for a while. If you get caught for anything these days, the worst you'll get is a slap on the wrist and told not to do it again.'

'It's not like in the USA where if the judge says ten years, you get ten years,' added Georgie.

'By the way, Georgie, you never did explain how you did away with your victim,' said Simon as he pulled the top off another beer. 'Will you hang for your little transgression?'

'Well, it's not really a way of murdering someone, just a way of increasing the chances of someone snuffing it. So, you really can't say it's murder,' she replied in an effort to decriminalise her method of murdering someone.

Simon decided not to beat around the bush and said, 'Georgie, has this anything to do with the death of poor old Dorothy?'

'No, not in the least,' Georgie protested. 'Maybe I'd better explain. As you know I was stuck with my book on trying to come up with a way to get rid of the victim without making it look like murder. Well, I gave up and decided to do a little gardening in the hope of inspiration. I went to the garage for my gardening tools and a rubbish bag and came across a spider; I think it was a huntsman, not that I'm an expert on arachnids. Anyway, it was a big black one, looked like it was on its last legs. Definitely not a funnel web, I know one of those when I see it. As I was placing the poor thing in a jar I wondered if…' Simon placed a hand over his eyes and shook his head.

'No, no no, you didn't, please?'

Noel and Sue immediately looked at Simon with the same blank expression on their face. Georgie looked at Simon and knew straight away she didn't have to go on. He knew. He mightn't know the details, but he knew. 'Go on, you may as well tell us the whole story,' said Simon with a groan. 'Just wait a tick; I think I'll need a few more beers.' Simon soon returned with two six packs, giving one to Noel.

'Hell, this must be some story,' commented Noel as he took a tinny from the pack and placed the remainder into the Esky.

Georgie downed a full glass of wine in a couple of gulps and poured herself another. 'Look, how was I to know stupid Dorothy would die. I didn't know she had a heart problem and how was I to know she'd bring in the washing?'

'You put the spider in the washing?' Simon asked for no particular reason as he already knew the answer.

'No. See, there you go jumping to conclusions again. Actually, I put the spider in the peg basket. Well, how was I to know it would stay there. And how was I to know she would see it, or feel it, or do whatever she did. Maybe the spider wasn't there at all and she just had a heart attack. All I know is that Dorothy hated spiders, lots of people hate spiders but they don't drop dead when they see one. Who knows what happened?'

Sue, Noel and Simon all stared at Georgie in a stunned

silence. It was Sue who broke the tension. She threw her head back and roared with uncontrollable laughter. 'Oh Georgie, how absolutely delightful.'

'Well, bugger me,' was all Noel could muster.

'Christ, Sue, it's not a laughing matter,' said Simon trying to suppress his laughter while at the same time aiming a rebuke.

'No, it's absolutely appalling the poor lady's dead. It just seems ironic that a purely harmless spider can be so lethal when it's in the wrong hands. Of course, we will never know if it was in Dorothy's hands,' said Sue, her amusement now under control.

'Well, you can't blame me. I didn't kill the old girl,' Georgie protested.

'I've probably seen more blatant homicidal maniacs running around, but this is up there with the best of them. If it ain't murder, it's as close as "damn it" is to swearing,' quipped Noel, braking into a smile as he began to see Sue's point of view. 'You know, I think that's worth another beer or two. Mind if we invite ourselves to dinner as I think this could be a long afternoon, and I'm driving?'

'No, no problems at all. You won't get anything too complicated, maybe fish fingers or something just as erotic,' Georgie replied. Her fifth glass of wine was taking effect and, on the whole, she felt pretty happy, even if she couldn't get her tongue around her words precisely as intended. Heavens, poor Georgie had just confessed, if not to murder, at least manslaughter and, even if it would be difficult to prove in court, Georgie felt she needed the few wines, purely for medicinal purposes to ease a guilty conscience.

'Well, you're right on one thing Georgie, you did find a way to kill off your victim without it looking like murder,' Simon said. 'But where does that leave us? I suppose all of us are now accessories to a felony, but stuffed if I know which particular felony, but a felony all the same. Irrespective of what she says, Georgie knew Dorothy had an aversion to arachnids and she used this knowledge to her advantage. She might not have known to what extent Dorothy would react, but she did know, or at least had a good idea, Dorothy would react in some way, even if she hadn't planned on Dotty dropping dead. So, Georgie did have intent, irrespective of the outcome. Noel, you went through College later than I did. What do you think?'

'To be honest, Simon, I think we just changed sides,' said Noel with a shake of the head and a shrug of the shoulders.

Sue looked at her husband, perplexed. 'Changed sides? Hey, Noel, what's with this "changed sides" business? You mean all this talk about becoming criminals isn't just a joke?'

'Come on, Sue, take it easy,' replied Noel with a grin. 'We've been playing on the goodies side for umpteen years and all we have to show for it is a dirk between the shoulder blades by the hierarchy. I for one believe it's time to change sides, be one of the baddies for a change. You know, Batman and Robin, the goodies, the Penguin and the Joker the baddies. I've always thought it would be good experience, career wise, to see what life is like from the other side.'

'Oh, shut up you two,' said Simon, although even he was beginning to see the humor of the situation. Construction of the pyramid continued in a somewhat more jovial manner than earlier in the day.

The dinner that night turned out to consist of a Chinese take-away delivered by a long-haired youth riding a Vespa motor scooter. Discussion around the dinner table was somewhat stilted, everyone waiting for someone else to raise the antici-pated topic. Having already over imbibed on the beer and wine, everyone was now content with coffee. It was Simon who finally broke the ice, it probably the expectation of the others that, as the senior person present, he would be the person to take charge of the discussion.

'Okay, the question is, do we change sides? At the moment both Noel and I have jobs with the police force, albeit with no apparent future in store, both of us probably headed for nothing better than traffic duty in some God forsaken place out the back of Woop-Woop. Irrespective of whatever the Force may have in store for us, any decision to change sides may not necessarily mean we have to chuck in our jobs, at least not right away. The way I see it, a move to the baddies may not be irrevocable; maybe just long enough for us to dirk the Chief Inspector.'

Noel sat back and examined the dregs of his coffee in the bottom of his cup. 'Well, I know the more time I have to think about it, the less inclined I will be to change sides. I'm all for it at the moment but, being a total wimp, the longer I sit and cogitate about it the more I will probably adopt the sensible and responsible attitude and do nothing.'

Sue rested her elbow on the table and supported her head with a clenched fist under her chin. She looked at Noel with a bewildered look. 'Noel, my sweet, I don't know if anyone else at this table understood all you just said, but it seems you're hedging your bets and looking for a way out if you make a wrong decision.'

'Hey, be nice, Sue. Don't pick on him. Noel's only trying to make a decision based on both the facts that he has and the facts he might have sometime in the future,' said Simon in support of his colleague.

'Oh, for heaven's sake. Let's cut the Freudian crap and get to the point.' Georgie was not really hostile but the tone of her voice and sharp words had a profound effect on the other three sitting at the table. 'We have a question that warrants nothing more than a "yes" or a "no" answer, so get on with it. Who's for changing sides and who's not?'

'Just one point before we vote,' sounded Simon. 'Georgie's little revelation should have some impact on your decision. As far as I'm concerned, I changed sides when I became an accessory to either a murder or manslaughter. Needless to say, I think Georgie is probably one of the baddies already, considering the circumstances. So that's two decisions. Noel, Sue, it's your turn to decide.'

Sue raised her eyebrows, pushed her chair back from the table and folded her arms. 'And if you've become an accessory to whatever, what makes you think Noel and I aren't accessories just as much as you are? It's not like we didn't hear any less of Georgie's little revelation than you did. Apart from that, whether Noel knows it or not, he's been like a bear with a sore head, and been that way for months. He's stuck in the mud and bored stiff, and that's not meant to have any reflection on you, Simon.'

'Thanks, but now you've mentioned it, I probably feel the same, to some extent at least. Chief Rose is determined to kill both of us off with sheer boredom,' replied Simon.

'Hey, hang about. What about me?' responded Noel indignantly. 'Sue, I didn't know I was like a bear with a sore head, and if I am, I'm sorry. In any case, it sounds like you've already made up my mind to change to the bad guys.'

Sue shrugged and crossed her long legs. Simon noted her posture was one of dignified intimidation, a look of stern authority on her face. 'Sorry, Noel, my love,' she said, 'but that's the way it's been for a while now. I'll be happy with any decision you make, as long as you're happy with it and it coincides with the decision I make for you. I just thought you'd like to know that I'm all for you being a bad guy for a change. You need a spark and something exciting in your life to get you going again, and I'm prepared for anything.'

Noel took a deep breath, his hands raised in a gesture of submission. 'Okay, all right, already. I concede, I surrender. I'm happy to become Jack the Ripper or the Boston Strangler, or whatever. That about makes it complete, doesn't it?'

CHAPTER 8

*S*imon and Georgie walked hand in hand along a windswept Collaroy Beach towards Narrabeen. Although late September, the southerly wind was cold, the accompanying bleak, overcast clouds smattering the coast with the occasional gusty shower. A few surfboard riders were taking advantage of a small but consistent surf, the waves protected from the wind by the distant bulwark of Long Reef. For the first time in months Simon appeared relaxed, the leave Sergeant Mathieson had fortuitously arranged proving a perfect tonic for his current dejected state of mind.

'And have you and Noel decided on just what you're going to do to become baddies?' Georgie asked matter of factly. 'I suppose the list of things you could do is endless, burglary, blackmail, extortion, robbery.'

'No, not really,' replied Simon, as he picked up a stick and stabbed a beached bluebottle. 'Your idea of a bank job seems to be the most feasible, or appropriate, if there's a word for such a decision. With so many ifs and buts to be considered, it will take a good lot of thinking to do it properly, and it's not until you start thinking about it that you realise just how difficult it would be. And don't forget, the object of the exercise is to discredit Rosie. Somehow I think it's a case of easier said than done.'

'What's so difficult about robbing a bank? From what I've seen on the telly, it all seems very easy. "Stick 'em up mister, this is a heist. Hand over your cash and nobody will get hurt". What's so difficult about that?' questioned Georgie.

Simon tossed the stick into the surf only to see a wave wash it back onto the beach. He turned to Georgie and smiled, 'Georgie, I have this vague idea that robbing a bank isn't quite so simplistic. For starters, which bank do we rob? If we choose just any old bank, Rosey will delegate the job to someone down the line and he'll have no involvement in the investigation. No, we have to select a bank where we know Rosey will be directed to conduct the investigation himself, or at least have his hands on the case.'

'You haven't spoken to Noel about this?'

'No. He's getting himself organised to go back to general duties and I still have some time off that will give me a chance to do some thinking.' Simon picked up the stick and threw it back into the surf, this time choosing to ignore the results.

'Well, have you any ideas?' asked Georgie, pulling the hood of her jacket over her head as another squall of gusty rain blew along the coast.

'Not really, 'though I do recall Chief Superintendent Paxton used to play golf with some bigwig from the Bank of New South Wales. I don't know whether he still does, but it may be something to work on. If we did rob a bank within our baili-wick that had a connection with Paxton, you could bet your life he would oversee the investigation, probably giving it to Rose to conduct. I'll ask Noel to see if he can find out if Paxton still plays golf with the banking boffin.'

They turned, having just passed Shipmates, one of the few high-rise residential buildings on the Collaroy to Narrabeen strip of coast, and started back towards Collaroy. Georgie took Simon's hand and snuggled against him as the cold southerly wind continued to whip along the beach. Even the seagulls had given up any thought of taking to the sky, preferring to nestle into the sand for some protection against the blustery conditions.

'So, if we knock off this bank that belongs to Paxton's friend, we assume, or hope, Paxton will direct Rose to conduct the investigation,' said Georgie, trying to foresee some of the ifs and buts. 'And what about Fisher? He stands between Paxton and Rose, so wouldn't he be involved?'

'Yes, he would be,' replied Simon. 'But Fisher's too senior to do the hack work, and I've yet to see him get his hands dirty. An investigation would normally be conducted by an inspector, and in this case we hope a chief inspector. We'll get Noel and Sue over on the weekend to have a chat and see what we come up with. If we're turning to bad guys, it's time we made up our minds just how bad we want to be.'

Typical of Sydney weather, by the Sunday afternoon the wind and rain brought by the cold southerly had cleared to be replaced with mild conditions and temperatures more commonly expected for September. Noel and Sue had driven over to Collaroy from Mona Vale just after lunch for the meeting that would probably decide the imminent future of the two couples.

'You were right, Simon,' said Noel after he had made himself comfortable next to Sue on the three-seater sofa in the Webster lounge room. 'Old Paxton has the occasional round of golf with a bloke named Howard Milner. Turns out he's head of one of the departments within the head office of the Bank of New South Wales in George Street, you know, the one that looks up Martin Place. Seems they're both on the committee of some charity organization and tend to concentrate their business towards the more affluent in society.'

'Well, that is interesting,' mused Simon. 'I think that may be very helpful.'

Sue looked and Georgie with an inquisitive look only to receive an "I haven't a clue" shrug of the shoulders. 'You have something planned, Simon?' asked Sue, raising her eyebrows.

Simon, sitting in his large comfortable lounge chair, pursed his lips, folded his hands on his lap and arched his thumbs together. 'Well, it would be a rare job to go and rob the Head Office of one of the biggest banks in the country. Be that as it may, I think it would be a great idea and I've always had this wild fantasy of how to do it. But before we start throwing around any notions on the hows, whens and whys, we have to decide if we want to rob a bank. All in favour?'

Three hands went up simultaneously. 'Well, I'm all for it,' said Georgie as she uncurled her legs from underneath herself and rose from the chair opposite Simon. 'Just one thing,' she said and sat back down. 'I take it Sue and I will be involved in whatever you plan to do?'

'If Noel thinks for one minute he's going to rob a bank without me going along with him, he's nuts,' rebuked Sue before Noel had a chance to open his mouth.

'Hey girls, calm down, okay,' entreated Simon. 'There's no question as to whether you'll be involved or not. Do you think my little bank robbery fantasy would be a fantasy without beautiful women being involved? Noel, you seem very quiet on the subject. Any thoughts?'

'I think it's a great idea, to rob a bank, I mean. It's just that I had this stupid notion it would be some small, out of the way bank, like the one at Mona Vale, not the Head Office in the middle of Sydney.'

Simon shook his head and smiled. 'Noel, I know it's a bit of a disappointment for you, but you ain't Jessie James and we're not knocking off a Wells Fargo Bank in Dodge City. Okay, so we've agreed to rob a bank, but we must not lose sight of the fact that we are not robbing a bank for the pecuniary advantage. We're doing it to try and stuff Chief Inspector Rose's career, as he's stuffed ours.'

'Damn,' said Noel and immediately received a friendly punch of admonishment from Sue, sitting beside him.

Georgie got up from her chair and crossed to the kitchen door before turning. 'Come on Sue, let's organise some coffee and bikkies while the boys plan the heist.'

Noel stretched and gave a yawn before kicking off his sneakers and putting his feet up on the sofa. 'So, by doing a job in the middle of Sydney, you think Chief Superintendent Paxton will get all bitter and twisted, especially if it's his mate's bank that's been robbed?'

Simon folder his arms and hunched his shoulders in a shrug of uncertainty. 'Well, the bank's in the Day Street response area and I'm counting on Paxton being involved from the start, only if it's to appoint an investigating officer, hopefully Rose. I don't think he would pass the investigation to Fisher, he and Fisher don't get on too well, which is understandable.'

'No, it's strange, isn't it?' replied Noel, who was now comfortable ensconced on the sofa. 'We don't like Rose, Rosey doesn't like us, Fisher loves Rosey, Rosey crawls to Fisher, Fisher seems to keep a low profile with Paxton and I think Paxton sees Rosey much like we do. It's all terribly unhealthy. At least you're on leave for a while and won't be going back to Day

Street, thanks to Sergeant Mathieson, and I'm out of that clique and pounding the beat.'

At that moment Sue and Georgie entered the lounge room carrying all the essentials required for a tea party. 'Noel, get your feet of the sofa,' scolded Sue as she set a tray on the coffee table before pushing Noel's feet out of the way to sit beside him. 'And have you got it all planned out yet?' asked Sue with more than a hint of sarcastic expectation.

'No,' replied Noel, 'we were waiting for the attendance of your astute and perceptive brains before we got down to the finer points, if that's okay? Now, are we ready to proceed?'

'Ah, for Christ sake, cut the crap and get on with it,' commanded Georgie as she sat down with a cup of coffee and two Monte Carlos. 'Come on, Simon, let's hear your fantasy, and not the one you told me last night.'

CHAPTER 9

*S*imon always believed in the sayings "keep it simple, stupid", and "cow-poo baffles brains". Put these two sayings together, add Simon's bank robbing fantasy and the mixture is one that would, in all probability, hold the attention of a captive audience.

'To begin with,' said Simon leaning forward in his chair, elbows on knees and hands clasped, 'now we've decided to do a bank job, we must get it right as we can't afford to be caught. The life expectancy of a policeman in jail is not long.'

'Amen to that,' broke in Noel. 'But let's be positive. We have a fair idea of how the police will go about the investigation so that puts us in the driver's seat. Now, about this fantasy of yours, Simon?'

Simon settled himself back in his chair, the hint of a smirk on his face. 'There are two attributes the police never seem to acknowledge in an investigation and yet they are attributes they possess in abundance.'

'And they are?' interjected Georgie who had never heard her

husband mention these qualities with which Simon would, no doubt, be endowed.

'Simplicity and stupidity, the two things police never consider,' replied Simon.

Georgie nodded, a smile on her face. 'I'll vouch for that. How does Noel stack up, Sue?'

'Definitely. Simon has described Noel to a T,' returned Sue, putting a placatory hand on Noel's knee. 'Don't worry, sweetie, I still love you. So, Simon, now we have the foundations for a bank job that's to be simple and stupid. It sounds like you're anxious to get to the slammer at Long Bay.'

Simon shook his head vigorously. 'No, no, no. The more complex the job, the more there is to go wrong, and the police look for the complex, it seems to satisfy their ego. My idea, or fantasy if you like, is to rob a bank, without the cash ever leaving the bank. That's why the Head Office of the Bank of New South Wales in George Street would be an ideal target.'

'Now this I've got to hear,' said Noel scratching the back of his head. 'Rob a bank and the cash never leaves the bank. Somehow I don't think that amounts to a robbery having been committed at all.'

'Please let me explain and the simplicity will become evident,' replied Simon. First of all, the bank itself. If I remember correctly, the bank's safe deposit boxes are located downstairs via an entrance right at the front door to the main banking chamber. The whole idea is, we rob one of the tellers and stash the cash in one of the bank's own safe deposit boxes.'

'You're going to rob, okay, *we're* going to rob the bank and put the money into one of the bank's own safe deposit boxes?' Georgie asked, a look of incredulity on her face.

'Why not? Who's going to look there?' said Simon simply. 'Apart from that, the more simplistic it is, the greater fool our Rosey will make of himself, hopefully.'

'Yes,' exclaimed Noel, 'simplicity and stupidity it is. And just how do we get the cash from the teller to the safe deposit?'

'Basically, we'll do a switch and handover job; that's where the girls will come into it. Noel and I will do the actual heist and the girls will do the cash stashing,' said Simon, with an air of excitement in his voice. The thought that they had finally reached the stage where the actual planning of a bank robbery was being considered prompted unexpected enthusiasm and excitement throughout the group of prospective bandits. Not the last person to exhibit these sentiments was Simon who was enjoying the unique opportunity to display an initiative for so long repressed by the seniority, notably Chief Inspector Damien Rose.

'It sounds like the actual robbery will require a lot of co-ordination and timing, even choreographed,' said Sue who, up to this point, had remained silent.

Simon nodded. 'Yes, and that's a good way to express it. The actual cash handover must be perfectly timed and executed otherwise we're really headed for Long Bay. Apart from the timing of the cash hand-over, I thought Noel and I would use a planned anti Vietnam march along George Street for our get-away so, again, our timing needs to be spot on. Noel, you need to find out the timings for the next march. Georgie, I want you to open an account and become one of their regular customers, at least to the extent the tellers recognise you. Sue, you have a look at the safe deposit area. You can even take out a safe deposit box, and make it about the size of a large corn flakes package. I know the boxes come in all sorts of sizes but we'll have a specific size requirement.'

'Why so specific on the size?' Sue asked.

'Well,' replied Simon, 'what if you took out a box too small for all the cash we're going to rob? That could prove rather embarrassing. A corn flakes packet should just about hold all the notes we'll be ripping off one of the tellers. Look, let's call it quits just now and do whatever we have to do. I suggest we all go and have a look at the bank, at different times, so we know the lay out. I've no doubt we will need a few meetings to get everything sorted and the whole thing choreographed, as Sue put it. Apart from that, Noel and I need to figure out how to actually rob a bank teller. Any questions?'

It was more than a week later before Simon called for the next meeting, many of the problems and unknowns relating to the proposed robbery having been addressed. Noel and Sue arrived at the West Bank Lane bungalow after dinner on the Tuesday evening to find Georgie had already made coffee, tea and snacks in anticipation of a long night. Simon, as the tacit leader of the group, had decreed that all discussion would be dry until after the event.

'Right,' said Simon as he pushed himself back into his favourite lounge chair. 'Let's get this underway as we have a stack to talk about. Georgie, you've opened a bank account?'

'Yes. I thought they would need stacks of identification but you were right; they didn't even ask. Seems the banks are eager to sign up anybody. There was no problem in obtaining a couple of the bank's cash bags either. I just asked the helpful teller for a couple and he handed them over. They're white calico with BNSW stamped in black on the side. I also took the opportunity to suss out the banking chamber and the safe deposit area.'

Simon smiled and nodded. 'Yes, I thought you wouldn't have problems with identification. There's so much competition and with so many banks around at the moment, one of these days the bigger banks will buy off the smaller ones, so all the banks are trying to expand their customer base and share market price as much as possible before that happens. Sue, how'd you go?'

'You were right. The entrance to the safe deposit box area is just inside the main door to the bank and just outside the main entrance to the banking chamber. There are actually two doors, the main door to the street which gives access to the bank's vestibule, and another door leading from the vestibule into the banking chamber. There's a stairway leading from the vestibule down to the safe deposit box facility. I made a few enquiries then arranged for a box about the size of a weeties packet. I have one key and they kept one. You need two keys to open the box, so the bank attendant unlocks his and then leaves you to it.'

'I hope you didn't give them your real name and address,' said Simon.

Sue shook her head and made a face. 'Come on Simon, all they needed was a signature. The very nature of safe deposit boxes is to maintain anonymity. See, I have done my homework.'

'Right.' Simon took a deep breath, clasped his hands behind his head and stretched. 'I'll go through how I envisage we go about the robbery. If there are any glaring blunders, please point them out straight away because a minor hiccup could have dire consequences. Basically, the idea is Noel and I go to the furthest teller from the main door to the bank and I rob him of all his ten-pound notes. The teller places the notes into one of the cash bags and gives it to me. I slide the bag down behind the counter where Noel takes it and hands me a cash bag full of scrap paper. We then head down the banking chamber towards the front door. Noel accidently bumps into Georgie who is currently heading out of the bank after doing some of her own banking. She's carrying a similar looking cash bag which only contains scrap paper. During this brief encounter, another switch is made meaning Georgie now has the money bag while

Noel and I each carry a bag full of scrap paper. Hopefully, anyone taking any notice of us will think both bags contain cash. Meanwhile, Georgie heads towards the front door and makes another switch with Sue who drops the money-containing bag into a briefcase and immediately heads for the safe deposit area.'

'Now just back up a bit,' said Noel as he swung his feet off the sofa where he and Sue had been lounging. 'Why the teller furthest from the front door?'

'Because,' replied Simon, 'you and I will be dressed in opposites, me in black trousers and dark blue shirt, you in dark blue trousers and a black shirt. Not necessarily those colors, but you get the general idea. We will both be wearing wigs, one black and the other blond. The idea is that people generally only recall what they think they see, so dressing like that will cause a whole number of different witness reports.'

Noel nodded in acceptance. 'And you've mentioned the size of the safe deposit box. Is that why we rob the teller of his tenners?'

'Yes. Enough of those to fill a corn flakes box, or whatever, will amount to quite a large sum of money.'

Sue frowned, a dubious look on her face. 'Okay, so you and Noel walk up to the teller and ask him for all his tenners, just like that?'

'No, not really. I'll have to produce an incentive for him to hand over the cash,' replied Simon.

'And that incentive?' Sue asked although anticipating the likely answer.

'Okay, I'll produce a gun, obviously a replica but the teller won't know that.'

The frown deepened on Sue's face. 'All right, the teller won't know it's a replica, but neither will the security guard sitting halfway down the banking chamber. He's got a real gun and if he sees you with some sort of pop-gun, replica or real, he might come out shooting.'

'Woooa. Just stop there.' It was Georgie intervening with her usual flare for the dramatic. 'No guns, replicas, real or otherwise. Once you start using guns you're inviting trouble.'

'Totally agree,' said Noel. We'll have bought ourselves enough trouble just robbing a bank in the first place. Let's not compound the problem by turning it into an armed hold-up.'

Simon turned to Sue. 'Sue?'

'Gangsters and thugs need guns. We can rob the bank with brains, not guns.'

'Okay,' conceded Simon. 'No guns.'

Before the conversation continued, Georgie got up and said, 'anyone for another brew?'

'Cripes, I thought you'd never ask,' said Noel. Within a few minutes Georgie, with Sue's help, had organised the brews while Noel and Simon chattered about Noels current employment; back in uniform and plodding the beat. 'Thanks Georgie,' said Noel as he took a mug of coffee. 'You know, I think I've seen enough Vietnam demonstrations to last a life time,' he said with a sigh. 'And half the people who turn up wouldn't know what they're demonstrating for, even if they are university students or members of the CPA, which most appear to be. We're used for crowd control and to make sure it doesn't get out of hand. Special Branch seems to be more surreptitiously involved, taking photos and hauling away known agitators.'

'Well, let's hope the demonstration march along George Street will be heavily patronized and noisy as we'll join them after we've robbed the bank. You have a date and time for this march yet?' asked Simon.

Noel nodded and said, 'Yes, it's on 14 October starting at two o'clock. They'll be marching from The Quay, along George

Street to the Town Hall where they'll hold a demonstration. That okay?'

'Sounds fine,' said Simon. 'That's a week before LBJ arrives in Sydney so everything will be so chaotic no-one will notice a simple little bank robbery.'

'You mean we actually have a date for our robbery?' asked Sue with excitement.

'Looks like it,' replied Simon, not knowing whether to be pleased or alarmed at the prospect of becoming a bank robber.

'If that's the case,' said Georgie as she placed her empty coffee mug on the table, 'I think we need to choreograph these cash switches and accidental collision we'll be doing.'

'Well, don't plan it for tomorrow,' said Simon. 'I'm heading off to Canterbury for some therapeutic gambling on the neddies. The only other thing we have to give some thought to is a rendezvous after we all clear the bank. Can I suggest we take a room at the Menzies for the night of the fourteenth and all meet back there?'

'Sounds like a good idea,' said Georgie. 'Sue, why don't you and Noel stay the night in town as well? I'm sure we'll all need a night of relaxation and a drop of wine after robbing a bank.'

CHAPTER 10

*S*imon didn't go to the races very often but when he did, he preferred the mid-week events held at Canterbury Race Course. The crowds were never huge and he found it far more relaxing than the bustle of the Saturday meetings at Randwick or Rose Hill. He took the train to Canterbury and arrived at the course a little before midday. After buying a ticket to The Paddock area, along with the obligatory race book and pencil, Simon wandered the betting ring taking in the odds of the runners in the first event to be run at twelve-forty. He enjoyed the atmosphere, the bookies barking the odds, the pencillers madly scrawling their incomprehensible scribble on the betting cards while the bookies' clerks recorded the details of each bet on their large pads.

After collating the details of all the runners and their jockeys, and taking into account the respective odds, Simon made his decision and placed a bet with a slight-framed bookie who, for some unknown reason, reminded Simon of Fred Astair. Having pocketed his betting ticket, Simon retreated from the betting ring and soon made his way to one of the numerous bars to be found at the course where, after buying a middy of beer, he settled back to watch humanity pass by.

'You got the big wheels out today, Simon?'

Simon turned to find the question had come from a small balding man aged in his forties, with dark friendly brown eyes and a face hardened by an outdoor lifestyle. His dress, which consisted of a pair of dark grey slacks, a beige open neck shirt and a brown sports coat, was neatly tailored and well fitting. It was unfortunately the gentleman wearing the attire was one of those people you could dress in a tuxedo and he would still look untidy.

Simon's face broke into a broad grin as he recognised the man. 'Ron, long time no see. You been keeping out of trouble lately?' Ron was Ron Lange, with the emphasis on the "e". As far as Simon was aware, Ron had been involved in petty crime for most of his life and could generally be found at any of the city race or trot meetings. Although a petty criminal, he was considered by police as harmless and, at times, had furnished the Force with valuable information relating to underworld activities. In truth, there was very little going on that Ron wasn't aware of, and if he wasn't, he had the resources to find out in very quick time.

'Of course. I'm squeaky clean now. After that last stretch I vowed I'd never go back. But I s'pose that means I don't intend to get caught again, right?' said Ron with a laugh. 'Hey, buy us a beer and tell me what's going on.'

'Helen, another middy, no, better make that a schooner, thanks love. Helen was a forty something bottled blond who had been serving behind the same bar at the course since God knows when. She smiled at Simon and gave a wink in acknowledgement. 'Now, what do you mean by "what's going on?"' asked Simon as Helen placed the schooner on the bar.

'Thanks, here's cheers,' said Ron, as he picked up the

schooner and took a long draught. Simon watched in horror as he realised the afternoon could become very expensive if Ron downed all his beers in the same fashion. He finally put the glass down and wiped his mouth with the back of his hand. 'Like, you being here. Sure, it's good to see you again, but I didn't expect to see you on a Wednesday, not with your Chief out here as well. There must be somethin' goin' on.'

'What, you mean Chief Inspector Rose is here, at the track?'

Ron nodded. 'Sure is. Saw him earlier. He was down talking to one of the rails bookies. Didn't say hello though as he seemed preoccupied. He comes here regularly, not every Wednesday, but often enough. I think he lives out this way somewhere.' Already Ron had provided Simon with the answer to the Wednesday afternoon conundrum of Chief Inspector Rose's whereabouts.

Simon shook his head in annoyance. 'Look, if you see him again, don't mention you've seen me. I've got a couple of days leave left before I head off to Cronulla and I'd prefer not to have him looking for me.'

'Sure thing,' said Ron. 'I heard you and your sergeant had both been dirked by your boss. Can't say I'm surprised.'

'What do you mean, you're not surprised?' asked Simon, his interest piqued.

'It's a long story, so buy me anotherie and I'll start at the beginning.'

Simon nodded to Helen, held up two fingers in the victory solute and dropped six shillings onto the bar.

Ron found a vacant table and drew up two bar stools. After putting the beers down, Simon turned to Ron and said, 'Before you start, you asked me what was going on. To be honest Ron, I haven't a clue. Both Noel, my sergeant, and I can't help feeling something's not right in the state of Norway but we don't know what that something is.'

'Denmark,' replied Ron

'What about Denmark?' Simon, who never liked Shakespeare while at school, was a little confused.

Ron smiled and shook his head. 'Doesn't matter. Just relax and I might be able to shed a little light on what you think you don't know,' a broad grin breaking his weather-beaten face. 'To begin with, it seems your boss's horse gambling is bankrolled now and then by your own CIB slush fund. I believe you have this fund for, how shall I put it, buying information from certain people willing to sell what they know, or at least pay people for a particular service rendered. You blokes wouldn't get anywhere without the bad guys selling their bits of info, you know that. Of course, it's all done on the hush hush as people can get a bit stroppy when they're ratted on. Still, a man has to make a living.'

'You're telling me Detective Chief Inspector Damien Rose helps himself to Police Force funds to finance his gambling habits?' asked Simon. 'Before you answer, Helen, I'll have a schooner myself this time, so make it two thanks.'

'Hey, it's not like he does it every day. The frequency of his attendance at the course might coincide with the topping up of the fund, but I wouldn't know about that.'

'I wouldn't be surprised if you did,' responded Simon with a wry smile. 'You seem to know everything else that's going on in the place.'

'Anyway, getting back to the story,' said Ron after finishing off the last of a schooner of beer and reaching for the fresh one. 'He goes and sees his mate, the rails bookie I saw him talking to earlier. Apparently this bookie gets inside information from a stable hand who then passes it on to Rosey. Rosey doesn't bet with the rails bookies, they're a bit out of his league, but once he has the good oil, he'll lay a few hundred quid, which he plainly can't afford on his salary. Hence the slush fund.'

The further the story went, the more Simon became confused. 'I take it Rose has something on this particular bookie for the bookie to be doing what he's doing, if you can understand that?'

Ron shrugged. 'I don't know the exact reason, but I believe Rosey did the bloke a favour, kept him out of jail for some reason or another. I don't know how long it will go on for, but it's been going on for some time now. Seems the info is pretty good as Rosey usually wins and has time to replace the police funds before they're missed. Trouble with Rosey is that he never builds up a bank to support his punting. As soon as he wins, he's off to The Taipan Club up in Forbes Street. He likes baccarat, though I can't understand why. Baccarat is a high rollers game and you can lose your money pretty quickly.' Ron scoffed the last of his beer and smacked his lips. 'Gees, that beer goes down well.'

'Helen.' Simon raised another two fingers then turned back to Ron. 'And does he ever win?'

'What, on the horses or at the casino? I don't suppose it matters as he'll lose at both in the long run. No-one can win all the time. Sure, he's doing all right at the moment, he wins enough on the nags to pay back the slush fund and have a few bob in his pocket to play the tables. But he's playing a dangerous game because one of these days the bookie will get it wrong and he won't be able to pay back the money he's temporarily removed before it's discovered missing.'

'Does anyone else know what's going on?' asked Simon, appalled at what he was hearing.

'Rumour has it your Superintendent Fisher knows. But that's the odd thing. If the Super does know, he's in a position to take Rosey down, but he hasn't, yet. Of course, the question must be, why not? Just maybe, and it's a very big maybe, someone is paying him off so he won't take any action against either Rosey or the casino. And just by sheer bloody coincidence, Fisher, unbeknownst to Rosey, is a regular visitor to The Taipan Club.'

Simon, struggling to keep pace with Ron's revelations, was endeavoring to sort the information into some sort of order, and failing dismally. 'You're telling me Superintendent Fisher is being paid by the owner of an illegal casino to turn a blind eye?'

'Hey, hang on. I'm not saying he *is* being paid, just might be being paid. Even so, the owner of the Taipan Club, where Fisher has been seen more than a few times, must feel pretty cocky having a superintendent of police as a patron. Funny thing is, I hear Fisher doesn't play the tables, so who knows what he's up to,' replied Ron with a broad grin.

'So, let's assume Fisher does know what Rosey's game is but chooses not to do anything about it,' said Simon, a look on concerted concentration on his face. 'Do you think Rosey knows if Fisher knows?'

Ron shrugged. 'He might as anything is possible, but I'd say probably not. You see, Rosey thinks he has Fisher eating out of his hand, and that Fisher is a sandwich short of a picnic. Fisher is happy to let Rosey think whatever he likes as Fisher's really in control of the situation. He doesn't have to do anything, just take a bit off the top from the casino, if he is receiving a kick-back, that is. Fisher believes the CIB hierarchy can't, and won't, find anything untoward going on. If what I hear is correct, your report on illegal gambling may have been illuminating at the top echelons, but it was binned before it got that high.'

'Hey, how'd you know about that?' said Simon suitably miffed.

'Come on, Simon, you know better than to ask a question like that,' responded Ron with a hurt look on his face. 'But getting back to the story. Irrespective of what's going on, I think Fisher wants to keep things as they are, you know, maintain the status quo. Seems his income from his salary doesn't quite match his expenses at the moment, but don't tell his wife that.'

'So, what you're saying is that Fisher must be supplementing his salary?' asked Simon, the look of stunned surprise now permanently etched on his face.

'Certainly looks like it and that would lend credence to the casino kickback theory,' replied Ron casually. 'You see, Fisher and his old lady have been married some twenty years now, and with his promotion to superintendent, Agnes, his wife, firmly believed the promotion automatically pushed them a few rungs up the social ladder, which I suppose it should, to some extent, anyway. Trouble is, Agnes likes to be seen in the presence of the "A List" people, you know, the best restaurants, social gatherings, fund raising events, those sorts of things, all of which cost money. Naturally it's easy for the real "A Listers", they have money whereas Agnes doesn't, and never will while hubby's a policeman. Maybe if he ever made commissioner, but he won't,' Ron reflected.

Simon sighed and rested his chin on his fist, his elbow on the table. 'So, we're supposed to feel sorry for Fisher who's not paid enough to keep his wife in the manner she clearly expects to become accustomed?'

'Good God no,' responded Simon. 'We're all in the same boat. Most of us try to make do with what we've got without trying to skim a little more through nefarious means.'

'Hang on, Ron. You're telling me that if you had a regular salary, you wouldn't do anything untoward to supplement that income, albeit through illegal means?' Simon asked with the sudden thought Ron may not necessarily be the shady person he thought he was.

Ron ignored the question only to tap the side of his nose with a forefinger and give a sly smile. 'There's more than one reason we shouldn't feel sorry for Fisher. While Agnes has her social life, so does Fisher. He's not into gambling, per se, but he does like the women who do, and that means the casinos and Randwick Race Course, mainly for the bigger events when the socialites come out of the woodwork. Agnes talked him into becoming a member of the AJC and she loves to be seen in the members' enclosure; who wouldn't? As I said earlier, Fisher is a patron of a casino but doesn't gamble. Well, I suppose he does in a way, but when he wins it's certainly not money.'

'Good grief,' exclaimed Simon. 'So, Fisher is stuffing around on his wife at the same time?'

'Yes, it seems so,' replied Ron, mater of factly. 'So you see, we have Rosey addicted to gambling and couldn't give it up even if he wanted to, and Fisher taking a kickback from an illegal casino, maybe. But even if Rosey knows what Fisher is up to, there's not much he can do about it without declaring his own little indiscretion. I think it a safe bet that, irrespective of who knows what about the other person, neither Rosey nor Fisher will say anything and would prefer to keep it that way. In any case, Rosey wouldn't be capable of compiling enough evidence against Fisher to make it stick. And let's face it, Rosey isn't doing that much wrong; just borrowing from a police fund. Geeze, that beer was good,' exclaimed Ron draining his glass.

"Well, I hope you're pleased with yourself. You've well and truly stuffed my quiet afternoon of relaxation. One question. You needn't have told me any of this, so why did you?' queried Simon, a frown on his face.

'Oh, that's easy. I heard you've been posted down to Cronulla, which isn't a career enhancing move. You can bet your life Rose and Fisher are behind that, both with a different motive, Rose because of long standing antagonism between you two, and Fisher because your report on illegal gambling was probably too close to home.'

'The whole thing's ludicrous, but I appreciate it, Ron. I can't see that I can do anything about it but it's nice to know both of those turkeys have a weak spot. Maybe I can use it one day.'

'Sorry about trashing your day for you, but you did ask. If ever you want another chat, you know where to find me,' said Ron and waved his hand in a friendly farewell.

With that, Ron vanished into the crowd leaving Simon pondering the conversation. Christ, as if I haven't enough on my plate as it is, he thought. Simon sat for a few minutes going over what Ron had told him and, on reflection, it started to make a modicum of sense, the more he thought about it the clearer the picture became. 'Well, I'll be buggered, no wonder my report was trashed,' he said to himself. He nodded to Helen, grabbed a stool against the bar and settled himself to watch the first race that had been run and won some twenty minutes earlier.

CHAPTER 11

*I*t was night time. Noel, Sue, and Georgie sat around the Webster's dining room table while Simon organised four mugs of coffee. It was planned that this would be the last meeting before the four attempted to conduct a robbery of the Head Office of the Bank of New South Wales in George Street, Sydney. Discussion, so far, had covered a multitude of topics, none of them pertaining to the purpose for which the meeting had been called. The main topic of idle chatter was, as usual, the Vietnam War and whether we should be participating or not. Everyone had a point of view and the conflict was the focal point of many violent demonstrations, some even led by politicians. To break the impasse, Simon raised his voice and said, 'Well, are we ready to rob a bank, or not?'

'Hallelujah, at least someone hasn't forgotten why we're here,' Georgie declared, a trifle exasperated by the chit chat when there were far more exciting things to talk about.

'Okay, okay, keep your shirt on, woman,' chided Simon, raising his hands in submission. 'Georgie, how have you been getting on doing some banking there?'

'Fine. I've been in a few times and made some deposits. I've got to know some of the tellers, by sight I mean, and also the guard, old Charlie, who usually sits on a chair half way down the banking chamber. I've spoken to him a couple of times and, although he has a pistol on his belt, I think he'd have a heart attack if he ever had to use it. Oh yes, I bought in a couple of the cash bags to show you what they look like.' Georgie removed the bags from a beach bag she had next to her and placed them on the table.

'Sue, your turn,' said Simon

'I've been in a couple of times and have got to know Adam, the head supervisor downstairs. I thought it a good idea to get into his good books just in case we're pushed for time to lodge the cash. I've no doubt the bank will slam the front door shut once they realise they've been robbed, and I don't want to be caught holding a bag full of stolen ten-pound notes.'

'Good point,' exclaimed Simon with admiration. 'Noel and I have worked out our dress and we've even bought a couple of wigs. It doesn't matter people can tell they're wigs, it's just to add a little to the confusion. Once we do the handover of the cash to you Georgie, we'll head outside the bank and join the demonstration that should be marching up George Street, if our timing's right. During the march we'll discard most of the iden-tifiable dress; with the rabble going on, nobody will take any notice, we hope. When we get to Town Hall, we'll catch a train back to Wynyard and go up to Menzies Hotel.

'Anyone for more coffee?' asked Simon, looking at the three others in expectation. 'Noel, come and give us a hand to organise this.'

Noel didn't have to be asked twice as he knew instinctively his boss, or ex boss, wanted a word. Having reached the kitchen, Simon filled the electric water jug, switched it on then turned to Noel. 'Noel, I had an interesting talk to a bloke while at the races yesterday. It involves Rosey and Fisher, and it's not squeaky clean. I'm not due back at Day Street until Monday week and, with any luck, I'll have at least another week there before Cronulla. I'll get in touch with you and we'll organise a brew up on George Street and I'll fill you in. Noel nodded and restrained from asking questions now his inquisitive nature had been piqued.

On returning to the dining room, it was Georgie who reopened the conversation. 'Simon, just confirming, it is the teller at the far end of the chamber, furthest from the front door that you propose to rob?'

'Yes,' replied Simon. 'Is there anything wrong with that?'

'No, it's just that the teller there couldn't be much more than twenty years old and it looks like he's been on the counter for no more than five minutes. He's certainly not confident in handling cash at this stage, but I s'pose he has to learn somewhere.'

'Well, that's all the better. He shouldn't give us any trouble then,' said Noel.

Georgie stretched back on her chair and clasped her hands behind her head. 'And what do you propose to do when you're his next customer. Just ask him to hand over all his ten-pound notes, just like that?'

Simon pursed his lips and frowned. 'Well, yes, I suppose I will.'

'Oh, I see, said Georgie skeptically. 'All bluff. You hope to scare the little bugger into handing over all his tenners?'

'Well, how would you do it, smarty-pants? We've decided on no guns, and I agree with that. Hell, the last thing we want is old Charlie Rambo blasting away with a six gun or having a coronary,' Simon replied.

'Who's Rambo, anyway?' asked Sue enquiringly.

'Don't worry about it, I was referring to the security guard,' replied Simon shaking his head. 'So, apart from us all having to remember what role we are taking in this little venture, is there anything else we need to do or consider before we turn to a life of crime?' he asked before adopting a serious look and awaited the inevitable response. When none was forthcoming, he heaved a sigh and relaxed back into his chair as if a great weight had been taken from his shoulders.

CHAPTER 12

'*G*ood morning, sir. May I be of assistance?' Georgie had been right. The teller behind the counter couldn't have been much more than twenty years old, immaculately dressed in a dark grey suit, and wearing a pair of metal framed spectacles. His physical stature couldn't prevent Simon thinking that here was the skinny kid at the beach who had sand kicked in his face by Brutus in his attempt to impress Olive. Simon felt a twinge of contrition, aware that the lad was going to be confronted, in the very near future, by two resolute bank robbers with a demand for his cash.

'Yes, I think you may be able to help,' said Simon with a confidence that belied his nervous state. 'You haven't been on the counter for very long, have you?'

'No,' replied the teller. 'I've only been on for a couple of weeks, but it's working out really well,' he said proudly. 'The accountant, Mr Grimble, says I will probably be appointed permanently as a teller. You see, I'm on probation just at the moment to see if it works out.'

'Well, we certainly hope it turns out well for you, don't we

No…Norman?' said Simon turning to his associate, his embarrassment already evident with his face taking on a bright shade of pink, a monumental blunder having been averted, just.

Noel, or Norman, turned to Simon then back to the teller. 'Yes, we hope you do real well.' Noel, looking a trifle annoyed, leaned closer to Simon. 'For Christ sake, get on with it. This isn't supposed to be a social call,' he whispered.

'Ah yes, to business. Look, you're a young bloke with good career prospects, and the rest of your life in front of you. Now, if I was to say to you, just for argument sake, that I had a gun in my pocket pointing directly at your chest, and asked you to hand over all your ten-pound notes, what would you do?'

Neither Simon nor Noel had given much thought to the possible response from the teller, once confronted. Irrespective of their expectations, the reply they received would most likely never have been considered. The teller looked thoughtful as he removed his spectacles and started to clean them with a small white cloth. After a few more seconds of deliberation, he replaced them on his thin, pale face, looked at Simon and said with calm alacrity, 'Well now, that presents us with a conundrum. If you were to say you had a gun pointing at me, I'd probably do what you wanted and hand over the money you asked for. But as you haven't said that you do have a gun pointing directly at me, the question is purely hypothetical, isn't it?'

The two aspiring bank robbers could not quite believe what they were hearing; to both bandits, the question posed was succinct and to the point, requiring a simple response. Obviously, somewhere along the line, the teller had encountered some difficulty in understanding the fundamental gist of the question posed as he continued his analysis. 'Regrettably gentlemen, until you make a definitive statement one way or the other, the best I can do is evaluate the information you have provided, and endeavor to make a calculated assessment of the situation based on that information. Once I have completed an assessment and come to a conclusion, I would need to review that conclusion to determine if some sort of reaction would be necessary on my part. Of course, the very characteristics and nature of the extreme circumstances which you have regrettably prevailed upon me may negate the opportunity to consider the ramifications of any such reaction as you will, no doubt, appreciate.

'So, let's make an arbitrary decision, just for the sake of argument, as you put it. You don't really have a gun and you're trying to deceive me into handing over all my ten-pound notes. Looking at you two gentlemen, with your extraordinary attire and demeanour, which I doubt are typical examples of underworld gangsters, I would, in all probability, take a chance and say you were bluffing. As a consequence, and not wishing to put a finer point on it, I would tell you to get stuffed. However, due to the fact that I place a great value on my life, and considering the fact that I cannot be certain one way or the other if you have a gun or not, I would probably play it safe and accept that you do. Of course, the situation is still at the hypothetical level, so I can only give a hypothetical answer.'

'Oh, for Christ sake. Of all the tellers in the world you had to pick this, this philosophical Einstein. Get on with it,' Noel said, exasperated to distraction.

Simon frowned and dropped the coin bag onto the counter. 'Look here, you stupid boy, just hand over your bloody tenners and nobody will get hurt, okay?'

'Ah, so now we come to the crux of the matter. You're going to rob the bank. Yes, we were told on the last day of our teller's course this might happen once, or at best twice in your career as a teller, and so soon in my career too,' the teller proudly proclaimed.

'Come on, get on with it, just hand over all your tens,'

demanded Noel, who was by now feeling that things weren't going quite to plan.

'Yes, by all means,' replied the teller, who dropped down behind the counter of his teller's box only to quickly reappear with a bundle of ten-pound notes neatly bundled and secured with a rubber band. He continued to disappear and reappear with a rhythmic bobbing action while Simon stuffed the money into the coin bag. Eventually the bag was full, but the teller continued to draw the ten-pound notes from behind the counter. Simon, unable to stuff further notes into the bag suddenly realised that if they took any more, they would be unable to fit them into the safe deposit box, let alone get any more into the cash bag.

'Hold it there, sonny, we have just about all we want,' he said to the teller on one of his bobbing appearances. It was clear the teller hadn't heard Simon's instruction as he continued to pile ten-pound notes onto the counter. 'Look, you imbecile, I just told you, we have enough, thank you very much. We don't want any more of your cash.'

The teller baulked, a bundle of ten-pound notes in each hand, an incredulous look on his face. 'What do you mean, you have enough? You're robbing a bank, and now you say you don't want any more money?'

As the high drama with the teller continued to gain momentum, Georgie and Sue had both independently come to the same conclusion that Noel had arrived at; things were not going according to plan. Georgie, already in the banking chamber and having made a deposit with one of the tellers, started to leave with the expectation the planned sequence of events would unfold, as so often rehearsed. However, instead of a brazen collision with two brutish bank robbers eager to make their getaway, she had made her way through the banking chamber without incident, only to pass Sue eagerly waiting at the top of the stairs to the safe deposit area in anticipation of a bundle of cash being dropped into her briefcase.

As she reached the steps to the George Street footpath, Georgie decided she and Sue should consult as to what they could do about the calamity now developing. As she turned to go back to talk to Sue, Georgie noticed the increasing crowd in George Street as the anti Vietnam War demonstration approached from the direction of Circular Quay. She could see placards held above the crowd demanding the withdrawal of Australian troops and a cessation to Australia's involvement in the war, and hear the chanting and whistle blowing that accompanied the march.

In the meantime, Sue, having decided to take the weight off her feet as she waited patiently for the robbery to get back on track, had taken a seat on one of the stone lion statues that reclined in the bank's vestibule. The thought crossed her mind that it might have been a good idea to have brought a book to keep her occupied as she waited; War and Peace would seem appropriately time consuming in view of the obvious time wasting going on inside the bank.

Somewhat perturbed by the lack of progress in the execution of a simple bank robbery, and the proximity of the anti Vietnam demonstration in George Street, Georgie approached Sue and asked, 'What the hell's going on and what are those two idiots up to? For heaven's sake, how much time do they need to rob a bloody bank? If they don't get a move on, the demonstration will be dead and gone and Simon and Noel will be left looking like a pair of garden gnomes stranded in the middle of George Street.'

'I can see them,' said Sue, as she stood and peered into the banking chamber. 'They seem to be in discussion with the teller, probably talking about football or the weather. How about you go and take a seat in the chamber and keep an eye on the boys. Once they start moving you could start walking towards the door. If anyone ever asks why the delay after your banking business, just say you'd been to the loo. I'll stay here and wait for you to make the drop.'

To the girls, the wait was an eternity. However, at last there was progress as Simon and Noel made their way with feigned nonchalance through the chamber towards the front door, both men carrying identical cash bags, one full of ten-pound notes, the other full of old newspaper. The first exchange of the cash bag had already been successfully completed with Simon passing the bag of tenners to Noel below the counter and out of sight of the teller. Simon was unperturbed, conscious as he was of the many bank customers passing furtive glances at the two gaudily dressed gentlemen making their way through the chamber towards the front door of the bank.

'Oops, sorry love, didn't see you. You okay?' Noel had made contact with Georgie, nearly knocking her off her feet with far more vigor than Georgie had expected.

Georgie turned, a look of anger on her face. 'Bloody lout,' she said, her voice raised in an aggressive verbal attack on the retreating bank customer. 'Next time, why don't you watch where you're going? Bloody men; no manners these days,' she fumed. Having just about vented all her immediate annoyance, Georgie turned and walked from the banking chamber, stopping just outside the entrance to readjust her disheveled dress and comb her hair after the brutal attack by some weird looking idiot.

CHAPTER 13

*D*etective Chief Inspector Damien Rose, dressed in mufti, arrived at the Head Office of the Bank of New South Wales some two hours after the report of an alleged robbery. Local uniformed police and two plain clothed CIB detectives, a sergeant and a constable, had made preliminary enquiries and had established a crime scene. It was from these officers that the Chief received a general outline of events. The sergeant, Sergeant Stuart Romaine, had made an arbitrary decision in selecting a number of witnesses for questioning, all of whom had been present in the banking chamber at the time of the alleged offence, while other witnesses were in the process of making statements to the uniformed police.

There were two significant justifications for Chief Inspector Rose to take control of the investigation. The first was that he was the senior CIB officer present at the crime scene. The second was a not too polite direction issued by the Chief Superintendent, Neville Paxton, to Superintendent Nigel Fisher ordering Fisher to get his senior inspector over to the bank.

Paxton had received a phone call from Howard Milner, head of the Foreign Exchange and Investments office of the bank soon after the robbery, asking Paxton for his personal intervention into the matter. Chief Inspector Rose had dutifully picked up his coat and headed for the crime scene, thus destroying any preconceived ideas he may have had of knocking off early, taking into account it was a Friday afternoon.

On arrival at the bank and surveying the scene, Chief Rose set about making up a list of people he considered may be of help in his investigation, most of those on the list being bank employees. 'Sergeant Romaine, do you know of anyone in particular I should start my questioning?' Detective Chief Inspector Rose asked officiously.

Sergeant Romaine extracted his notebook from his coat pocket and flicked the pages. 'Ah, yes sir. Here it is,' he replied after ceasing to flick. 'There's a Mr Paul Slater who appears to be in charge of things at the bank. He said he'll see you in his office up on the seventh floor. Apparently, he's the Chief Operations Officer and goes under the acronym of The COO. The staff refer to him as The Pigeon, for some unknown reason.'

'Oh, so he'll condescend to see me, will he? That's nice of Mr Slater. Thanks, Sarge, I'll go and see him now. In view of it going on five, I'm anxious to get as many statements before we release the witnesses. Apart from this bloke Slater, I'll talk to the teller and the security guard before calling it quits.'

'Right, sir. I get right back to taking some more statements,' replied Sergeant Romaine, eager to impress a chief inspector.

Entry to Paul Slater's office was policed by a tall, pretentious looking brunet in her mid twenties who sat at a desk strategically positioned beside a large oak door. The sole function of the secretary appeared to be nothing more than to prohibit entrance to the inner sanctum without the credentials of the visitor being thoroughly scrutinised. 'Mr Slater sir, there's a gentleman to see you, a Chief Inspector Rose,' the secretary announced in a very husky voice via a small white intercom system.

'Thanks Sonja. Please show him in.' The secretary stood and gave Chief Rose a look of contemptuous superiority before opening the door to Mr Paul Slater's office. The first thing the Chief noticed on entering was that he was walking on a plush beige carpet. Geez, and I thought I was doing okay when they gave me a mat, he thought as he eyed the voluptuous décor of Mr Slater's office. Apart from the mahogany desk which was at least twice the size of the pine desk located in the Chief's office, all the considerable seating was strictly leather, not a trace of vinyl to be found. Another aspect Chief Rose readily identified was the freshness of the air, a freshness he could never expect at Day Street in light of an air conditioning system that would spring out of action on more occasions than it would spring into action.

After the general salutations had been dispensed with, the COO cordially invited the Chief to take a seat. Detective Chief Inspector Rose, with a spurious cool nonchalance, sat down and folded his arms in an attempt to convey his superiority and dominance over a mere bank clerk. It was probably unfortunate for the Chief that as he settled himself into the leather chair, his pale pink shirt finally yielded to the inexorable strain from within. Nevertheless, Mr Slater, being a man of refinement and good taste, chose to remain silent while trying, with difficulty, to ignore the disconcerting sight of a protruding hairy stomach.

Detective Rose, totally oblivious of his dress malfunction, looked across at the man sitting behind the ornate desk. Paul Slater was a man in his early forties, tall, muscular and immaculately dressed in a dark blue suit, white shirt and a pale blue tie.

He sat back from his desk, his elbows resting on the arm rests of his plushy high back leather chair, his hands together, fingers steepled. 'I really don't know why you should want to talk to me. I've already told the sergeant downstairs all I know, which isn't much. Although I may be the Chief Operations Officer for the branch known as George Street Head Office, I'm also responsible for the operation of all our metropolitan branches. I think you will find the staff on the ground floor will be in a far better position to help you than I am.'

'Yes, I quite understand. We're taking statements now and I'll be conducting some interviews this evening,' replied Chief Rose as he mopped the perspiration from his face with a handkerchief and shifted uncomfortably in his chair. 'However, I believe you have been provided with an internal briefing of the events already.' The comment was a statement, not a question so the COO didn't bother to offer a response.

'You say the teller, what's his name?' The Chief referred to his notebook. 'Ah yes, Bentley, Bruce Bentley. You say he didn't raise the alarm until the robbers had made their getaway?'

'I'm sorry Chief Inspector, but I haven't said anything about the robbery. However, I'm led to believe that the answer to your question is no, that's right. According to all accounts, Bentley was unaware if the robbers were armed or not, so he worked on the assumption that they might be. With all due regard to the situation, he probably did the right thing.' Mr Slater now had his hands folded on his lap, slowly rocking back and forward on his chair.

'You mean, "no, he didn't raise the alarm until after they were gone", or "no, he did raise the alarm before they were gone"?'

'He did not alert anyone of the situation until the robbers had decamped the building,' replied Mr Slater with the sudden feeling he may not be dealing with the most intellectual member of the CIB.

'Getting back to the gun. You say Bentley didn't actually see a gun?'

'Not that I'm aware. Maybe you should speak to Bentley,' replied Mr Slater with a shrug of the shoulders.

'I take it the bank has conducted a cash count to determine how much cash was stolen?'

'Of course. We believe they got away with three thousand two hundred pounds in ten-pound notes. Of course, the bank would ask you not to release that figure to the press as we would prefer to keep it confidential; doesn't do our image any good.'

Chief Inspector Rose raised his eyebrows and, as an afterthought, asked, 'You didn't happen to witness the robbery?'

'Good lord, no. You don't think I'd work on the ground floor, do you? The accountant has an office down there, but I believe he was in conference on the sixth floor at the time of the robbery. Anyway, Bentley was the only person to have contact with the robbers. No-one else had a clue what was going on until Bentley started yelling the place down, and that was after the robbers had left the building. Go talk to him,' Mr Slater said testily, his calm demeanour rapidly deteriorating under Chief Rose's tedious questioning.

'Yes, that might be a good idea. Thanks for your time Mr Pigeon, you've been a big help.' With that, Chief Rose left the office, nodding to the sweet young secretary as he made his way to the lifts, totally ignorant of the impact he had made on Mr Slater who was well into his second Glenfiddich before Rose had pressed the "down" button.

∾

The accountant, John Grimble, had thoughtfully allocated one of the offices off the banking chamber for police use. It was in this office that Detective Chief Inspector Damien Rose had comfortably ensconced himself, delighting in the high-backed leather chair located behind a beautifully polished desk. This is more like it, the Chief reflected, as he ran his hand over the strikingly grained mahogany table. Why the hell can't I get stuff like this, and this office only used for interviews when some poor sod wants some money? A knock on the door interrupted the Chief's daydreaming. 'Come,' he responded.

'You wanted to see me, sir?'

'I don't know. Who are you?'

'Sorry, sir. I'm Bentley. Bruce Bentley. The teller. The teller who was robbed.'

'Ah, yes. Come in. Come in. I'm Detective Chief Inspector Rose and I have some routine questions I would like to ask. Sit,' said Chief Rose gesturing to a comfortable looking armchair. 'Now Bruce, tell me exactly what happened.'

'Well, it was around two-thirty, don't know exactly but thereabouts. I had taken in a fair few deposits, as you do on a Friday afternoon. Anyway, my next customers were these two gentlemen, quite conspicuous by their dress, might I add, who approached the counter. The taller of the two did all the talking, well, the talking to me, that is. I was quite surprised when this bloke posed a purely hypothetical question which, in all honesty, took me aback somewhat. After giving the question some thought, I found I couldn't give a definitive answer. You see, usually people come up to the counter and get on with their banking, not ask you some stupid question.'

'Yes, I can appreciate it would be rather off-putting,' responded the Chief, eager to get on with the details. Before Bentley could continue, Chief Rose's curiosity got the better of him and he said, 'Hang on. Just what was this hypothetical question?'

'I'll probably never forget it. He just asked what I would do if he said he had a gun pointed at me and asked me to hand over all my ten-pound notes. Well obviously, I couldn't answer because the circumstances would be entirely different if he said he did have a gun pointed at me. As it was, he only said "if I said I had a gun," he didn't say that he did have a gun.'

'So, he didn't have a gun?'

'No. You miss the point. He wouldn't say if he did or didn't have a gun. It was a hypothetical question. If he said he did have a gun - which he didn't,- it wouldn't have been hypothetical as it would have been a statement of fact.'

'So, he did have a gun?

'Well, maybe he did and maybe he didn't. At no time did he say he had a gun and at no time did he say he didn't.'

'Oh, yes, I see,' lied Chief Rose. 'Let's forget about the gun for the moment. You said they looked quite conspicuous in their dress?'

'Quite ridiculous really. The tall gentleman wore jeans, lime coloured sports coat and a black hat. I think he had a white shirt on, maybe it was green. Oh yes, he wore a moustache, and I think he may have had dark hair – not too sure on that because of the hat. The short gentleman wore jeans, a white tie and a white hat. Blonde hair.'

'Cripes. How could anyone not see them? Seems like they wanted to be spotted,' said Chief Rose.

'Yes. And considering there were fifty million people just outside the bank involved in that anti-Vietnam rally, there must be hundreds of witnesses,' Bruce added.

'Let's get back to the actual robbery,' said Chief Rose as he delighted in the novelty of pushing his high-backed chair away from the table. His office chair at Day Street didn't have wheels.

'The tall bloke, sorry, gentleman, placed a coin bag on the counter and asked me to fill it with nothing else but ten-pound notes. No, I tell a lie. By now both gentlemen were getting quite exasperated and the tall gentleman didn't ask for the money, he just told me to fill up the bag with tenners. I was quite offended when he called me "a stupid boy".'

'Now why on earth would he do that?' asked the Chief.

'Probably because he couldn't understand the position he had placed me and I had tried to clarify my situation.'

'Totally understand. I would have been offended too.'

'Anyway, for a number of reasons I had decided to do as I was told, none the least being that there were a lot of people in the chamber and a gun battle was the last thing on my mind, not that I knew if he had a gun or not, you understand. So, I started bringing out my ten-pound notes and putting them on the counter while Mr Tall placed them in a coin bag. Eventually, when the bag was full, Mr Tall told me he had enough.'

'Enough what?'

'Money.'

'You mean to say you'd given them enough tenners. He didn't want any more?'

Bentley shrugged his shoulders. 'Yes, that's right. He just said he didn't want any more. I had a lot more he could've taken, but he didn't want them.'

'And they just walked off?'

'Yes. I'm not sure who was holding the cash when they did. I seem to think it was the short guy, er, gentleman, but I suppose it could have been Mr Tall. After all, he was the one I handed the cash bag over to. As I said, he was the one who seemed to be in charge so maybe he held onto the bag, although they both held bags on their way out. I did see the little bloke collide with a lady further down the banking chamber while on their way to the front door. She was leaving at the same time. She really gave him heaps for being so rude, which he was, of course. The lady seemed okay though. She's one of our customers, and real friendly too. Comes in once or twice a week to do her banking. I can't recall her name, but such a nice lady and treated so badly by that gangster.'

'Well, thanks, Mr Bentley. You've been very helpful with our investigation. I have your details should I need any further information or clarification. That okay with you?' asked Chief Rose, unsure if there were more questions needing to be asked.

'Yes, no problems. I'm pleased to have been able to help,' replied Bruce.

On Bentley's departure, Chief Rose reflected on what he had learnt. He wasn't quite sure if Bentley should be considered a hostile witness because, after persistent questioning, he was still unaware of whether a gun was involved or not.

Next to be interviewed was Charles Milner, a fifty something, employed by the bank as a security guard. It was clear the bank's resolve to deter prospective robbers was not a consideration when they employed old Charlie. He may have been fit, once, but it seemed Charlie now had a penchant for the odd nip of gin and no longer did he appear to have a great deal of respect for his physical condition. As a consequence, Charlie was walking a tight rope having been warned by management on at least two occasions for conduct the bank considered prejudicial to its interests. Still, everyone who worked on the ground floor liked Charlie and they would be sorry to see him leave.

Charlie, having decided to become a security guard after nearly thirty years in the army, never gave a second though to the possibility that he may be confronted with a situation requiring some sort of physical exertion. From what he had been led to believe, the job of a security guard was solely to be seen, and that was sufficient deterrent to prevent any improper activity. As a consequence, the situation Charlie now found himself was, according to Charlie at least, quite galling.

'Ah, you must be Charles Milner, the security guard,' Chief Rose said as Charlie entered the office. This bit of successful detective work may have been attributed in no small way to Charlie's neat grey uniform prominently embroidered in several locations with the words "Security Guard", a peaked cap, and the gun on his hip.

'Why yes, yes I am. Pleased to meet you, Detective Chief Inspector.'

'I won't take up too much of your time, Charlie. There are just a few questions I would like to ask so please, take a seat,' said Chief Rose, offering the armchair with his hand.

Charlie sat and said, 'Now, how can I help you?'

Chief Rose adopted the superior position by sitting back in his seat, his arms folded. 'Now Charlie, at what point were you alerted to the fact that something was amiss in the banking chamber?'

'Sorry, I'm not sure. Probably not until Bruce, I mean Mr Bentley, alerted everyone that there had been a robbery.'

'You mean you didn't actually see anything relating to the robbery; nothing suspicious?'

'No, not really. You see, there was all this yelling and chanting and whistle blowing from a mob of anti-Vietnam protesters outside the door in George Street, so I went to have a look, break the monotony, you see. It can get pretty boring sitting on your bum all day, and you're not allowed to read a book or do anything like that.'

'Yes, I quite understand.' Nevertheless, Chief Rose closed his eyes and slowly shook his head. 'What did you do after Mr

Bentley finally got around to letting everyone know there had been a robbery?'

'I immediately closed the main doors. That's the standard procedure when you get robbed, not that we're robbed very often. Come to think of it, I can't remember having been robbed before.'

'Yes, thank heavens. The robbers have been identified as wearing bright clothing and hats. Did you see any such persons leaving the bank prior to Mr Bentley's alert?'

'Well, yes. Just before Mr Bentley shouted out that he'd been robbed, these two blokes, one short and one tall, walked out of the bank. The tall bloke was wearing jeans, a black sports coat and a white hat. He was also carrying a coin bag that appeared to be quite full. But then again, so did the smaller bloke. He wore this bright green coat with blue jeans and looked like a real ponce.'

'Did you see which way they went?'

'Yes. The tall bloke turned left out of the bank, so I s'pose he was headed off towards Circular Quay. The other bloke turned right and headed along George Street. I didn't see how far they went 'cause at the time there was no reason to watch them. Like I mean to say, it wasn't like they'd just robbed a bank.'

'Could they have joined the rally march once they left the bank?'

'Well, yes I s'pose so. Just because they turned in different directions when they got outside doesn't mean they had to keep on going in their separate directions, does it? Like, it was a pretty long parade so they could have joined in, or they could have continued their separate ways along George Street. As I said, I had no reason to keep an eye on them, and even if I did, I would've only been able to watch one of them.'

God give me strength, why me? Chief Rose thought. 'Yes, of course,' he said in a condescending manner. Charlie was either oblivious to the nuance of the Chief's comment, or chose to ignore it. 'Anyway, thanks for your time Charlie. Sorry to have detained you for so long.' After Charlie had departed, Chief Rose rested his elbows on the table and rubbed his eyes with the balls of his hands, a drop of sweat falling from his chin to pool on the mahogany table. Chief Rose had seen better days.

CHAPTER 14

*I*t was seven-thirty in the Friday evening of the robbery. Simon, Georgie, Noel and Sue occupied a booth in Cahill's Clipper Room Restaurant on Market Street, Simon and Georgie opting for the chicken maryland, Noel and Sue the vienna schnitzel.

'Everything seemed to go according to plan,' said Simon expecting someone at the table to make some snide remark.

Sue looked at Simon and pulled a face that reflected her obvious disagreement with the statement. 'Okay,' she said. 'I suppose it was successful in the end, but only by sheer good luck. It wouldn't have come close to being successful if we had relied only on good management and if Lady Luck hadn't intervened when she did. And don't forget, we still don't know if the robbery was a success. If you recall, the whole aim of the exercise was to make Rose look like a complete idiot.'

'Okay. I'll concede things got a little out of hand, but that was beyond our control and couldn't have been anticipated. Anyway, you haven't explained what happened after Georgie dropped the cash into the briefcase,' said Simon, anxious to turn the discussion away from any appropriation of blame for the hiccups encountered, especially as he considered himself completely blameless.

'Well, it was just sheer luck I was able to get back downstairs and even more luck to get the money into the safe deposit box,' said Sue as she unfolded a serviette and placed it neatly across her lap.

'Yes, I thought you'd be pushing it,' said Georgie. 'When I put the money in the briefcase, I had the idea you wouldn't have much time to lodge it in the safe deposit box before the alarm was raised. I suppose I left you stranded, but as soon as I gave you the cash, I took off out the door and into George Street. The last thing I wanted to do was hang around in the banking chamber. I saw the security guard standing on the front steps watching the demonstration go by, so everything in the chamber must have been okay at that stage.' The conversation ceased as the waitress, dressed in a black dress uniform arrived and started to distribute the meals around the table. Georgie waited until the waitress had left and then said, 'Anyway Sue, you were saying?'

'After you made the drop, I went back downstairs and had just reached the safe deposit counter when an alarm sounded and all hell broke loose. It was quite evident the people down there didn't know what was happening, but the officials ordered everyone out. I was passing through into the safe room along with a bank official, he had the other key to the box, when he stopped and ordered me out. Fortunately, he was the same official I had spoken to earlier and he recognised me. I explained that it was imperative that I gain access to the box before the weekend, and that it would only take a second. He relented, ran to the box and unlocked his key then withdrew to the door and waited after telling me to make it snappy. I did. After that I just went upstairs to the banking chamber, and sat around until the police arrived. As I had not been in the chamber at the time of the robbery, a sergeant told me to go home.'

'So, all our ill-gotten booty is safe and secure in one of the bank's own safe deposit boxes?' said Noel as he plied his bread roll with butter.

'Well, if it's not, we're in big trouble,' replied Sue with a grin. 'The police didn't even ask me any questions, not that I could've helped, of course. Anyway, after I was told to leave, I just wandered down George Street, cut through Wynyard and went up to Menzies. I sat in the lounge just off the reception area and had a scotch and dry, purely for medicinal purposes, and that's when Georgie came down from the room she'd taken. I suppose you boys were up there getting changed and cleaned up. And how did your getaway work out, Noel?'

'No problems, all went according to plan,' said Noel. 'After I bumped into you, and I'm sorry, Georgie, if I was a bit more robust than needed, I took off after Simon down the steps and out into George Street. He turned left, and I turned right for a few paces and then we both joined the rabble. Simon soon caught up with me and we strolled along together discarding our disguises. We used curb-side garbage bins to dump the newspapers from the cash bag as we went. Regardless of the earlier debacle inside the bank, the timing turned out perfectly with the demonstration just passing the bank as we left. I saw the old security guard standing at the top of the steps having a look at what was going on outside and he looked totally preoc-cupied. I don't think he would have been distracted even if the Saint Valentine's Day Massacre had been going on inside.'

'Did you really need to dress as you did?' asked Georgie, with some embarrassment. I'm just glad I wasn't seen with either of you. You both looked like, like… Georgie gave up on a suitable simile and shrugged her shoulders.

'I reckon they looked like two little Irish elves or pixies, something you might see at the bottom of your garden,' said Sue with a giggle.

'Okay, okay. But I felt right at home once we had joined the demo,' responded Simon with indignation. 'No-one turned a head or even gave us a second glance. If they did give a thought to us, they probably had the idea we came from Nimbin. It was easy to get rid of the disguises and clothing as we moved along George Street. By the time we got to the Queen Victoria Building we were down to the normal clothing we were wearing under the colourful stuff. After that, it was easy to leave the demonstration and hop a train from Town Hall to Wynyard, and you know the rest.'

'And next time we rob a bank,' said Noel pushing a potato chip around his plate to get the last of the gravy, 'I choose the bloody teller. What an absolute debacle. And if I hear the word "hypothetical" again, I'll scream.'

'Okay, I'm sorry,' said Simon raising his hands in resignation and adopting a feigned pout on his face. 'How was I to know the teller was an academic with an IQ of Mensa proportions wanting to analyse every word I said? Hells bells, give us a break.'

Georgie leant over and kissed Simon on the cheek. 'It's okay, sweetie, I still love you.'

'Gee thanks,' responded Simon. 'One thing I'd like to be is a fly on the wall when whoever interviews the teller. Let's hope to heaven it's Rosey because if it is, he'll never be able to understand the little bugger.'

'So, what now?' asked Noel raising his eyebrows inquiringly.

'That's easy,' responded Georgie. Simon and I are off back to the Menzies for a night of lecherous debauchery, aren't we sweetie?' Simon gave a coy smirk and said nothing.

'That's okay,' replied Sue. 'We took your advice, Georgie, as it sounded like a really good idea. We're booked into the Travelodge just across the road. How about we meet in Wynyard Park tomorrow morning around nine-thirty? Is that too late?

'No, but I'm hoping I'll find it a little too early,' replied Georgie.

CHAPTER 15

*B*y the middle of the week Chief Rose had collated all the reports from notes taken by the police in attendance at the robbery, along with all the written statements provided. These were now contained in a file held firmly under the Chief's arm as he proceeded to Superintendent Fisher's office, where he stopped and knocked on the door.

'Come in, Rose,' called the voice from within. As he entered the office, he couldn't help but notice the disparity between the office occupied by Mr Pigeon and the one occupied by Superintendent Fisher. If this is a superintendent's office, I don't suppose I have much to grumble at, thought Chief Rose. Instead of the mahogany table was a pine desk, the leather chairs now vinyl chairs, the lush paintings replaced by framed certificates of achievement and various police plaques. Gone were the window curtains, now replaced with venetian blinds, the plush carpet now linoleum, and the clean fresh ambience replaced with the smell of stale tobacco, Fisher currently in the process of contributing to the unpleasant smell by stubbing out another cigarette in an ashtray already filled with burnt out butts.

Chief Rose handed the file to the Superintendent, sat down and watched his boss skim through the file before throwing it on the table in front of him. 'I've already received a copy of your report and, needless to say, I'm not overly impressed. I thought there were only two robbers?'

'Yes, sir, that's right, only two.'

'Well, I'm not a mathematician, but if I count up the number of different descriptions given by various people who claim they were witness to the event, the whole Kelly gang could have done the job. Rent-a-Mob could have been involved.'

'Yes, sir. We're following up a few leads, but we haven't got much to go on at the moment. It seems the robbers may have used the cover of an anti-war demonstration to make their getaway, so no-one took any notice of anybody once they left the bank. In fact, it appears no-one took much notice of them while they were in the bank, apart from their weird clothing. We did come across what is believed to be a jacket worn by one of the robbers, a lime green jacket found on the corner of George and Market Streets. We sent it to forensics but it seems everyone in the demonstration used it for a door mat. As I said, sir, we have very little to go on but every bit helps,' said the Chief, sweat now dripping from his face onto his shirt.

'I would hope it does. I would hate to think for one minute that any evidence, irrespective of how trivial it may seem, would not be helpful. Now listen, Rose, I've got the Chief Superintendent on my back right now. He's not at all happy that the head office of a major bank in the middle of Sydney can be robbed in broad daylight, and by two yobbos dressed as clowns. But what is getting right up his nose, and mine too, is the fact that these two clowns appear to have been successful. And one last thing. We both know promotion is not an easy thing to come by; too many people for too few positions. Your failures are also my failures and right at the moment Chief Superintendent Paxton believes we are achieving brilliant success in failing to get this case sorted. As it is abundantly clear you're lacking the competence and intelligence to bring this case to a satisfactory conclusion, I want you to hand everything you have over to Inspector Hanson and we'll see if he can do any better. Do I make myself clear?'

'Yes, sir,' replied Chief Rose, wiping the sweat from his face with a handkerchief. He suddenly became conscious of the fact that he had responded to each of the Superintendent's questions with a "yes sir". He was a dispirited and unhappy chief inspector as he left the Superintendent's office. Yes sir, yes sir, three bags full sir. Yes, you cretin, don't you mean my failures are my failures and my successes are your successes. He made his way back to his office and dropped disconsolately down into his chair. Something had gone wrong with the amicable relationship the two men had previously shared, but for some strange reason, Chief Rose didn't really care. Okay, you repugnant smart aleck, you do better.

'Hanson, my office, now,' bellowed Detective Chief Inspector Rose down the corridor. Inspector Hanson was a CIB detective employed on matters relating to corporate crime, or white-collar crime, as it was euphemistically known. Apart from conducting criminal investigations, he had been involved in criminal profiling in his earlier days before doing a stint in Police Intelligence. As a result of his broad experience, he was considered one of the most senior and knowledgeable detectives in the CIB, but for some unknown reason had not progressed passed the rank of inspector. Daryl Hanson was approaching sixty and had made up his mind to take things easy until his imminent retirement. He was a short, slight man, bald as a badger, and was never seen without a cigarette hanging from the corner of his mouth.

'You called, Chief?' as he stuck his head through the open door.

'Yes. Here's the file on the bank job. See what you can make of it and get back to me. The Superintendent's on my back and Paxton's on his back, and I'll be on your back if you don't come up with some answers.'

'Sure thing, Chief. Timeframe?'

'ASAP.'

Detective Inspector Simon Webster sat in the coffee shop on the corner of Bathurst and George Streets and gazed out the window. He still had a few days leave left and had taken the opportunity to take the bus into town to meet Sergeant Elliott. His attention was quickly drawn to a man in the centre of George Street, along with the sound of an urgent car horn. The man, Simon quickly identified as his friend Noel Elliott, was in the process of playing a game of Russian roulette with the speeding traffic, with the odds firmly in favor of the traffic.

For some unaccountable reason, Simon had the idea the scene must have been very similar in the Circus Maximus as the half-starved lions chase the slaves around the arena. Here, it was a case of the George Street traffic metamorphosing into a pack of demented, malevolent, metal beasts, all transfixed in a feeding frenzy as they tried to run down any human stupid enough not to avail themselves of the zones of sanctuary, usually define by the simple traffic light. Either by good luck or good management, Noel eventually made a non-fatal crossing of the street. He entered the coffee shop where, after spotting Simon, removed his cap and collapsed into the chair opposite.

'Holy hell, it's bloody dangerous out there; a man could get himself killed,' he said, still breathing heavily from both the physical and mental exertion.

'Yes, but that's why we have traffic lights, you moron,' said Simon without any sympathy. A young waitress dressed in a black skirt and white blouse soon approached the table, the four top buttons of the blouse inadvertently left undone. Notwithstanding a mouth full of chewing gum, the waitress asked for orders. Simon, his eyes riveted on the girl's eyes replied, 'one cappuccino and one flat black, thanks.'

'One cappuccino and one flat black,' she repeated in an extraordinary display of mental recall. Having failed to illicit any further response from either of the two men, she quickly wrote the order down on her note pad, turned and made her way back to the counter.

'My God, the younger generation. Girls never looked like that when I was at that age. What, she'd be no more than sixteen?' said Simon, shaking his head.

'Well, when I was at that age it seemed girls weren't allowed out without a chaperone,' quipped Noel with a grin. 'But getting right off the subject, I suppose you'd like to know what's going on?'

'Yes, sure would. A lot of water has passed under the bridge since I went on leave and I bet something's going on in Day Street,' replied Simon.

Noel took a deep breath and pursed his lips before answering. 'It seems the Chief has called in Daryl Hanson to look at the file on the bank job. He's a good detective, as you well know, but I have an idea the basic intelligence already collated is very light on. You were absolutely right about the clothing the robbers wore. It seems every witness saw something different and I doubt if anyone, including the teller, could give an exact description. As for Sue and Georgie, the police consider them a non-event as they have ignored them completely. No-one paid any attention to the girls, except when the robber ran into Georgie and there's nothing on the file to suggest any female involvement at all. The money is safe in the bank's own safe deposit box, and no-one but the four of us know where it is. Hanson has some lackeys going through the records trying to find a similar modus operandi, which they won't find, of course. He's also doing a check on known bank robbers which is a bit of a waste of time, but he has to go through the usual routine.'

'More to the point, how are things with Fisher? Thanks, mines the cappuccino,' said Simon as he tried in vain not to ogle the waitress, now leaning over the table to set the coffees down.

'How on earth you can perve on girls when we have the two best looking women on the coast is beyond me, you dirty old man. Now cut it out,' said Noel, as he watched the sugar cube sink into his coffee. 'It seems we're winning on that score. Fisher had the Chief up to his office recently. Naturally I haven't a clue as to what happened, but the Chief was not happy after the visit, and it was just after that meeting that Rosey hauled Hanson in and gave him the file. By the same token, Paxton had Fisher to his office and the betting is that they didn't talk about the weather. Rumour is Paxton is livid that anyone could pull off such an audacious robbery and appear to have been success- ful, so now he's putting pressure on Fisher.'

Simon drew of the frothy top of the cappuccino with a spoon then licked the froth from the spoon before continuing. 'That's good. If Fisher is getting up Rosey, it means someone is getting up Fisher, and that would have to be Paxton. I know Paxton is well thought of in the commercial field and I wouldn't be surprised if his golfing buddy in the bank hasn't already been on to him. If nothing else, Paxton will demand results, which is good for us, provided they don't catch us, of course. Anything else?'

'Yes, there are a couple of things. First. I took the time to read the police report on the death of Dorothy. The autopsy showed she did have a wonky heart and her doctor's records confirmed this. The coroner's report stated she did die of a massive cardio infarction. There was nothing to suggest she had been bitten by a spider, and I dare say it couldn't be confirmed if she died of fright, so it seems Georgie's in the clear. The second thing is odd. I was approached by Sergeant Mathieson who quizzed me about Chief Rose. Nothing specific mind you, just general stuff; what was he like to work for, did he drink or gamble. Well, we all drink and gamble to some extent, a question like that is very subjective. I got the idea he was searching for something more specific but didn't want to come straight out and ask. Just struck me as odd,' said Noel with a shrug of the shoulders. 'Anyway, I have to get back to work. I'll give you a ring if I hear anything. See ya.' Simon ordered another cappuccino and watched the world go by.

CHAPTER 16

*S*imon edged his way past the bookmakers' umbrellas, looking at the odds of each of the horses running in the next event. It wasn't a day for the favorites, three of them going down in the first four races. But then again, Simon thought, it can only be expected with weather like this, which was not good. A strong cold south-easterly wind bringing blustery showers scurrying across the racecourse made it highly uncomfortable for the meager crowd of punters in attendance. He paused to refer to his race book and, after reading the form guide, took his pencil and put a circle around a horse said to be a proven wet track specialist.

'No, mate, I wouldn't back him with your money. He likes it wet but it's only his second run back from a spell. He needs about four races before he remembers what he's s'posed to do.'

'Oh, hi Ron. I was hoping to see you here.'

'Yeah, likewise. I've got a bit of info you might be interested in.'

'Right,' said Simon. 'Look, here's twenty quid. Go put a brick on for me and one for yourself. I'll go with whatever you back then we'll have a beer and you can tell me what's going on.' Simon handed over two ten-pound notes and watched as Ron spoke to a bookie before receiving two betting cards. He kissed one of the cards, for luck Simon surmised, and placed it in his pocket before handing the other to Simon.

'Thanks mate. That was real kind of you. Now, let's go and have that beer, I'm as dry as a Temperance Party piss up,' said Ron.

Simon left Ron sitting on a bar stool while he went for the beers. He smiled at Helen who, on recognising him, raised her eyebrows questioningly and gestured with two fingers in the victory salute. Simon nodded and within a minute two beers had been placed on the bar in front of him. 'Thanks, luv.' Simon dropped a ten-shilling note on the bar, picked up the beers and returned to Ron. 'Okay Ron, what have we got?'

'Your boss's back with a pocket full of money. Word is he's going to lay it all on Tara Lad in the sixth.'

'So, our slush fund is pretty empty at the moment?' suggested Simon.

'Bone dry, I'd say. But then you'd have a better idea of how much should be in it and how much cash our Chief Inspector Rose has on him.'

'No, not really. I've taken a couple of weeks leave before starting down at Cronulla, but I dare say he's got a few bob.' Simon hadn't realised just how thirsty he had been and his beer was soon empty. 'Anotherie, Ron?'

'Thanks, ta.' Ron gulped the last of his beer and handed his empty glass to Simon.

On Simon's return with the beers, Ron said, 'Look, as soon as I finish this beer, how about I go and confirm what horse your boss intends to back and we'll stick around and see how it runs?'

'Good thinkin' Ron. But right now I'm a bit more interested

in the next race. Hey, by the way, what horse are we on?' Simon could never understand the bookies scrawl on a betting ticket.

'Trevors. It's being ridden by Jack Thomson so I give it a good chance. Got fives so if it comes in that's fifty quid each, and that's more money earned legally for a long time. Well, for me, anyway.'

'Don't tell me. I don't want to know,' replied Simon with a grin.

Ron disappeared into the crowd, probably in search of the rails bookie who had been furnishing the Chief with the names of horses that always seem to win, Simon presumed. He nodded to Helen, raised one finger and was acknowledged with a sweet smile. 'Quiet day? Must be the weather,' said Simon as Helen placed the beer on the bar and moved a bowl of peanuts closer to Simon.

'Yes, terribly quiet, but I suppose it's to be expected with weather like this. Even so, there are punters who are just as crazy as golfers; they still get out in it even if it's raining cats and dogs, and no, I'm not casting aspersions on *your* sanity,' Helen said with a smile. 'It'll be fine by Saturday so there'll be a big crowd at Randwick to make up for today. Apart from that, it's hard to pick a winner with the track condition as it is.' Simon handed Helen a couple of bob for the beer and sat back up on the stool and looked at the TV screen above the bar.

The runners in the fifth race had made their way to the starting gates for the nine furlong event as Ron sidled up to Simon, water dripping from him. 'Bloody wet out there. Much better to watch the race on the telly in here,' Ron said as he tried to shake the water off like a shaggy dog. 'And yep, our Rosey has plonked his bet on Tara Lad at seven to two with a rails bookie, and not the one who gives him the tips. All the same, for Rosey to back a horse with a rails bookmaker is certainly a first for him. He must have bet a lot of money because those rails bookies don't bet with chicken feed.'

'Bloody beauty, mate. Here's your fifty, and thanks,' said Ron after taking the winning tickets back to the bookie with whom he had placed the bets to collect the winnings. Simon couldn't quite figure out just how Ron knew Trevors would win. After the race, Simon had taken the time to look at the form guide in the race book to see if there was anything to suggest the horse would win. There wasn't, so Simon just accepted the fact and decided not to ask Ron the secret of his success.

As the two men watched the rain tumble down and drank their beers, Ron finally said, 'You know, Simon, there are some good coppers and there are some bad coppers and it seems like you've become known as one of the good coppers, irrespective of what Rosey and Fisher may think of you. It's easy to be considered a good copper by other coppers, but when the bad guys regard you as being a good cop, you know you must have something goin' for you. There are some coppers who want to punch your lights out first, and then ask the questions, or arrest you for jaywalking, or for just being wherever they think you shouldn't be. And some coppers must be morally bankrupt. Like, we know Rosey and Fisher are both as corrupt as an ambitious politician, not that there's any collusion between the two. That makes it worse because they're both independently corrupt individuals working on their Pat Malone. It's hard to accept that a bloke like Fisher is probably earning more money from a casino than what he's being paid as a policeman. But then again, Rosey gets himself caught in the gambling net and can't get out, while Fisher has a wife who spends money like a political party at election time.'

Having been alluded to as one of the good coppers, Simon felt a chill run down his spine and his stomach muscles contract. Yeah, I'm a real good copper who's just robbed the Bank of New South Wales, he thought. 'Thanks for the kind words, Ron, but I just try to do my job. Anyway, I don't expect you to answer this question, breach of confidentiality and all that, but how do you know about Rosey and the slush fund, and I suppose about Fisher, as well?'

'Sorry, mate, but you're absolutely right and you know the rules. These things aren't going to go on forever, so when it's over we'll all get together, have a few beers and have a good laugh.' The words Ron had used impacted on Simon who tried to recall exactly what Ron had said. Maybe I'm paranoiac, but he did say "we'll all get together." He wouldn't have used "all" unless there were other people involved. How very strange, Simon thought.

With more than twenty minutes to the next race, race six, and with probably nothing more exciting to talk about, Simon casually asked, 'Ron, have you heard anything about the recent bank job in town?'

'Strange you should ask,' said Ron with a shake of the head, 'cause the answer is no, not a whisper. And that's the strange part of it. Two clowns walk into the bank, rob the place, walk out and just disappear without anyone knowing a thing about it. Usually someone knows something, but not this time, not a murmur. It's really quite refreshing to see a couple of pillocks put it up the police like they have.'

'Yeah, I was just wondering because Fisher initially gave the case to Rosey. Seems Rosey wasn't going anywhere fast with it so Fisher directed him to hand it over to Daryl Hanson, who isn't doing any better.'

'Well, I'm not surprised,' said Ron. 'The Chief really hasn't enough sense to come on in out of the rain so I think whoever did the job should send Fisher a Thank You card.' Simon just smiled.

By the sixth race the rain had become even heavier and if it hadn't been bucketing down earlier, it certainly was now. There had been talk of the race program being abandoned but the stewards, after doing an inspection of the track, had decided to make a further assessment after the sixth event. There were very few spectators taking the opportunity to view the horses as they paraded in the mounting yard, and even fewer taking up spots on the running rails to view the event. The majority had probably arrived at the same conclusion reached by Simon and Ron and were now crowded into the various bars throughout the course eager to view the event in a warm and dry environment.

Tara Lad looked fit and well as he made his way with the other runners onto the track and headed for the starting gates. Simon looked around, half expecting to see Chief Inspector Rose who was obviously somewhere waiting in excited anticipation of another winner and the bundle of winnings he would soon collect. The view of the horses was much clearer for those watching on TV than for those who opted to watch from the rails or the grandstand. Although the stand was covered, it provided little respite from the driving rain for the few unfortunate spectators who had chosen the stand to view the race.

'Rather be here than outside,' commented Ron as he gazed at the TV screen. 'Hey look, isn't that Rosey?' The TV camera, scanning the meager number of people huddled under umbrellas against the running rails, settled on one particular spectator caught in a losing battle to control his umbrella which had been turned inside out by the howling wind.

'Cripes, it's either Rosey or Mary Poppins and from the size of the bloke, I'd bet it ain't Poppins,' said Simon, feeling vaguely sorry for his boss. Ron tried to suppress a smile, gave up and broke into side splitting laughter.

'See, I told you. He hasn't got the sense to come in out of the rain. Sorry, Simon, but it couldn't happen to a nicer bloke,' Ron lied after he gained control of himself. 'Hey, they're ready to jump,' he said, drawing Simon's attention back to the race. The horses were plowing through the heavy going along the back of the course with Tara Lad well positioned, tucked away in third place. As they turned into the straight, Tara Lad found firmer ground towards the centre of the track and made his dash for the wining post.

'Looks like Rosey's on another winner here,' said Simon.

'Not yet. Look at Sir Miles, he's finishing off stronger than Tara Lad.' As they passed the furlong post, Tara Lad was half a length in front, his stride shortening. Ron was right. Sir Miles was finishing over the top of Tara Lad but the winning post looked like it was close enough for Tara Lad to just make it. Head to head, Tara Lad and Sir Miles were involved in a classic racing duel, neither horse willing to concede defeat, both jockeys striving to get as much out of his mount as possible.

The crowd in the bar was shouting encouragement as the horses crossed the finishing line locked together. Photo finish. 'Tara Lad has held on,' said Simon, surprised at just how excited he had become watching the spectacle.

Ron broke into laughter again. 'I wonder how Rosey's feeling right now. He's probably having palpitations. Serves him right'. Clearly, Ron had no compassion for Detective Chief Inspector Damien Rose.

~

'They're a long time with the photo, aren't they?' asked Simon, unaware of the mechanics involved in a photo finish.

'No, when it's as close as this race, the judge will usually call for a second print, just to make sure he's made the right decision. The numbers should go up in the frame shortly.' Correct to his word, the numbers were soon in the frame and the course announcer gave the judge's decision declaring Sir Miles the winner by a short half head.

'Holy hell. I bet Rosey's feeling a trifle ill right at the moment, poor bugger. Apart from falling off the planet, I wonder what he'll do now,' Simon asked, more to himself than anyone in particular. Just at that moment, an ambulance maneuvered through the crowd outside the bar and headed for the rails where a body lay prostrate on the ground, a small group of spectators gathering to see what was happening.

'Hello, hello. What have we here? Isn't that pretty close to where Rosey was standing,' Simon asked as he shouldered his way through the bar patrons to get a better view.

'Yes, maybe we should get over and have a closer look, just in case,' replied Ron as he felt a twinge of apprehension. The rain had eased from the bucketing down to become a steady downpour as the two men made their way across the lawn to the scene unfolding by the running rail. Two ambulance men were kneeling over the unfortunate soul, one with an oxygen mask in his hand, the other pounding on the chest of the prostrate racegoer.

'Crikey, it is Rosey, and he doesn't look really well at the moment,' exclaimed Simon as he drew his warrant card from his coat pocket and pushed his way through the small crowd of onlookers. He showed the card to the ambulance men who nodded and continued to work on Chief Inspector Rose. The feeling Simon was beginning to experience was a combination of both shame and pity, shame in that he was quite prepared to do everything possible to make the Chief look bad in his boss's eyes, and pity because the sight of someone fighting for their life is extraordinarily distressing. But hell, thought Simon, Rosey got himself into this, and Rosey can bloody well get himself out of it.

'You'll excuse me sir, we just need a little space,' said one of the ambulance men to Simon as he opened the back doors of the ambulance and withdrew a stretcher and a blanket.

Simon felt a cold shiver down his spine. 'He's going to be all right?' he asked as they placed Rosey into the back of the ambulance.

"You know him?' asked one of the medics, slamming the back doors of the ambulance shut.

'Yes, he's Detective Chief Inspector Damien Rose from the Day Street Police Headquarters.' Simon was going to add that Rose was his boss, but thought better of it.

'I'm sorry then, officer,' the ambulance man said, in no particular hurry to get their patient to hospital. 'Looks like a massive heart attack. I'd say he didn't stand a chance and was probably dead before he hit the ground.' Simon and Ron stood there in the rain and stared at each other, appalled at what they had just witnessed.

'Well, I'll be buggered,' said Ron, gazing after the ambulance as it drove slowly off into the crowd, its blue light flashing. 'Like, I mightn't have liked the bloke, but this is a bit stiff, if you'll excuse the pun. Sorry Simon, but God works in mysterious ways.'

'Yes, he does, Ron. He certainly does,' Simon replied, his mind in turmoil.

CHAPTER 17

'Now let's get this straight. You're telling me we go to all the trouble of knocking off the Bank of New South Wales in the middle of Sydney for the sole purpose of making Chief Inspector Rose look bad, and he goes and has a fatal heart attack. Simon, you've got to be joking?' said Noel, trying to come to terms with the enormity of the event.

'I'm sorry,' said Simon with a shrug. 'But what can I say. It wasn't a pretty sight seeing Rosey lying there with two medicos trying to resuscitate him by beating the life out of him.'

Noel frowned. 'Well, I think it's bloody inconsiderate. He could've died before we pulled the bank job. As it is, we went to a lot of trouble for nothing, let alone putting our lives in jeopardy of a ten year stint in Long Bay.'

The three others sitting around the small round garden table in the Webster's back yard on a sunny Saturday could empathize with Noel's irritation and share his frustration. Simon took a cold beer from the Esky, cracked the lid and took a long draught. 'God, what a mess. Look, Rosey handed the investigation over to Hanson because Rosey wasn't going anywhere with it. From what you tell me, Noel, Hanson isn't doing much better. The current thought is that it had to be an interstate job, probably because they haven't got anything better to go on. Let's not get panicky just yet. However, we still have a problem with Fisher who is, after all, just as responsible as Rose was for stuffing up our careers. We know Fisher is on the take and is an out and out sleaze, not that that matters, but he's still a crook and needs to be brought down. I think we have him offside with Paxton who is demanding results on the bank job, and somehow I don't think Hanson will retrieve the situation for Fisher.'

Noel crunched an empty beer can in his hand then threw it into a nearby garbage can specifically placed for such purpose. 'I reckon you should have been at work yesterday, Simon. The shit really hit the fan when they carried out an audit of the slush fund and found no cash in the tin and the payment vouchers looking very suss. It's odd, they rarely do an audit and as soon as Rosey pegs out, they do one. And guess who did the audit?' said Noel, working on the cork of a bottle of Ben Ean for the girls.

'Let me guess,' replied Simon, shutting his eyes tightly and feigning deep concentration. 'Ah, yes. It had to be Sergeant Mathieson.'

'Right in one,' replied Noel.

Sue frowned as she poured two glasses of wine. 'You know, I've got a bone to pick with you two. Georgie and I sit here in complete ignorance as you two men chat away as if there's no tomorrow. We're in this thing just as much as you, so how about telling us what the hell is going on.'

'Totally agree,' said Georgie, taking her wine and sitting back on her chair.

'Okay, okay, keep your knickers on. We don't know much more than what you've already heard from Noel and myself,'

Simon replied, holding his hands up in surrender to the girls' verbal tirade. 'This friend of mine at the races told me that both Rosey and Fisher were playing both ends of the stick. Rosey had a gambling problem which he funded from a police slush fund. Fisher, on the other hand, is more corrupt in that he's being paid-off, I suppose you can call it protection money, for want of a better word, by the owner of at least one casino. The pay-off is to guarantee the police refrain from shutting the place down. And that's about it. God knows if Chief Superintendent Paxton knows what's going on, but this bloke at the races seems to know everything. I could be wrong, but I think it would be safe to assume Paxton at least knows something about it, surely.'

'And you think Fisher may have trashed your report on illegal gambling for that very reason?' asked Georgie.

'Yes, well at least on the recommendation of Rosey although Rosey had his own motive for having the report trashed. He's always known what I think of him, sorry, thought of him, both as a person and a police officer, and that goes back to the beginning of my career at The Rocks station. I've no doubt he'd always been on the lookout for the opportunity to plant the dirk and the report gave him a helping hand. You see, any report that isn't endorsed by the next person in the chain gets trashed.'

'So where does that leave us?' asked Sue as she poured herself another glass of wine.

'Well, there's not much we can do to make Rosey look any worse than what he looks like right now,' said Simon. 'The whole idea of trying to make Rosey look incompetent to his superiors appears to have been nullified by two events. First, the fact Rosey's and Fisher's illegal enterprises have both been compromised, and second, and probably more significantly, Rosey's dead. In view of what's happened and the upheaval Rosey's death will cause at the station, I think it might be a good time to give the bank its money back. What do you think, Georgie?'

Georgie rested her elbow on the arm of the chair and studied the wine in her glass. After a moment's contemplation, she replied, 'Yes, I would feel far more comfortable knowing the money's where it should be.'

'And you, Sue?' Simon asked.

'Yes, I agree with that. While it was a lot of fun, I'm really not a bank robber. And to tell the truth, I'm worried we could still get caught.' Simon then turned to Noel with an enquiring look.

'I'll go with the consensus, but I think we have definite potential here. The job we did was contrary to all good robbers' code of conduct. I've always liked the idea of giving the money back to the bank, but in the process we've demonstrated a huge weakness in the bank's security, irrespective of the actions of the security guard. Even if he had been alert, he wouldn't have spotted anything untoward until it was too late. The establishment just isn't prepared for the unusual, and we have that commodity in abundance. We could always hire out those attributes where people want to improve security.'

'Sort of crime awareness scheme. Show a company, or business just where it may be vulnerable to criminal attack,' said Simon, his interest aroused.

'Yes, that sort of thing. Could be a lot of fun.'

'Okay, okay, let's not get carried away. We haven't finished this job yet,' said Simon coming back to the problem at hand. 'And how do we get the money back to the bank? Take the money out of the safe deposit box and go make a deposit?'

'Oh, shut up, you goose,' came the caustic response from Georgie. 'All we have to do is write a letter to the bank, tell them where the money is and, at the same time, apologise for the inconvenience we may have inadvertently caused. We enclose the key to the safe deposit box with the letter, and that's the end of the story. Too easy,' said Georgie who had clearly given the mater some thought beforehand. 'And if you're going to organise that, Simon, I suggest you refrain from signing the letter,' Georgie added sarcastically.

'Sounds good to me,' said Noel as he pulled the top off a can of beer and accidently spraying Sue who just happened to be sitting in the wrong place. 'Bugger, sorry sweetheart,' he said and offered her a dirty handkerchief from his Stubby shorts pocket. Sue ignored him with a frown.

'Okay, that sounds like an excellent idea,' said Simon enthusiastically. If we can get the letter to the bank advising where the money is, the case of theft would be pretty hard to prosecute even if they do catch us. Two of the proofs of robbery are that we intended to take the money permanently, which we didn't and that the money was removed from the premises, which it wasn't. In fact, I'll send the letter priority mail up to Paddy Scanlon on the Gold Coast. We were both in the class of '63 and we've always kept in touch, even though he's no longer in the Force. I'll ask him to post the letter to the bank seeing they already believe the job was done by an interstate gang. That will just add grist to the mill.'

CHAPTER 18

*D*etective Inspector Simon Webster was in the process of clearing out personal items from his desk when he was interrupted by a knock on the door. 'Come in, it's open.'

Sergeant Mathieson, dressed in mufti, entered the office, his brown checked sports jacket slung over his shoulder. 'Sorry to bother you, sir, but Detective Chief Superintendent Paxton would like a word in his office.'

'So, he doesn't need me for that.'

'A word with you, sir.'

'Oh, I see. Just the two of us?'

'No, I've already spoken to Detective Sergeant Elliott and there'll be at least one other there.'

'Can you tell me what this is all about?' asked Inspector Webster, well aware there were a number of topics that could be the subject of discussion.

'No, that'll be up to the boss, but I'm sure you must have a few ideas as to what it's about,' responded Sergeant Mathieson as he held the door open for the inspector.

'Well, that's a good start. Since when have you been calling Chief Superintendent Paxton the boss?'

Sergeant Mathieson ignored the question as he led the way up the stairs to the fourth floor, along the corridor and stopped outside Chief Paxton's office where he knocked twice. It was Chief Paxton who opened the door and ushered the inspector and the sergeant into his office where Inspector Webster immediately saw Sergeant Elliott sitting in conversation with another man. Inspector Webster nodded to Sergeant Elliott while the man with whom he had been speaking stood and turned to face Inspector Webster.

'Simon, good to see you, and in a different environment too, for a change.'

'Ron. What the hell are you doing up here? You know this is a police station, don't you?' asked Simon, perplexed.

Before Ron could reply, Chief Paxton, who had seated himself behind his large cedar table, said, 'Gentlemen, if we could all be seated please, we'd better get on with it as this may take some time.' Whatever "it" may be, thought Simon.

Chief Superintendent Paxton leaned forward and rested his clenched hands on his table and looked at the four men sitting in front of him. Sergeant Elliott was in uniform, minus his cap while Inspector Webster was dressed in a dark grey lounge suit. Sergeant Mathieson was wearing a pair of light brown trousers with an open necked white shirt without a tie, in fact, very casual for an attendance at the Chief Superintendent's office, thought Sergeant Elliott. 'Before we get into the nuts and bolts of what I want to talk about, I think it best to clarify a few things.'

'What a bloody good idea, because I'm utterly confused,' remarked Inspector Webster who now regarded his position in the Police Force as a lost cause.

'Now, now, Simon. Just a little patience, please,' pleaded

Chief Paxton. Hang on, thought Simon, he's calling me by my christian name. Something is very rotten in the state of Norway. 'To begin with, Sergeant Mathieson works directly to me, and no-one else. I employ him where there is a requirement for a more discreet internal investigation concerning improprieties, or alleged improper conduct, the investigations sanctioned at commissioner level. Generally, they cover matters of administrative fraud, corruption and a host of other offences that you would normally find committed in society. Fortunately, I can say that for most of the time he is under employed. However, there are instances where I have the need for a little discreet digging.'

'And you've been doing a little digging here at Day Street,' interjected Inspector Webster.

Chief Paxton ignored the remark and continued. 'Sergeant Mathieson is well equipped for his role as he is suitably qualified in many aspects of white-collar investigations, including company fraud. Naturally, the nature of his work is strictly confidential, very demanding and is, to some extent, career limiting. Notwithstanding these minor inconveniences, there are fringe benefits which I will not go into. Simon, I think you already know Ron?'

'Yes, I've met him a few times, although it's now obvious I don't know him half as well as I thought,' said Simon looking at Ron. Ron just smiled.

'I think Ron has already bought you up to date on a couple of transgressions within Day Street,' said Chief Paxton, clasping his hands behind his head and rocking slowly back and forward on his chair.

'You mean, you knew Ron was feeding me snippets of information?' asked Simon becoming somewhat aggrieved. 'So that makes Ron an informer, and I'd hazard a guess that it's your Sergeant Mathieson who tells Ron what to tell me.'

'Yes, I know it sounds a little complicated, but it had to be that way. I understand Ron has helped you out on a number of occasions and you know Ron as a petty criminal who's done time for some minor offences. But actually, Ron is one of us,' said Chief Paxton. 'What I mean is, he's a paid informer, not a member of the police force.' Inspector Webster shook his head in disbelief, not so much that Ron was "one of us", but for the fact he should have worked it out long ago.

'And apart from being "one of us", he probably wasn't what you thought he was,' said Chief Paxton, pushing his chair back to stretch his legs straight out in front of himself. 'Ron was a petty criminal up in Queensland where he got himself caught up in a pay-roll job that went wrong. One of the gang pulled a gun and a shot was fired. Unfortunately, there was a fatality which was enough to make Ron decide he was way out of his league and getting into big trouble. To cut a long story short, Ron went to the police and told them all he knew of the gang which resulted in several arrests and successful prosecutions. Ron was granted immunity from prosecution and was covered under the police protection scheme. He came down to Sydney with a new identity while still maintaining his role as a petty criminal. Naturally we have to turn a blind eye to much of his goings-on as the information he provides is generally high-grade stuff and we don't want to blow his cover.'

'So, sir,' said Simon, wishing the conversation would stop for a moment's reflection, or at least slow down, 'on those occasions when Ron has provided information to assist in an investigation, he's done it with your knowledge?'

The Chief Superintendent nodded. 'Yes, and that was particularly so in the case of your investigation into illegal gambling.'

Simon turned to Ron and shook his head. 'Well I'll be buggered,' he exclaimed 'No wonder you knew what was going on. And that answers the question why you were providing only snippets of information. For you to have provided any more may have led me to think you were receiving inside information, which may have compromised your cover.'

'Exactly,' replied Ron. 'The Chief, having read your report on illegal gambling, thought things were getting out of hand, especially as Rose and Fisher were of the belief the report had been trashed which, of course, it hasn't.'

Simon gave a shrug. 'I'd like to talk about my report later, but right now, what are you proposing, sir? Chief Rose's slush fund indiscretions are behind us leaving only Fisher's little get rich scheme, and it's for sure neither Noel nor I have a clue what's going on in that regard.'

Noel looked at Simon and pulled a discreet face which conveyed a lot, like, what the hell is going on here. We're posted out anyway.

Chief Superintendent Paxton rested his elbows on the table and cupped his chin in his hands. 'Well, that about puts you on a par with what we know, which isn't much. We do know that a Mr Graham Lee, who owns the Taipan Club in Forbes Street, has been paying Fisher insurance money to negate any possibility of a police raid closing him down. And as for your report, Sergeant Mathieson happened to come across a copy which found its way to me. I found it to be very comprehensive, probably too comprehensive for Fisher and too well investigated and written for Rose. Rose wanted it trashed because he was trying to cast aspersions on your professional ability, and Fisher wanted it trashed because it was too close for comfort.'

'So, neither knew of the other's motive for trashing the report?'

'Good God, no. Fisher couldn't very well tell Rose why he wanted the report trashed, could he?'

'No, not really.'

The Chief continued. 'Anyway, Chief Rose occasionally

played baccarat at the Taipan Club, not that we were too concerned with that. We were more concerned with where he got the money to play. As he was in control of certain police funds, we started to take an interest, and you now have the gist of the matter. But getting back to Mr Lee. While we know he's paying Fisher, we have no proof, only circumstantial evidence. We need solid, irrefutable evidence, something like a photo of Fisher receiving his money from Mr Lee, something that will stand up in court. Hey, how about a brew before we go on, tea or coffee?' Chief Paxton pressed a button on his intercom and was greeted with a woman's voice.

'Yes, Mr Paxton?'

'Joyce, could you organise tea and coffee for five please?'

'No problems, luv. Be there in a tick.' True to her word, there was presently a knock on the door which Sergeant Mathieson opened for Joyce loaded with a tray of cups and saucers, tea and coffee pots and all other brew time necessities.

'Thanks, Joyce. Just leave it on the table.' The meeting adjourned while the seating was rearranged around the coffee table in the middle of the office, the teas and coffees poured. This was the first time either Sergeant Elliott or Inspector Webster had been in the Chief Superintendent's office, and although both had spoken very briefly to the Chief in the past, this was their first serious encounter with the Detective Chief Superintendent. In fact, Chief Paxton had made quite an impression on the two detectives who found the Chief amicable, friendly and, notwithstanding the exulted rank, very easy to get on with.

'So, what did you have in mind, sir?' asked Inspector Webster with a touch of indifference. 'You obviously didn't invite us up here for a chat and a cup of tea.'

'Haven't a clue and that's why you're here, but first things first. Simon, you have every right to be pissed off. Rose never did like you, ever since that night in George Street.'

'You know about that, sir?'

'Good God, Simon, I know everything about my staff, well, nearly everything. I wouldn't be much of a chief superintendent if I didn't. I know about your application for transfer and the reasons behind it. I also know why Rose knocked it back, so just relax and let me get on with it. I've made a couple of telephone calls and it's all been sorted, so forget Cronulla. You're staying here.'

'Gee thanks, sir. Naturally I would prefer to work here than at Cronulla, apart from the obvious.' The obvious, as far as Chief Paxton need surmise, was the travelling of zillions of miles from Collaroy to Cronulla. The obvious, as far as Inspector Webster was concerned was that he would be in a better position to keep tabs on how Inspector Hanson was progressing with his investigation into a particular brazen bank robbery.

'And you, Sergeant Elliott, get yourself back upstairs. You both work well together and it would be shame to break you up.' Sergeant Elliott exhaled a deep breath and dropped his shoulders in relaxation, a faint smile on his face. The Chief settled himself back in his chair and looked at Inspector Webster. 'I'm giving you and Sergeant Elliott a free rein to do whatever it takes to fix Superintendent Fisher. I want to be in a position to charge him for corruption, and I don't care how you do it as long as I get results. The only alternative I'll settle for is for you to have Fisher present himself to me and have him confess to his corruption; and by hell, wouldn't I love to see that. Either way, confession or evidence, I'll have Fisher. In view of the environment you'll be working, I thought it might be advisable to have Ron along today. If you need him, he's all yours. That okay with you, Ron?'

'No, that's fine. I hope Simon can use me.'

'Oh, one last thing,' said Chief Superintendent Paxton, more as an afterthought, 'you wouldn't happened to have heard anything about that bank robbery in town a few days ago, would you? I asked Fisher to get right onto it and I think he gave the case to Chief Inspector Rose who palmed it off to Inspector Hanson. It seems that if we wait long enough, Joyce will be the investigating officer.'

'No, not a thing, sir,' replied Simon. 'I've been on leave for a while and have been out of touch.'

'That's okay, just asking,' replied Chief Paxton. Christ, the bugger knows, thought Simon.

CHAPTER 19

*T*here were five people sitting around the dining room table; the Websters, the Elliotts and Ron Lange. Simon had arranged the gathering at Collaroy in order to conduct a think tank on how to satisfy the Chief Superintendent's simple requirement; get Fisher. 'Ron, I hope you don't mind the girls being present for this discussion. I've found women's logic and intuition can often be very helpful.'

'No, that's fine. I don't often have the company of two such good looking women.' The girls looked at each other, both rolled their eyes and smiled at Ron.

'Okay, let's get on with it. Has anyone any idea of just how we are to bring down Superintendent Fisher? Chief Paxton wants evidence of corruption, or have Fisher front him with a confession, and we want to bring him down because of his collusion with Rose to stuff up our careers. It sounds like an easy task, not like robbing a bank I suppose.' As Ron was oblivious to the recent history of the Elliotts and the Websters, Simon was immediately the target of a silent rebuke from the girls and Noel.

'We could photograph him taking a bundle of money from Mr Lee,' said Sue, just throwing the idea into the pot.

'No,' said Simon. 'We're not going to achieve our aim with a simple ploy, although taking a compromising photo of Mr Fisher would be helpful. We have to think about this. What do we know about Fisher? How and when does he get paid off? Does he get paid, in cash, cheque, chips at the table, or favours? Does he have a weakness? Like, what do we know about the man? Ron, you probably know more about him than anyone else here, but just before you start, anyone for a beer, tea, coffee?'

'I could really go a coffee right now,' said Ron. 'Don't like to mix work and pleasure, and I would hate to be picked up for a DUI with my record.'

'Give us a hand Georgie,' Simon asked as he got up from the table. 'Coffee okay for everyone?' About five minutes later, the coffees distributed, the discussion on how to undermine Superintendent Fisher resumed.

'Ron. You were going to tell us what you know of Mr Fisher,' Simon said.

'Right. To begin with, Superintendent Fisher is not a nice person. He'll go through the personnel files of those officers with whom he works, irrespective of rank, in an effort to see if he can come up with any weakness he can exploit. And it doesn't matter what type of weakness, be it professional or personal. He prefers if he can nail someone with a personal weakness because that person usually wishes the weakness to remain hidden. Fisher found Chief Inspector Rose's weakness in Rose's gambling, and it didn't take him long to establish how he was financing his problem. He therefore had Rose vulnerable on two counts; his gambling and the slush fund.'

Simon frowned. 'But it seems Fisher wasn't exploiting Rose's weaknesses.'

Ron took a sip of coffee then smiled. 'As I said, Fisher would try and find out if there was a weakness he could exploit, not would exploit. You see, Fisher went to see this Mr Lee, the owner of the Taipan Club, which just happens to be the same place Rosey goes, or should I say, went, to play baccarat. And no, Mr Graham Lee is not Chinese, he's Caucasian, born and bred in Oz. Anyway, Fisher approached Lee to offer immunity from police harassment or even closure of his Club, for a price. Clearly, Lee thought the offer quite attractive, especially as he had the distinction of having both a detective superintendent and a detective chief inspector as clients of the Club.' Ron paused, deep in thought. 'I s'pose having the law as clients of an illegal casino is something one might call a contradiction in terms.'

'Okay, Fisher knew Rose was using the slush fund for his horse racing addiction, but did he know Rose was a client of the Taipan Club?' asked Noel.

Ron shrugged. 'Almost certainly. It seems Mr Fisher hit upon the idea of extorting money from the Taipan Club as soon as he found out what Rosey was up to. However, we don't believe Rose knew of Fisher's little escapade involving the Club, but obviously Fisher knew of Rose's involvement. It just provided Fisher with another string to his bow should he ever need to blackmail Rose. All Fisher had to do was make sure he and Rose never ran into each other at the Club. Mind you, a lot of this is pure speculation. There's a lot of work to be done to corroborate or refute what we have, which isn't much.'

'And how much is Fisher receiving from Mr Lee?' asked Georgie.

'Don't know,' Ron replied. 'It seems he goes to the Club every second Friday night of the public service pay week, has a couple of beers, ogles the women and goes home, unless he gets lucky, that is. The actual handing over of the cash is quite discreet and is paid direct from Lee to Fisher.'

'You said he ogles the women?' Sue enquired.

'Oh yes. Our Mr Fisher believes he's God's gift to the fairer sex. He's been married to Agnes for close on twenty years. She's a definite "would be if she could be", you know, a real Madam Muck. Fisher must be somewhere around fifty and she's about the same age, maybe a year or two younger. They live over at Waverley, which is as close as they could afford to living at Vaucluse. They dine at least once a week at an expensive restaurant, and she likes to socialise and be seen at functions far above her social status. Fisher does whatever Agnes tells him while she spends his money. I think that while he keeps her in the lifestyle to which she has become accustomed, he's free to do as he pleases. I really doubt they could maintain their current lifestyle if they were living off his salary alone. Clearly Agnes has never stopped to ask herself where the money comes from as she probably thinks he's so far up in the police ranks he's being paid a fortune.'

'And she spends a fortune,' added Sue, shaking her head. She then leant forward and placed her folded arms on the table. 'And Ron, does Mr Fisher play up on Agnes?'

'Well, I'm glad we finally got off the finance wagon and onto the juicy bits,' responded Georgie eagerly.

Ron smiled. 'I'm sure he does. As I said, he believes he's God's gift to women and he's always trying to chat up women at the Club. He's got something of a reputation there as a marauding sleaze who believes all females are falling over themselves trying to get him into the sack. Most women just ignore him, although I suppose he must make more than his share of conquests,' Ron said as an afterthought, wondering just how successful Fisher was.

'So,' said Simon with an air of finality. 'Do we try to obtain enough evidence for Chief Paxton, or do we blackmail Fisher into providing Paxton with a confession?'

'Who said anything about blackmail?' asked Noel with surprise. In fact, Noel's question had pre-empted the same question from three others at the table.

'Ah, come on,' said Simon mockingly. 'How else would you obtain a confession? We know Fisher could blackmail the balls off a bandicoot and anyone else he could get his slimy claws into, including old Rosey, God rest his soul. He's so adept at blackmailing other people the last thing he would expect is for someone to blackmail him.' Simon frowned and shook his head. 'But I honestly don't know why Paxton wants either evidence, or a confession; they both mean the same to Fisher in the long run, and that's being hung up by his short and curlies. I just think it might prove a lot easier to gather suitable evidence that we could use to blackmail the bugger.'

Ron stretched his legs out in front of him and put his hands in his pockets. 'I have my doubts as to Paxton's motives. He's a very smart man, a lot smarter than most give him credit and I doubt he wants evidence or a confession just to satisfy a whim to string up the Superintendent. Simon, you mentioned that it wouldn't make any difference to Fisher, one way or the other. Well, it may as we have no idea what motive Paxton has for providing us an alternative as to how we nail Fisher. Let's face it, we can't make Fisher confess to anything unless we force his hand. Obviously, this means any blackmail has to be based on whatever errors of judgment Fisher has committed that we can dig up.

'On the other hand, the complexities of compiling admissible evidence and the preparation of a case that will stand up in court. Either way, I think Paxton will just sit back to see how, or if, Fisher falls on his sword.'

'Right,' said Simon. 'So let's go for the blackmail angle. I suppose it doesn't really matter which way we go because we'll still have to get into the Club as that's where he commits his little transgressions, at least those we know of.'

'Yes, but it's what happens once we're inside that determines if the evidence is sufficient and reliable enough to use as blackmail material. We can attack him on two fronts; his extortion of money from the Club and, secondly, we can exploit his Achilles' heel which is his womanising. That's the one thing I know we can capitalize on,' declared Sue as she raised her eyebrows at Georgie and gave a knowing grin.

'No. Definitely not me, Sue, and I'm adamant on that. There's more chance Fisher will have spotted me with Simon at some function. Besides, you're tall and slim and have all the attributes Fisher probably looks for. And you'll look perfect in one of those short dresses whatsaname wore to the races.'

'Hang on, hang on, what the hell are you two talking about?' asked a totally confused Simon.

Georgie rolled her eyes and shook her head in disbelief. 'Bloody men. Absolutely as slow as a wet week. You explain Sue.'

'Well, I only have an idea in the back of my mind, but I think Georgie's been thinking along the same lines.'

CHAPTER 20

*S*ue was dressed in a long black dress cut low enough to reveal just enough cleavage to create interest. Her high heeled shoes made her look even leggier than she was, but that was as it should be. Sue always worked on the adage "if you've got it, flaunt it", and Noel was never backward in encouraging Sue to comply with the adage; except this time he was not too keen on seeing his wife dressed so provocatively, especially as he was not her escort.

It was the first time in Sue's life that she had set foot inside a casino, legal or otherwise. The initial impression that struck her was the entrance to the casino, off Forbes Street. Any person visiting the club for the first time would need to have very clear instructions in order to find the front door. Contrary to many other similar premises, such as The Spinning Wheel with its garish red neon sign, here there was nothing overtly displayed to suggest a casino existed anywhere in the street at all. The second impression struck Sue as she and her escort walked through the front door where the tuxedo dressed doorman, having welcomed sir and madam to the Taipan Club, wished them both an enjoyable evening; all very polite. Once inside, it was the opulence that took her completely by surprise. Sue hadn't given much thought as to what a casino might be like. Any preconceived idea she may have had was probably based solely on what she had seen in B grade movies where the clientele, all unsavoury characters, if not criminals, moved in a dark and dingy environment with guns tucked away in shoulder holsters. What Sue hadn't anticipated were the bright chandeliers, the neatly dressed croupiers, the unobtrusive waitress serving free drinks to the players at the tables, and the well-dressed clientele. A blue haze and the smell of tobacco smoke hung in the air and this was the only distraction Sue could think of.

The man escorting Sue was short and rather stocky, the small amount of hair on his head brushed forward in an unsuccessful attempt to conceal a bald patch. He was neatly dressed in a dark navy blue suit, a white shirt with a light blue tie. In fact, it was probably the best Ron had looked for years. 'Just relax, Sue, they're not all criminals,' he said, appreciating Sue's apprehension. 'In fact, see that gentleman over there playing pontoon? He's a solicitor and the bloke next to him is a doctor. There are blokes here from all walks of life, most of them professional people taking home very big pay cheques. Not what you expected?'

'No, not quite what I had in mind. Do the women play the tables or are they here just to add spice?' Sue asked after noticing a good percentage of the patrons were women who all appeared to be suitably attired for a part in a James Bond movie.

'Good grief, no,' replied Ron, shocked by the question. 'Many of the high rollers are women who'd think no more of putting a grand on buying one card to an inside straight as you would leaving ten-bob out for the milko.'

'Okay, so my education's been lacking. Who are the tennis

umpires?' asked Sue nodding to the several strategically placed seating towers, similar to those used by tennis umpires.

'The blokes sitting up there just keep an eye on the tables. In legal casinos overseas they have the luxury of cameras in the ceiling to monitor the tables for any sign of irregularities whereas here they just keep an eye open for any dodgy activity that might occur. It rarely happens as most of the patrons here like the place and bending the rules could get them thrown out. Before we do anything else, how about we go and get a drink? There's a couple of stools over there,' said Ron nodding towards the far end of the bar.

'Great idea,' replied Sue, her nerves beginning to soothe following her initial fear of the unknown. After they had settled themselves and Ron had ordered a couple of drinks, Sue turned to Ron. 'Ron, I know I'm naïve on matters of this sort, but this place seems to be more than just a casino. I've seen a lot worse night clubs around Sydney and this place appears to be catering to both the night clubbers and the gamblers. The whole setup seems to be very permanent. If it's so illegal, why don't the police shut it down?'

Ron fumbled for his wallet and withdrew a pound note as one glass of white wine and a light beer arrived on the bar. 'Oh, it's illegal all right, but it's a case of the devil you know. See, Mr Lee knows the police are aware that he's running an illegal business, and he thinks the police won't shut him down because he's paying Fisher to keep them off his back. If the truth be known, even if Mr Lee wasn't paying Fisher, or anybody else for that matter, it would still be unlikely he'd be shut down. It's quite logical, really. If the police raided Mr Lee, he would just close up and move to another location and start all over again. The police would then have to spend both time and manpower to find the new location and the same thing would just keep on happening. As it is, the police know where Mr Lee is and they can keep an eye on him, albeit a blind eye. Let's look at it objectively and accept that Mr Lee is running a very respectable illegal business catering to the specific demands of a wide cross-section of society. He runs his business well and pays his taxes, at least I suppose he does, and he doesn't tolerate any trouble on his premises. As long as he doesn't push the boundaries too far, the police will let him continue to operate.'

'Sounds reasonable when you put it like that,' said Sue as she surveyed the clientele. 'Have you seen anyone yet?'

'Yes, I saw Mr Lee talking to the barman as we came in. It's only nine-thirty so I suspect Mr Lee won't be looking for Fisher to turn up for at least another half hour. I only hope he does show up tonight.'

'And you ain't whistlin' Dixie there, Ron. If you think we're going to do this again, you're dreaming. And yes, I know it was my idea, well sort of, but I honestly didn't know what I was letting myself in for, and the night hasn't even started.'

Ron smiled. 'You'll be right,' he said reassuringly. 'Noel knew what you were getting into and he was willing to let you do it. It seems you blokes really have it in for Fisher.'

'We didn't initially set out to get Fisher, but circumstances changed, as you are no doubt aware. But right now, how about another drink or two? And this time I'll have a scotch and Coke.'

'Sorry.' Ron looked towards the barman who raised his eyebrows questioningly. 'One light beer and a scotch and Coke thanks, mate,' Ron said amiably.

'I suppose you do have film in the camera?' Sue asked, knowing it was probably an unnecessary question.

'Do I have to answer that?' replied Ron. 'And I suppose you have batteries in the recorder?'

'Touché,' replied Sue and patted her handbag.

Ron frowned and said, 'Hey, while we have a bit of time, can you explain something that's been on my mind? When Simon called us together for that meeting at Collaroy, there was never any doubt of Georgie's and your involvement in the scheme of things; it was tacitly understood and accepted by everyone concerned. I felt like a new boy in town trying to break into the local society. I can see the professional rapport between Noel and Simon, and I expect that. But the four of you seem to have an understanding, a connection or am I being too sensitive?'

'Well, we have been good friends for some time now, and the current circumstances have probably strengthened that friendship. You know what they say; a common enemy makes for close allies. When this is all settled, no doubt we'll all get together for a chat where everything will become clearer,' said Sue as she continued to scan the patrons over the rim of the wine glass. 'Do you know Mr Lee personally?'

'Yes, I've met him a couple of times in here. If you were to meet him anywhere else you would never pick him as a gangster. In fact, I don't consider him as such but see him more as a business man and a gentleman who knows how to treat people. As long as you do the right thing by him, he'll do the right thing by you. If you don't, he can get nasty, or so they tell me. Anyway, looks like you're going to meet him as he's headed this way.'

Sue turned to see a tall, thin man, probably in his late forties, dark complexion with long black hair, neatly cut in the Beatles style. He was wearing a dark suit and tie, and wore a gold wrist chain on his right wrist. His blank face broke into an affable smile as he approached. 'Ron Lange, it's nice to see you again. And you really have improved the décor of the club with the presence of this beautiful lady.'

'Mr Lee, I would like to introduce my niece, Sue. She's over from Adelaide for a short stay and, unfortunately, I'm the only person she knows in town. Under the circumstances, I thought it appropriate to volunteer my services to show her around, under great duress, might I add,' said Ron with a wry smile.

'Of course, a lucky girl to have such an accommodating uncle,' replied Mr Lee, who turned and addressed Sue. 'I do hope you enjoy your stay in Sydney and that you have the opportunity to call in at the Taipan Club again before returning to Adelaide. If there is any way I can make your evening more enjoyable, please do not hesitate to ask.' Mr Lee nodded to the barman and took his leave of Ron and Sue.

'Seems like a nice gentleman,' said Sue. 'And I see what you mean. He doesn't exactly fit my preconceived ideas as to what a criminal should look like, or how he should act.'

'As they say, you can't judge a book by its cover. You know when he nodded to the barman? Seems like all our drinks are on the house tonight. Like I told you, he does know how to treat people.'

'Ron, as I've answered what was on your mind, there's some-thing I've been meaning to ask,' said Sue, ceasing her surveillance of the clientele and turning to Ron with a serious look on her face. 'You're a nice enough bloke, but you've never mentioned your wife?'

'No, I don't talk about Ellen very often. Very few people know the exact story, but the short version is that she was shot by some useless thug in an attempted hold-up. We were living in Brisbane at the time. I was a small time petty crim, you know, non-violent stuff where nobody got hurt. Anyway, I let myself get caught up with some so-called friends in a payroll robbery of a pub down in the Valley area that went horribly wrong. Ellen was with us although not actively taking part in the robbery. Anyhow, one of the so-called "friends" went nuts, drew a gun and started shooting everything that moved. Unfortu-nately, for all the shots fired, Ellen was unlucky enough to be the only casualty.

'It put the wind up me to the extent I went to the police and told them everything I knew. Having a good knowledge of the underworld characters and their associates, I was able to provide names, places and a stack of information that was of interest, all free gratis. They police must have thought all their Christmases had come at once. They asked me if I wanted to become an informer and I thought it a good way of coming to terms with Ellen's death, so I said yes. They provided a new identity and concocted a criminal background to go with the identity before sending me down here to Sydney to work for the New South Wales Police.'

'So, not many people know the true story?' asked Sue.

'Apart from Chief Superintendent Paxton and maybe one or two other senior officers, you're the only person who knows. And I would really like to keep it that way.'

'What story, Ron?'

CHAPTER 21

I know, a watched pot never boils, thought Sue, but if Fisher doesn't get here soon, I'll be drunk as a skunk. At the same time, Ron's attention was equally divided between his watch, the door and the glass of beer in front of him, the thought having already crossed his mind that the decision to opt for light beer was probably a good one. It was closer to ten-thirty before Ron suddenly turned to Sue and raised his eyebrows. 'Well, look what the cat just dragged in. The bloke over in the lobby, I mean,' said Ron, nodding towards the front door.

'Is that Fisher?' replied Sue, swiveling her bar stool around to see the door more clearly.

'Who else? And please, do try to be a bit more discreet.' Sue turned back to the bar, suitable admonished. While desperately wanting to get a view of Fisher, Sue realised all she had to do was look in the mirror behind the bar to gain a good view of anyone she wished, and right at that moment that anyone was Superintendent Fisher. Fisher stopped and chattered to the doorman before he gave him a pat on the back and entered the club with an air of arrogance and confidence of one knowing exactly what he wanted. Sue's first impression of Fisher was not favourable. Sue lived on the northern beaches and had always done so. To see anyone with their hair plastered down with Brilcream had to mean that there was a good chance that person came from the Western Suburbs and, more than likely, rode a Harley.

On closer inspection, her thoughts returned to Simon's description of Fisher as a sleaze, and from outward appearances the description fitted Fisher to a T. God, he must be going through a mid life crisis, she thought. Fisher was probably five eleven, thick set with a conspicuous paunch that buried the belt holding up a pair of stovepipe, pinstriped dark blue trousers that matched his dark blue pinstriped coat and white tie. The white pointy toed shoes, gold bracelet and large gold ring on his right middle finger completed the ensemble, making Fisher look something more like a pimp from downtown Manhattan than a superintendent of police.

'Oh God, Ron. What have I done? Quick, a double scotch and Coke, and keep 'em coming. Geez, I've really blundered this time. Bloody Georgie, it's all her fault. She should be sitting here, not me. Fisher is closer to her age.'

Ron laughed. 'Oohh, look at them claws. Thing is, Sue, our Mr Fisher prefers his women blond and a bit younger than Georgie, no offence to Georgie, of course. But he is willing to compromise if the prospects are encouraging, and he does like tall women.' This fact was borne out almost immediately as Fisher engaged in conversation with a tall, leggy brunette, provocatively dressed in a black backless evening gown that clung to a body Jean Harlow would have been proud of. Sue concluded that Fisher had to be a tactile person as he was soon running his hand slowly down the brunette's bare back. The brunette closed her eyes and swayed against the hand before she turned and smiled sweetly at Fisher. She ran her hand softly down his arm and took his hand and squeezed it gently. Suddenly, and without warning, the flirtatious smile was gone, the eyes now blazed in anger. The hand she had been so fondly holding a second earlier was thrust, with considerable force, into Fisher's groin, a gasp of pain drawing the attention of the casino patrons; conversation over.

'Goodness,' exclaimed Sue. 'She doesn't beat around the bush, does she?'

'No,' said Ron, shaking his head. 'That's one woman I wouldn't like to meet in a dark alley, she's a real amazon. Hey boss,' called Ron to the barman, 'who's the lady?'

The barman turned and smiled. 'That lady is Louisa Porter. She's married to a politician and definitely not someone to mess with. Men don't initiate conversation with her; she does the selecting and initiating, if you're lucky. You feeling lucky?'

'No, not that lucky,' replied Ron emphatically. 'How come Mr Fisher knows her?'

The barman touched the side of his nose with his index finger. 'All very hush hush, at least it's supposed to be. But between you, me and your lady, and probably everyone else in the place now I come to think of it, she and Fisher were an item not so long ago. They used to meet here, have a few drinks and then go off to his flat at Potts Point for a night of sexual shenanigans. He'd come in next night and brag about the sessions they had, in detail. No wonder she'd like to have his balls for book-ends now. Lovely if you can get it, as long as you don't boast about it,' said the barman with a knowing smile.

'Good heavens,' exclaimed Sue. 'I've heard of women like that but I never knew they really existed, and I'm no prude when it comes to that sort of thing.'

'I'm sure you're not,' Ron responded. Sue blushed.

'Excuse me, Mr Barman, another scotch and Coke, double,' Sue demanded.

After the altercation with Louisa Porter, Fisher, red faced, made his way to the bar where he ordered a schooner of beer, clearly glad to be rid of the amazon. He appeared to be surveying the club, paying little attention to the goings on at the tables where the gamblers were settling in for some serious gambling. Sue guessed he was searching for a possible liaison or, more bluntly, a predator on the prowl looking for a woman for the night, any woman, she thought before realizing that she just might be that woman. 'Ron, I feel ill. And, by Christ, if you don't get some decent shots of Fisher and Lee, I'll make Madam Louisa Lash look like a…, well, I don't know what,' she said, as she downed her second double scotch in one gulp.

'Don't worry about me, you just look after yourself. If things look like they're getting out of hand, Noel is parked opposite the Club so you just hop it and get over to him. Look, I'd better make myself scarce. Fisher isn't a patient man and he'll want two things in pretty short order; his money and a woman. I'll try and get photos of him chatting you up as well as the pay-off. Just be careful, and good luck.'

It didn't take Fisher long to spot Sue sitting alone at the end of the bar. She had discreetly kept him in view and was not surprised, after his furtive glances in her direction, that he should decide to change his position at the bar. Ron's bar stool was still warm when Fisher, together with his ego and self importance, nonchalantly sidled up next to Sue and sat down. Holy hell, she thought. What a thoroughly odious cane toad.

CHAPTER 22

It was well after midnight before Noel's Holden pulled up outside the bungalow in West Bank Lane. Both Noel and Sue had initially planned on driving straight home to Mona Vale, taking Ron along with them so they could all meet at Collaroy the following morning to discuss the night's outcome. As it was, neither Simon nor Georgie had any intention of retiring for the night without a full expose of events.

'Well?' demanded Simon after they were all comfortably seated in the lounge room.

'I think we got what we were after, but we won't know for certain until we get the photos developed and printed. I've a friend teed up to do the work for me first thing in the morning and he'll do it while I wait,' said Ron, looking a little worse for wear. 'To tell the truth, I wasn't sure if Mr Lee was going to pay Fisher, and I was starting to get a bit anxious. I finally saw them together in a small alcove off the main gambling room and suspected it wasn't for a romantic tryst. That's when Mr Lee gave Fisher his cash; well I hope it was cash because that's when I photographed them.'

'Come on, Ron. I shouldn't think he would be giving Fisher a recipe for muffins,' remarked Georgie, eager to get to the exciting bits.

Ron yawned and stretched. 'No, I suppose not. I must say I did feel pretty uncomfortable taking photos of Fisher trying to chat up Sue. Honestly, some women must be either nuts or frustrated out of the knickers not to see Fisher as anything but a sleaze out for anything he can get.'

'Yes, come on Sue, don't leave me in suspense. What happened? Did anything happen? Could anything have happened?' It was Georgie, all a twitter with expectation of a sordid story, who was eagerly seeking the scandalous revelations.

'As soon as Ron left me to the vultures, I think it took Fisher fully ten seconds to park himself on Ron's stool. He started off with the usual pick-up rhetoric, and even introduced himself as Nigel Fisher, which was odd. Usually when a man plays up on his wife, they'll use some exotic name designed to impress, something like Spencer Mann, or Errol Flynn. It's never Brown, Jones or Fisher.

'You speaking from experience?' asked Noel, his voice tinged with a touch of jealousy.

'Oh, shut up Noel,' came Sue's aggravated response. 'Although he introduced himself as Nigel Fisher, I think it must have been the only thing he got right. He had the temerity to tell me he was a yacht broker, of all things, and he produced a business card which I have in my bag, somewhere.'

'Yeah, I bet he's got a pocket full them, and all different,' Noel broke in, sardonically.

Sue continued with her story. 'Apparently his so-called yacht broking business is at Rushcutters Bay and he claims to drive a Porsche. He also said he owned a flat at Potts Point. Anyway, he eventually asked if I wanted a drink so I asked for the most expensive one I could find, seeing he was paying. It was while he was buying the drinks I took the opportunity to turn on the tape recorder. It had a one-hour tape, so I think I got all the interesting bits. We could listen to it now, but most of it is small chit chat stuff, so I'll leave the playing to another time. All in all, unless a girl was completely naïve or just plain dumb, our Mr Fisher wouldn't have a hope in hell of successfully chatting up a prostitute on a rainy night, even with a handful of tenners.'

'Oh, for Christ sake, Sue. Did he put the hard word on you, or not?' asked Georgie, getting annoyed at the lack of substance in the telling.

'Okay, okay, I was coming to that. We chatted for about half an hour before he made his first move, you know, first base stuff, hand on the knee, shoulder rubbing. All the little things a girl likes when it's the right bloke and a real pain in the bum when it's not, and Fisher's definitely not, so Noel, forget it. When I asked Fisher if he was married, he said he'd been married for a few years but the marriage was on the rocks with the wife seeking a divorce. He said she had a regular boyfriend and they had, for all intense and purposes, gone their separate way. Unfortunately, I didn't know how Ron was going with taking the photos, so I had to play along with Fisher. He finally put the hard word on me and suggested we go back to his flat at Potts Point, which apparently does exist.'

'So, he actually asked you to go to bed with him?' asked Georgie, wide eyed in anticipation.

'Well, not in those words exactly, but I'm sure he must have felt he was on a sure thing as I had to keep him interested,' responded Sue. 'Fortunately, before I had time to answer I saw Ron who gave a nod towards the Ladies. I excused myself from the predicament I had got myself into and started walking towards the loo. That's when Ron came up behind me and whispered that he had what he was after and that we should get the hell out of the place. I didn't need him to tell me twice so I bolted and made a beeline for Noel's car. A couple of minutes later, Ron arrived. End of story. And no, Georgie, I'm not going to tell you the answer I would've given Fisher if Ron hadn't given me the nod. You already know the answer to that.'

Simon frowned. 'The aim of the exercise was to gather sufficient incriminating evidence on Fisher that, once he becomes aware of its existence, he will do anything to save both the embarrassment of exposure to his lovely devoted wife, and his career. We'll see how the photos turn out and also listen to the tape. We'll need an anonymous note to go to Fisher with a copy of the evidence advising that if he doesn't go to Paxton and bare his soul, his wife and the press will receive copies of the evidence. The question is, do we have that evidence?'

Ron nodded. 'I'm sure we have sufficient, but one never knows if enough is enough, especially when it comes to blackmail. Let's face it, Fisher might not give two hoots about Agnes and couldn't care less what we do with seedy photos and recordings of him on the make. The one question I would be asking is, if I was Fisher, why go to Paxton with a confession at all? And what does Paxton want Fisher to confess to; playing up on his wife, or the fact he's on the take from the Taipan Club. And let's face it, Fisher isn't the only cop screwing around on their cheese and kisses. There's something screwy here and I don't know what it is, if you'll excuse the pun.'

'Maybe Paxton is the only one who knows. He seems a pretty smart bloke, so I'll back him, even if I can't see the point of it all,' said Noel with a big yawn and a stretch.

Simon rubbed his eyes with the balls of his hands. 'Yes, it's way past my bedtime and we're not going to come up with anything constructive at this hour. Let's call it a day. Ron, how about you bunk down here for the night while Noel and Sue make tracks for Mona Vale? And I think it might be an idea if we do nothing over the weekend and just let the dust settle?'

Simon's suggestion was met with a chorus of agreement.

CHAPTER 23

The knock on the door to Chief Superintendent Paxton's office ten days after the Taipan Club incident was more of a hammering than a knock. 'Okay, alright. I hear you. Come in and stop that bloody banging,' came the irritated response from Chief Paxton. 'Ah, Superintendent Fisher, you no doubt want to see me?' he enquired, peering over the rim of his reading glasses. 'How absolutely delightful to see you. I suppose I can take it you have something on your mind, and from your knocking, I'd say it must be something important. Take a seat; I'll be with you in a moment.' After signing and dating the document in front of him, Chief Paxton put the pen down, removed his spectacles and sat back, elbows resting on the sides of his chair, his hands clasped on his stomach. 'Now superintendent, tell me, what's on your mind?' Superintendent Fisher chose to remain standing.

'I'm being blackmailed,' snarled Fisher.

'I'm sorry to hear it. Going to cost you much?'

'That's not the point. I've been set-up. I received a note saying I have to make a confession to you, so you obviously know all about it.' Fisher was angry, his demeanour now in total contrast to the imperturbable, composed character he was, generally, at length to portray.

'Haven't a clue what you're talking about. Look, calm down, take a seat and start at the beginning.'

'I won't calm down. You had me set-up for a blackmail scam.'

'I didn't do anything of the sort and I can guarantee no member of the Force set you up, as you so politely put it. Well, no-one under my command anyway. But to blackmail someone, that someone must have done something that he doesn't want a third party to know. And you haven't done anything so remiss that some third party would like to know, have you?'

Fisher threw his hands in the air and collapsed into a chair. 'Look sir, no-one is squeaky clean. And sure, there are things in my life I would prefer Agnes not to know.'

Chief Superintendent Paxton pushed his chair back from the table, crossed his legs and folded his arms. 'And are there things in your life you would prefer the police not to know? Really, what you do behind Agnes's back is your business, although it does raise some doubt as to your integrity, honesty, discretion, and morality, just to list a few of the attributes one thought a superintendent of police should possess. Yes, we may have to look into that, but I really don't understand. You say the note passed to you said you had to confess to me, personally. Well, honestly, Fisher, as I don't give a rat's proverbial about you and your wife's personal life, maybe there's something else you might like to confess.'

Fisher leant forward, one hand on his hip, the other holding his head as he unconsciously examined the floor. 'God, what a mess,' he said, despondently. 'Undoubtedly someone has evidence of a transgression I would prefer them not to have, and if I don't confess to you, a copy of that evidence will go to Agnes and the press. And those evening newspapers would love to have a scandal spattered across the front pages.'

'Ah, the nature of blackmail, a truly insidious crime. I take it you're here because you don't want Agnes or the papers to get their hands on this so-called evidence?' said Chief Paxton, inwardly enjoying Fisher's predicament.

'Hell, she'd kill me. You know Agnes. She leads a double life herself, always trying to be a cut above her station. If the evidence was released to the public, it would destroy her. She likes to think she's part of Sydney society. She can cope with many things, but being ostracized by the society clique would be the worst thing that could happen, even worse than a marriage break up.'

'Superintendent Fisher, it is only by the Grace of God that you are the only officer beating a track to my door to confess your sins. I have no doubt the majority of the Force have secret indiscretions they prefer to keep secret; it's obvious you just weren't discreet enough. I'm sure the blackmailer couldn't give a stuff as to your infidelities, they're a dime a dozen. I'd even hazard a guess and say it was probably a little bonus that just happened to fall into the blackmailer's lap. You know, I can't help thinking there is a little more to the story than you're telling, and I bet the evidence backs up my theory. Care to comment?'

'I may as well,' said an unhappy Superintendent Fisher. 'To use the vernacular, I'm the one that's screwed, either way. To cut a long story short, I've been on the take.' Fisher put his hand inside his coat pocket and withdrew a large brown envelope which he placed on Paxton's table. 'Here, someone took these photos inside the Taipan Club about ten days ago. There's also an audio tape of my conversation with a girl. And honestly, sir, I'd never seen her before in my life.'

'On the take, eh?' Chief Paxton's manner changed dramatically from a somewhat flippant attitude towards the whole event, to one of all seriousness. He replaced his reading glasses on his nose and scanned through the photos, occasionally pausing for closer inspection.

'Yes, from the Taipan Club.'

'You mean Mr Lee. I take it he's the one in the photo?'

'Yes.'

'And how long has this been going on?'

'Several months, I suppose.'

'Don't suppose. How long has this been going on?' Paxton riled, dropping his glasses onto the table.

'Shortly after Detective Chief Inspector Rose arrived. It didn't take me long to find out he was using money from the funds we have to pay our informants. He used this to bankroll his gambling at the races and at casinos, notably the Taipan Club, although he had been to others. I went to see Mr Lee and we came to an arrangement.

'Ah yes, the arrangement,' said Chief Paxton. 'He pays you, not an insignificant amount I'd wager, and the police turn a blind eye. 'How much?'

'Let's just say it was enough to finance Agnes's life style. Look, Agnes and I have been married for twenty odd years now. We both need a little excitement in our life and she can spend money like there's no tomorrow. She has her social life and what she does is her business.'

'And you never saw Rose at the Taipan Club,' asked Chief Paxton as he picked up his reading glasses and pen and started jotting notes on a pad.

'Hell, no. He'd only go on a Wednesday or Saturday night after the races.'

'Does Agnes know you're out at illegal gambling casinos chatting up stray women?'

'I really don't think she could care less what I do.'

'So, what's on the tape that might upset her if she's so ambivalent to your goings on?'

'Well, I don't think she'd be too impressed to hear me asking a young lady to spend the night with me back in my flat at Potts Point.'

'Why?' asked Chief Paxton, now interested to see just how big a hole Fisher could dig for himself.

'Two things. First, I think she wouldn't be overly impressed with my chat-up technique, as I probably exaggerate or stretch the truth, just a bit. But really, most women appear to like a braggart and appear eager to believe anything you tell them. It must create a bit of excitement in their otherwise bored existence. The second is that Agnes knows nothing of the flat at Potts Point. I started renting it years ago but eventually found that to have a nice private place that nobody knew about was very convenient.'

'And did the lady in the photos agree?'

'Agree to what? Ah, you mean did she agree to go back to my flat. No, and that's what makes the whole thing stink. The little bitch must have had the audio tape in her hand bag. Just after I had put the hard word on her, she said she was going to the loo, and never came back.'

'Clearly the lady was more astute than you gave her credit for,' said Chief Paxton, now enjoying Fisher's humiliation. 'You know you do have something of a reputation for women around Day Street.'

'Oh, well seeing there aren't many women around Day Street, I'd say I didn't have much of a reputation at all.'

I'll ignore that, thought Chief Paxton. 'I'll put that a little more succinctly, Fisher. The junior ranks within the Day Street station refer to you as The Sleaze because of your reputation of trying to get every second woman you meet into bed. Anyway,

I'm anxious to hear this tape of yours, it must be absolutely pornographic.'

'You'll be disappointed, sir. Okay, so I invited a girl back to my flat. So what? That's not a crime,' replied Fisher petulantly.

'No, not a criminal crime, but maybe a moral one depending on your moral standards,' returned Paxton.

'Look, sir, I admit I screw around on my wife. But so do the majority of married men.'

'Well, you might, Fisher, but there are a lot of married people, including myself, who don't. Does Agnes sleep around then?'

'Good grief no. Well, how the hell would I know? Maybe she does, but who in their right mind would take the time and effort? Good God, she's almost in her fifties and past that stage in life. Hell, just the thought of it is appalling.

'And you're not?'

'Not what? Oh, you mean "passed that stage". Come on, sir, it's different for a man.'

Chief Paxton sighed and shook his head. 'Fisher, your wife knows what a pillock you look like when you go hunting and I've no doubt she has a good idea as to what you're hunting. Do you ever consider how she might feel?'

'No sir, and I really don't care. I jeopardize my career so she can go swanning off on the social scene. No sir, I really don't give a damn how she feels.'

'Well, that's your business. But taking kick-backs from the Taipan Club is my business. And what do you think Mr Lee is going to think when you stop frequenting his club to pick up your money? And you will not be picking up any more money from Mr Lee. Do I make myself clear?'

'Yes, sir, and I haven't a clue, sir. I never stopped to think about what Mr Lee might do,' replied Fisher, a thoughtful look on his face.

'Well, I have, and guess what? The first thing he'll expect is for the police to close him down. And if the police, for one reason or another, don't close him down, our Mr Lee might justifiably ask what the hell has he been paying you for. And we both know it's not in our interest to raid the Taipan Club. So, when nothing happens Mr Lee will be one pissed off criminal for having paid you for nothing in return. But if you don't happen to turn up for work one day, at least we'll know where to start our investigation,' said Chief Paxton, his demeanour reverting to his earlier flippancy. In fact, he was enjoying seeing Fisher squirm.

'Well honestly, sir. I really don't think the situation is as bad as all that,' replied Fisher.

'I'm glad you see it that way, but you probably haven't considered the situation from our point of view. I suppose the judge may be lenient in view of the fact that you came to me. After all, extortion is an offence which, in this State, carries a maximum of ten years, and you have made a confession,' said Chief Superintendent Paxton, showing little sympathy for Fisher's plight.

'So, a couple of years in Long Bay, if I should last that long, or run the chance of being taken out by one of Mr Lee's gunmen. Gee whiz, they say you never reach crisis point while you have options. With those options my future looks assured,' said Fisher despondently.

Detective Chief Superintendent Paxton sat back in his chair and folded his arms. 'Well, Ollie, looks like you've gone and got yourself into one hell of a mess this time. The blackmailer wanted you to confess your little arrangement with Mr Lee to me, or he'd tip off your wife and the press of your extra marital shenanigans and unauthorized income from the Taipan Club. Just a thought, but I take it you're not declaring this income to the Tax Department?'

'No, sir.'

'So, tax evasion. And the flat at Potts Point. It's rented in your name?

'No, sir.'

'False pretenses. How long did I say your stay in Long Bay would be, a couple of years? Better make that a few. But let's get back to the blackmailer. It appears the blackmailer gets stuff all out of this, so why go to the trouble. Maybe he just wants to see you squirm. Have you upset anybody lately?' Chief Paxton asked with complete indifference.

'No, no-one I can think of. Chief Inspector Rose would get up people's nose at times as he was closer to the coalface but…' Fisher shrugged.

'As I said earlier, I don't think for one minute the black-mailer is in the Force.' Chief Paxton looked at his watch and got up from his chair. 'Unfortunately, I have an appointment with the Assistant Commissioner and, much as I would like to continue our little discussion, I'm afraid it will have to wait. For the moment you will consider yourself under an administrative warning and you will confine your police duties to administrative matters only. And I would strongly suggest you go nowhere near the Taipan Club. I will need to bring this matter to the attention of both the Assistant and Deputy Commissioners. Do I make myself clear?'

On his way out of Detective Chief Superintendent Paxton's office, Detective Superintendent Fisher closed the door with conscious gentility. He was not a happy man.

CHAPTER 24

*S*imon and Noel sat by the window in the George and Bathurst Streets coffee shop. Both men were unusually quiet, both pausing to reflect on recent events.

'I hear Fisher has been to see Paxton,' said Noel, absently tearing a napkin to shreds, one little piece at a time.

'Yes,' replied Simon. 'Paxton called me up and gave me the gist of the conversation. Apparently, Fisher did confess to both the womanising and the pay-off from the Taipan Club. I don't think he was too pleased with our methodology of obtaining the evidence, although he did say that in view of the circumstances, he would overlook the small matter of blackmail.'

'Well, bully for Paxton. How else did he think we could get Fisher to confess his sins? So, what now?' asked Noel as he pushed the scraps of paper into a tidy pile.

'I think we've achieved what Paxton wanted, so I guess it's back to business as usual. We still don't know how successful Hanson has been, so maybe we're still headed for the Long Bay Jail. Now, that would be something. You and me incarcerated in one cell with Fisher in the next,' remarked Simon, taking on a reflective mood.

'Come on, Simon, Hanson's good but you don't honestly think he'll crack the case. The silence here at Day Street regarding the robbery is deafening, no-one has a clue,' said Noel, looking around the coffee shop in expectation. 'I thought Ron was meeting us?'

Simon looked at his watch. 'Yes, he is, but he's only a couple of minutes late. We'll give him another ten. Another coffee?'

'Yeah, why not. I'll pee all day, but what the heck.'

Simon nodded to the buxom young waitress who sauntered over with a broad smile on her face. 'I know, don't tell me. One flat black and one cappuccino, right? Becoming one of the regulars now, aren't you?'

'Better add another black coffee to that,' Noel said, as Ron entered the coffee shop and made his way over to the table and sat down.

'Morning Simon, Noel. What's new?' Ron asked, happy to get the weight off his feet.

Simon shrugged. 'Probably nothing you don't already know. I suppose you know Fisher has fallen on his sword and gone to Paxton?'

'Yes, so I heard. Couldn't happen to a nicer bloke. But that might be totally irrelevant now,' Ron replied dismissively.

'What do you mean, irrelevant?'

'Rumour has it Mr Lee has put out a contract on our Mr Fisher.'

Simon exhaled and relaxed. 'Phew. For a moment then I thought you said Lee has put out a contract on Fisher.'

'No, I didn't say that, Simon. I said rumour has it Lee has put out a contract.'

'You mean a contract on Detective Superintendent Fisher? You've got to be kidding?'

'Sorry Simon, but I kid you not. The word is Lee was ripped off by Fisher, and we all know that's exactly what he did. The unfortunate thing, for Fisher I mean, is that he didn't think he was ripping Lee off. You see, it seems Fisher held the belief that he was providing Lee with a watertight guarantee the Club was immune to police closure, albeit at a price. Lee now knows something has happened as Fisher hasn't been near the Club for a couple of weeks and the Club's still operating. The truth is, Fisher did rip him off and you shouldn't do that sort of thing, at least without some consideration as to the ramifications.'

'Oh, hell,' exclaimed Noel. 'And all we wanted was to bring him down a peg or two, not six feet down.'

'Is there any room for negotiation with Mr Lee?' asked Simon. At that moment the waitress arrived with the three coffees and the conversation came to an abrupt halt. 'Black there, black there, and…

'Don't tell me. I know where the third one goes.' The waitress placed the cappuccino in front of Simon. 'See, you're my regulars now.' The young girl turned and walked away, her hips swaying.

'Ah, the innocence of youth, while we sit around talking about someone getting bumped off. Ca la vie,' said Ron.

'And not just someone. You mean Detective Superintendent Fisher,' said Simon. 'You didn't answer my question, Ron. Will Lee negotiate?'

'Why should he? It's not as though we have something he wants, apart from not closing him down. Lee was under the belief the money he paid Fisher was for an insurance policy against being raided by the police. I know it's only been a fortnight which means Fisher hasn't been in to pick up his pay on the last two occasions. Suddenly Mr Lee believes Fisher has taken him for a ride as Fisher's not collecting his money and the police haven't been around to belt the door down, yet.'

'Cripes. A contract is a bit heavy handed though. You would have thought Lee would have discussed things with Fisher to see just what's going on before he put out the contract,' said Noel.

Ron shook his head. 'No, you see, Lee doesn't like Fisher, never has. Lee regarded Rose as a harmless nonevent with a brain the size of a sub-atomic particle, but then Fisher turned up with his proposition, you give me money or I'll close you down. Plain and simple extortion. However, Lee has eventually decided the money he was paying Fisher made no difference as to whether the Club would be shut down or not. Lee obviously came to the conclusion that he wasn't receiving the quid pro quo.'

Simon frowned. 'Yes, but surely Fisher must have known he was setting himself up to be blackmailed. Mr Lee is no fool so he must have had sufficient evidence on Fisher to blackmail him, if the need ever arose.'

'I'm sure he has, or did,' replied Ron. 'Irrespective of any material Lee has on Fisher, it's now useless since Fisher has been to see Paxton. I've no doubt Lee knows of Fisher's little visit to see Paxton and he probably thinks the future of the Club is now in the lap of the Gods. The last thing Mr Lee wants is to draw attention to himself. The Club is very successful due, mainly, to the fact that Lee has always played a straight game, the best clientele, no hoods or rough stuff. While he continues to play it that way the police are happy with the devil they know, and won't close him down,' said Ron simply.

'But Mr Lee has never known that little fact,' said Noel. 'So now he believes his beloved Club is insecure, through Fisher's action, and he's gunning for Fisher.'

Ron shook his head in disagreement. 'No, I think it's all rumour. Lee isn't the type of man to have someone shot, or whatever. When you meet him, and no doubt you will eventually, you'll find he's a perfect gentleman, definitely not the typical gangster, by any means. To be honest, for Mr Lee to have put out a contract would be contrary to everything we know about the man.' Ron looked at his watch and said, 'Look, I'd love to stop and chat, but I have an appointment. If I hear anything on the grape vine, I'll let you know.' Ron gulped the last of his coffee, and hurriedly left leaving Simon and Noel somewhat perplexed.

CHAPTER 25

'Hi boss,' Noel said breezily as he entered the office. He was glad to be back dressed in civvies and doing what he regarded as real police work; crime detecting.

'Morning, Noel,' returned Simon, sitting back in his chair, his feet up on the table. 'We haven't got much on today. It seems that with Rose's death and the sword hanging over Fisher, there's a lack of direction here at Day Street.'

'Any scuttlebutt on their replacements, assuming of course Fisher gets the bullet? Sorry boss, that was in poor taste, but you know what I mean,' Noel said, as he hung his coat on the back of the door.

'Not a whisper. I feel sorry for Paxton, losing his chief inspector and then this kafuffle with his superintendent within such a short time. I hear he's spoken to the Assistant Commissioner, and Fisher's problem may have even gone higher.'

Noel sat back in his chair and loosened his tie. 'And what about Hanson,' he asked as he unscrew the top off a bottle of water. Although the office was fitted with an air conditioner that worked sometimes, the November weather had finally brought consistently higher temperatures which were making severe inroads into the effectiveness of the antiquated cooling system.

'I don't think he's having any greater success than Rosey did, poor bugger,' said Simon flatly. 'I know Paxton was keen to get the case wrapped up quickly, but that seems a forlorn hope now. Somehow I think even Paxton's losing interest.'

'Well, Fisher is still alive and kicking. Hopefully Mr Lee isn't overly committed to doing away with him. But you're right. The place seems to be grinding to a halt, which brings me to the question, Simon. Are we the goodies or the baddies? I think I should get this clear in my mind whether we're policemen or criminals.'

'Good question,' replied Simon, pursing his lips and concentrating deeply. 'Let's be objective about it. We've robbed a bank, we've blackmailed a police superintendent, we're accessories to murder, although that could be debated, and we're accessories to fraud, just to run a few off the top of the head. I'm sure there are a few more that could be dragged up if we were to take a closer scrutiny. As some Roman poet said, "Disce Omnes".'

'Which means?' asked Noel, although not that interested in what some Roman poet had to say.

'Noel, your education is lacking. It means "From one piece of villainy judge them all", or something like that.'

'Yeah, okay, that's wonderful. But you haven't answered the question. Are we the good guys or the bad guys?' asked Noel, becoming a little frustrated.

'Right, I've listed the points which, on face value, would tend to suggest we're on the baddies side. Now, you list the points to put us on the goodies side.'

Noel settled back in his chair and rested his feet on the table. 'Okay, we robbed a bank, but we gave the money back, or at least we're in the process of giving it back, which proves we never intended to permanently deprive the bank of its cash. Isn't that one of the proofs of robbery that has to be proven?'

Simon shook his head. 'Don't go there, Noel. You'd be walking into a legal minefield because at the time of the robbery, it could be claimed you had every intention of taking the cash from the bank, permanently. But do go on.'

'Okay, there was no murder. It was a simple case of death by natural causes that could happen to anyone, even poor old Dorothy. As for the blackmailing of Superintendent Fisher, we were only doing what Chief Paxton wanted. He didn't provide us with the means to an end. He just left that up to us. And the fraud. Okay, as soon as we found out about Rosey and the slush fund, we should have reported it to the hierarchy, who clearly knew all about it anyway. I'd say that puts us with the good guys.'

'All right, all right,' conceded Simon. 'What side do you want to be on?'

Noel didn't hesitate. 'The goodies, of course, especially after confronting that bank teller, what's his name, Bruce, Bruce Bentley. He was enough to put Dillinger on the straight and narrow.'

'Yes, he certainly did have a way with words. Nice enough bloke, I thought,' replied Simon. The conversation on whether to be goodies or baddies was interrupted by a knock on the door.

'Password?' called Inspector Webster.

'Haven't a clue,' came the voice of Sergeant Mathieson.

'Close enough. You may enter.'

'Ah, such frivolity in the face of adversity,' said the Sergeant as he entered the office. My illustrious leader has extended a cordial invitation for you both to attend a meeting to be held in the third floor conference room at ten o'clock tomorrow morning. You will be in attendance?'

'Is that a question or a statement, Sergeant?' asked Inspector Webster.

'I'd consider it a statement, but then again, I'm just a lowly sergeant. No offence meant, Sergeant Noel.'

'None taken. Can you give us an idea what this is all about?' asked Sergeant Noel, in all innocence.

'Come on Sergeant, you're supposed to be a detective. If you haven't any idea, maybe you should be out directing traffic. I'm sure your boss knows, so ask him later. But let's just say you aren't the only recipients of an invitation. I even got one, as did Inspector Hanson and Superintendent Fisher. I've no doubt there will be others as Chief Paxton wanted the conference room booked.'

Inspector Webster picked up his diary and flipped through the pages. 'Ah yes, I think I may be able to attend. Yes, you can tell the Chief Superintendent my chronicle of forthcoming engagements, which may preclude my presence at the convocation to which I have been cordially invited, is currently deficient of any prearranged circumstance that may inhibit or, indeed, pose any significant impediment to my being able to assemble, along with other august recipients of such solicitation, as entreated by your honourable boss. Both my Sergeant and I look forward in anticipation to the convocation and the ensuing proceedings with baited breath,' said Inspector Webster in a theatrical manner.'

'Would I be amiss if I were to interpret that as an acceptance of the Chief's invitation?'

'No. Not at all.'

'Oh, how absolutely grand,' said Sergeant Mathieson, taking his cue and taking up the theatrics. 'Chief Paxton will be absolutely delighted. Thank you, gentlemen. I shall now take my leave and convey your acceptance to milord with all due haste.

Au revoir, mes amis.' With that, Sergeant Mathieson made a sweeping bow, and left the office.

'Well, that's a change; a bloke who can see the brighter side of life,' said Noel. Regardless of the recent levity, his friendly countenance rapidly changed to a worried look. 'Boss, this meeting tomorrow. The invitation list doesn't auger well for a friendly chit chat, especially with Fisher and Hanson attending. Do you think Hanson's onto something?'

Inspector Webster sat back in his chair and clasped his hands behind his head. After a moment of reflection, he said, 'I honestly can't say, but if I was a betting man, which I am, I'd say he's achieved sweet bugger all with the investigation, and that's probably why Paxton wants him at the meeting. As I said to Mathieson, I wait with baited breath for what will, no doubt, be a very interesting little get together.'

CHAPTER 26

$\mathcal{I}$nspector Webster and Sergeant Elliott were the first to arrive at the third floor conference room. The room, rectangular in shape with heavy blue curtains hanging along one wall, was one of the few rooms in the building with a carpeted floor that happened to be a motley green colour. Sergeant Elliott, his first time in the room, pulled back one of the curtains to reveal a set of windows overlooking a brick wall of a building a short distance away. He nodded in appreciation of the fine art work some clown had produced on the overlooked wall; a very large and meaningful painting of a finger. Sergeant Elliott smiled, closed the curtain and turned his attention to the rest of the conference room. The walls were adorned with plaques of different police forces and organizations from around the world, together with photographs of past senior police officers. Centered on the wall at the head of the room was an Australian Flag and a New South Wales Police Force flag. The rectangular conference table was of highly polished cedar and approximately ten feet long and four feet wide. There was a blue velvety chair at each end of the table, with another four similar chairs placed down each side. Several jugs of water had been placed at various intervals along the table and each chair had been provided with an upturned glass, a writing pad, a pen and an ash tray. In a corner of the room was a chair and a small table upon which a tape recorder had been arranged, a tape already loaded for operation.

'Ten to,' commented Inspector Webster after referring to his watch. 'Everyone else will arrive at two minutes to ten; bet your life on it.' Inspector Webster was wrong, for at that moment the door opened and a gentleman was escorted into the room by a uniformed constable. The man was tall and lean, impeccably dressed in a dark blue pinstriped suit, a white shirt and a dark blue tie. He wore a gold Omega watch on his left wrist and a gold bracelet on his right.

The constable looked around the room and, on recognizing Sergeant Elliott said, 'Sergeant, as Mr Lee needs to be escorted within the building, can I hand him over to you?'

Sergeant Elliott looked at Inspector Webster with a look of surprise before returning his attention to the constable. 'Yes, by all means. Thank you, constable. Mr Lee, I'm Sergeant Noel Elliott and this is my superior officer, Inspector Webster.' Mr Lee graciously shook the hands of both men and smiled.

'My presence surprises you and for that I apologise. I thought my being here might prove uncomfortable for some people.'

'Well, there's no discomfort on my part, Mr Lee. But I wouldn't mind betting it'll be bloody uncomfortable for someone else,' said Webster, with a knowing grin.

'Oh, no doubt you're referring to Superintendent Fisher,' responded Mr Lee.

'Well, I don't think he'll be overjoyed to see you, which I can understand in light of the local gossip. I would say you'd probably be the last person on earth he'd want to see.'

Mr Lee shook his head in disappointment. 'Gentlemen, I never have and never will put out, as they say, a contract on anyone. I run a legitimate illegal casino and could not afford any bad publicity. I have no idea where the rumour started and, if there is any reason to believe such a thing, it is a misunderstanding. However, while I do look forward to seeing Mr Fisher, I doubt my feelings are reciprocated.'

Next to arrive was Inspector Hanson, his short stature, bald head and habitual cigarette hanging from the corner of his mouth a dead giveaway as to his identity. Like Webster and Elliott, Hanson was in civvies, his shirt hanging out of a pair of trousers that appeared to be at least two sizes too big. 'Hi Simon, Noel. D'ya know what's goin' on?'

'No, not a clue,' replied Inspector Webster. 'I could hazard a guess, but then I could be wrong, so let's just wait and see. By the way, how's the investigation into the bank robbery going. I hear Chief Inspector Rose handed it over to you?'

Inspector Hanson put his hands in his pockets and shrugged. 'Simon, between you and me, it's progressing about as fast as a three toed sloth on sedatives. It's proving to be a difficult case as none of the usual informants know anything about it. What information we do have is all contradictive, although the name of one of the robbers is thought to Norman, which isn't much to go on. But don't tell Paxton that, he's eager for results.'

At that moment the door to the conference room opened and a group of people crowded into the room. Inspector Webster immediately identified Chief Superintendent Paxton, Ron Lange and Sergeant Mathieson. There were two others with the group, a female constable and a policeman in a uniform wearing the rank insignia of an assistant commissioner. After the congenial introductions and pleasantries, people found their seats and waited for proceedings to commence.

It was Chief Paxton, standing behind a chair at the head of the table who bought the meeting to order. 'Gentlemen, if you please, we'll get this show underway.' On taking his seat, Paxton looked around the table. 'It looks like we're only missing one person at the moment, and I think I can hear him now.' The door opened and Superintendent Fisher entered the room, the look of concern etched on his face quickly replaced by one of horror when his gaze fell on Mr Lee. Fisher's initial impulse was to turn and run, but the cool voice of Chief Paxton halted any action he may have been contemplating. 'Relax Nigel, no-one is going to shoot you, well, not here anyway. Just take a seat and let's get on with it.'

Chief Paxton continued. 'Gentlemen, may I introduce Assistant Commissioner Garside. The Commissioner is here to ensure everything is correct on procedural matters, and to answer any questions you may have at the end of the meeting. This get-together is rather important as it could possibly pre-empt a career change, at least for some of you. Also present is Constable Pauline York who will ensure the proceedings are taped and recorded appropriately. We will take a break after half an hour for coffee and comfort. One last point. For the sake of brevity, I will not be using ranks, only surnames.'

With that, Chief Superintendent Paxton put on his reading glasses and opened a manila folder. 'I have currently three topics listed on the agenda sheet; Chief Rose's fraudulent use of the slush fund, Superintendent Fisher's little extortion exploits, and the bank robbery.' Whether by design or by accident, Paxton's searching gaze over the rim of his glasses just happened to fall on Sergeant Elliott at the time he mentioned the topics.

For a moment Sergeant Elliott closed his eyes and let his head sink to his chest in despondency. Bloody Paxton. If Hanson doesn't know who did the bank job, Paxton sure does, bet my balls on it, thought the Sergeant. He then raised his head and looked at Inspector Webster whose face failed to convey any emotion.

Chief Superintendent Paxton continued. 'I'm not going to bore you with what has become general knowledge. We all know, and have known for some time, Rose was taking cash from the informant's slush fund to finance his horse racing and casino gambling habits. What some of you may not know is that Sergeant Mathieson here works directly to me and he has been conducting an investigation into the embezzlement of the fund for some time now.

'The way Rose did this was to present vouchers to Fisher for approval to pay informants who never existed. Normally vouchers are required to be accompanied by supporting documentation, a fact Fisher chose to ignore, thus contravening Police Administrative Instruction 42A. However, Fisher knew exactly what Rose was up to. Not to be outdone by a subordinate, Fisher decided to get in on the act by going to the Taipan Club and extorting money from Mr Lee. Mr Lee believed that by paying Fisher, the Club would be immune to being shut down. Have you any comments, Mr Lee?'

'Just a quick one,' replied Mr Lee. 'Naturally, after Mr Fisher came to see me I took steps to ensure his lasting support. On the night of his first pay packet, the whole transaction was photographed in detail thus providing me with an insurance policy.'

'Don't you mean you had the evidence you needed to blackmail Fisher, if the need arose?' asked Inspector Webster.

'Yes, I suppose so, but I prefer not to use words like extortion or blackmail; they sound so corrupt,' replied Mr Lee. 'And you are forgetting one thing. Although I may have been in a position to exact remuneration, pecuniary or in kind, for the non-disclosure of certain information which may have discredited Mr Fisher, the question as to whether I would have used that information is problematic. You see, in the legal sense, blackmail is a criminal offence and, regardless of what you may think, I am not a criminal. Apart from that, the blackmailer never ends up with a good reputation, and that's something money can't buy.'

Chief Superintendent Paxton took off his reading glasses and looked at Fisher. 'So, you've compromised yourself on two separate occasions, initially being photographed taking money from Mr Lee and, more recently, by doing exactly the same thing. It seems the only difference between the two incidents is that you were being photographed by two different photographers working for two different people with similar motives. I can take it, Mr Lee, you are not blackmailing Fisher?'

'No way in the world. I'll admit I don't like the man because it looks like I paid him his extortion money for nothing. I haven't paid him for a couple of weeks now and the Club's still operating. This leads me to believe I needn't have gone along with his proposition in the first place. Correct?'

'Probably,' replied Chief Paxton.

'Well, as I said, I'm not blackmailing Fisher, but best of luck to whoever is. If you ever find him, or her, you can tell them I'll buy them a beer or two. Are we allowed to know on what grounds he is being blackmailed, although I presume it's for extorting money from the Club?'

Paxton looked at Fisher, who sat with his head down making a conscious effort not to look at anyone. 'Everyone's going to find out sooner or later, Fisher, so I may as well let them know now. Fisher is being blackmailed on two counts, receiving cash from the Taipan Club, and he's been caught playing up on his wife.' The seriousness of the first blackmail issue was overshadowed by the amusement of the second, a ripple of laughter percolating through the room. 'Gentlemen, before we get any smart-arse comments, I think it might be a good idea to call a break for twenty minutes,' said Paxton, placing his spectacles on the table.

Thirty minutes later everyone was seated and ready to proceed. The familiar topic of discussion during the break was the future of Superintendent Fisher. There was little that could be done regarding Rose; he was dead. But Fisher was alive and kicking, notwithstanding the rumour of his imminent demise. Again, it was Chief Paxton who set the meeting off. 'Gentlemen, before cracking on to our third topic of discussion, Mr Lee has identified a potential problem with which we may be faced with in the near future. Mr Lee.'

'Thanks, Chief Paxton. As you know, marijuana has been readily available on the streets and is increasing in popularity. Regardless of this popularity, it seems a niche is being created for harder drugs, primarily heroin. Where I have no doubt marijuana will continue to be sold on the streets, heroin is a different kettle of fish. We are beginning to see establishments, such as nightclubs and casinos, excluding the Taipan Club at this stage, being targeted for the development of hard drug dealing opportunities.

'Chief Paxton, I'm aware the Police Department will shortly be setting up an independent drug squad and I would like to be involved with this squad in some way. Regrettably, the Taipan Club is located within a socioeconomic area in which the local environment may, and in no way do I wish to cast aspersions or denigrate the good inhabitants of the specific area, contribute to the development and even precipitate the expansion of the heroin trade, once established.'

Chief Paxton frowned and leaned back on his chair. 'Mr Lee,

to put it, how shall we say, more colloquially, the Taipan Club is located with a brothel on one side and a tattoo parlour run by a bikie gang on the other. You have the idea the nature of the clientele of these two establishments may prove detrimental to your club's standing within the community.'

'Chief Paxton, your foresight and grasp of the situation is inspiring,' replied Mr Lee, with a nod of appreciation.

'Okay, let's make some decisions. First off, Mr Lee's advice on the heroin trade. Ron, could you do with an undercover cop, someone to have contact between you and these places identified as potential dens of iniquity?'

'Could never have too many. Do you have anyone in mind?' replied Ron, drawing little circles on his pad.

'Yes, I do,' replied Paxton. 'Fisher, would you prefer two to four in Long Bay or go undercover?'

For the first time, Fisher looked up, the look on his face reflecting the distress of having just realised the precarious position his future was now in. 'Hell sir, that's a great option. Go to Long Bay and get rubbed out by some psychopathic killer who loves killing cops, or go undercover and end up at the bottom of the harbour.'

'Well, don't blame me,' replied Paxton. 'But I want an answer, now.'

'Undercover. I'll take my chances outside. You can't hide while inside.'

'Settled, and I think I can speak for Commissioner Garside when we acknowledge the fortitude and bravery you have shown in volunteering for such a hazardous position. Thank you, Superintendent Fisher. You'd better come and see me tomorrow morning and we'll discuss the matter. Ron, you'd better come along too. Oh yes, I suggest you and Mr Lee get together and have a chat as to the role Mr Lee may be able to play.'

'Excuse me, sir.' It was Inspector Hanson who finally got the chance to enter the conversation. 'All this has been very interesting, and you did mention the bank job was on the agenda. So far nothing has been in my bailiwick.'

'All right Hanson, let's talk about the bank job. How's the investigation going?' asked Paxton, satisfied that some meaningful decisions had already been made at the meeting. He abhorred meetings where nothing happened, or no progress made.

'It's progressing, sir. We have a few leads we are working on and I'm sure a breakthrough is imminent,' Hanson replied, sorry now that he hadn't kept his mouth shut.

'Bullshit, Hanson. Your investigation is going as slow as a tectonic plate and, even if it wasn't, I expect an answer, not some glib throw away response a journalist from the TV news could expect. I want you to collate all you have and pass it to Inspector Webster here. He'll take over the investigation and he will get results, won't you Webster?'

Inspector Webster sat with the shocked expression of a condemned man, the blood rapidly draining from his face. 'Sorry, sir, but I can't,' he blurted out before thinking.

'Why not? Anyway, I'm not asking, I'm telling, and you will get results.' Inspector Webster glanced at Sergeant Elliott who looked pale, a blank, faraway look on his face. 'One last point, and it's not on the agenda; the staffing of Day Street,' continued Chief Paxton. 'We are deficient one chief inspector, although we have a number of candidates for this position, and one superintendent now that the good Superintendent Fisher has volunteered his services to go undercover. I have already spoken to the Commissioner on this subject and our decision as to the appropriate action is pending. Sergeant Mathieson will conclude his investigation into the swindling of the slush fund, and I can confidently predict there will be nothing emanating from his report to tarnish the good name of Chief Inspector Rose. I think that just about covers all I wanted to say. Has anyone any questions?'

Inspector Hanson had, by his earlier question to Chief Paxton, appeared to have successfully negated any inclination anyone may have harboured to ask further questions, regardless of Paxton's cordial invitation. Chief Paxton looked around the table and, as none were forthcoming, he said, 'All right gentlemen, I think that just about does it. My thanks to the Commissioner for his attendance and to Constable York for ensuring everything has been recorded. Mr Lee, thanks for coming along and we shall see what we can arrange, keeping in mind you are running an illegal casino. Inspector Webster and Sergeant Elliott, I'd like to see you in my office at two o'clock this afternoon. Sergeant Mathieson, would you please escort Mr Lee from the building.'

As they were walking down the corridor towards the lift, Sergeant Elliott couldn't help but overhear Mr Lee ask Ron how his niece had enjoyed her trip to Sydney and that he hoped she got back to Adelaide safely.

CHAPTER 27

'Holy hell, I feel like I've been put through a washing machine. If I feel like this now, how will I feel by this afternoon? And you know, something tells me old Paxton is going to come down on us like a ton of bricks,' said Noel as he and Simon made their way back to their office.

'Yes, you can bet he knows more than he's letting on,' said Simon dejectedly. 'When he was talking about the blackmailing of Fisher, he looked at Ron a couple of times and he stole a glance at you, as if trying to see what your reaction was to certain statements he made. As for the bank job, he could have discussed that with Hanson in private. To raise the subject of the robbery was completely out of context with the rest of the meeting. Lunch at the coffee shop?'

At precisely two o'clock there was a knock on the door to the office of Chief Superintendent Paxton. The knock elicited a one word response. 'Enter'. On complying with the order, Sergeant

Elliott immediately recognised the implication of the seating arrangement; two chairs in front of the Chief's table. This was not a social visit, or even a cordial visit. This was a business only visit or, as Sergeant Elliott feared, a strips-off visit. 'Be seated gentlemen.' Chief Paxton had changed from the civilian clothes worn at the morning meeting and was now attired in his uniform, silver braid abounding, a sight of seniority and authority. He turned his swivel chair around and gazed out the window onto Darling Harbour. Without turning back to face the two detectives, he said, 'Gentlemen, I can't help thinking there's something very wrong going on here, and guess what? I'm about to find out, aren't I?'

Inspector Webster shifted uncomfortably in his seat. 'Yes sir.'

Chief Paxton swung his chair round to confront the two men, a look of outrage on his face. 'Listen here, you two, I may be out of order by admonishing you both at the same time, but I choose not to waste my precious time by repeating myself, especially when you two conspire to make my life hell. And I'm sick to death of "yes sir, yes sir, three bags full, sir". Do I make myself clear?'

Sergeant Elliott looked at Inspector Webster and gave him a "well, you're the boss" look. 'Absolutely perfectly clear, sir,' replied Inspector Webster, making every effort to avoid the "yes" word.

'Good,' replied Chief Paxton who, given credit, was adopting many of the techniques he had come to exercise in curbing his oft-vented rage. 'Now, I'm no mental giant when it comes to sleuthing, but it doesn't take too much grey matter to work things out, especially when you've just received a phone call from the Chief Operations Officer of the Bank of New South Wales. And this call only confirmed what I expected. You two imbeciles robbed the bloody bank just to make Rosey look bad in return for the treatment he'd been handing you both. And apart from that, it was you who blackmailed Fisher. I'll concede you successfully met my requirements to have Fisher confess, but you had a completely different reason to do so.

'Let's deal with the bank fiasco first. The nature of the robbery would make a very interesting court case. From what I've learnt, you didn't demand money, you bloody well just asked nicely for it with some hypothetical question that resulted in a lengthy debate with the teller. And then to tell the teller you had sufficient cash, and not to bother providing further bundles of notes, prompts the question; what sort of gangsters are going to rob a bank and not take all the cash they can get their grubby little hands on?'

Inspector Webster looked up at Chief Paxton, a look of guilt written all over his face. He was about to answer when the Chief put his hands up to stop whatever Webster was about to say. 'Don't say anything, because I'll tell you what sort of gangster. A couple of moronic cops out to make their boss look stupid, that's who. As I said, it would make for an interesting court case and I'm sure you know why. The only good thing to come out of this was the expression on your face, Webster, when I passed the case over to you at this morning's meeting. That was really worth something and even the Commissioner had a giggle about that.'

'You mean, the Commissioner knew?' asked Webster, appalled that even the Commissioner was aware of their guilt.

'Of course he bloody well knew,' replied Paxton. 'But let's talk about the Fisher blackmail case. Although I know neither of you were involved in the Taipan Club setup, I have an idea who the man was, and absolutely no idea who the woman was, and frankly, I couldn't give a stuff. I don't need to remind you that blackmail is an offence against the Crimes Act, but on reflection, you were probably forcing Fisher into making a confession to me about his little extortion racket. And seeing that is exactly what I asked of you, we'll just turn a blind eye to that little transgression. Agreed?'

'Agreed,' said Webster and echoed by Elliott.

Chief Paxton's demeanour had softened since his initial outpouring of rage and now took on a look of benevolent frustration. 'Crikey, fellas, I'm easy to get on with and if you have a problem you should come and see me. I told you at our previous meeting I knew of the animosity between you and Chief Rose, and I sympathise with you. Anyway, that's history. Now, is there anything else you'd like to raise?'

Inspector Webster leant forward and clasped his hands together. 'There is one thing I'd like to get sorted out, just for my own piece of mind.'

'That's fine, go ahead,' replied Chief Paxton.

'We know Chief Rose diddled the slush fund to bankroll his gambling habit. He did this by plonking the money on a horse, the tip given to him by a rails bookie. Fortunately, Rosey always seem to win, except for the last time when his horse didn't and he dropped dead; Rosey, I mean, not the horse. The question is, what would have happened if Rosey hadn't dropped dead and he just lost his money?'

'Now that is a very interesting question. Sergeant Mathieson and I were wondering the very same thing. Now what I'm about to tell you goes no further, understood?' Both Webster and Elliott nodded in acquiescence.

'We knew of Rosey's activities and the rails bookie who gave him the tips. The bookie's name is unimportant, just the fact that he is known to us. Sergeant Mathieson went to see the bookie prior to race one on the day Rose died. Mathieson and the bookie came to an arrangement where, for some consideration, the bookie would give Rose the name of a horse that couldn't win.'

Elliott frowned. 'Don't wish to be insubordinate or disrespectful, sir, but to put a finer point on it, aren't we referring to blackmail?'

Chief Superintendent Paxton pursed his lips and held his chin by thumb and forefinger, his elbow resting on the table. After a moment he said, 'Sergeant Elliott, you don't get to be a chief superintendent by blackmailing people. I'd call it the recognition of potential opportunities offered under certain circumstances and the development of those opportunities with consideration given to the objective. I'm sure your boss, Inspector Webster will help you develop these skills.'

'And the objective?'

'Screw Rosey.'

'Okay, that's all well and good, sir. But if Rosey's horse had won, Rosey may well be alive today.'

'Not necessarily,' replied Chief Paxton, becoming irritated with what he considered such obtuse questioning.

'Okay, I appreciate there is always a probability factor to consider. But even so, it could be construed that you may have contributed to the death of Chief Rose by giving him the name of a horse that couldn't win. After all, he died of a heart attack just after his horse had come second,' said Sergeant Elliott, as he felt himself sinking into an abyss from which there was no return.

'And there you have hit the nail on the head, Sergeant. He may or may not have had a heart attack. Rosey was certainly a candidate for one so you could presume it was on the cards even before the race started,' replied the Chief Superintendent, wondering just where all this was leading.

'But in effect, you may have contributed to his death?'

'Well, in a very small and round about sort of way, I suppose. But I'm certainly not going to lose any sleep over it.'

Buoyed up with his sergeant's persistent questioning of the Chief Superintendent, Inspector Webster launched into the discussion. 'To draw an analogy, sir, if you knew a woman was scared to death of mice and you put a mouse in her knickers drawer so when she opened the drawer and saw the mouse, she dropped dead in fright. Would that be murder, manslaughter, accidental death, death by natural causes, or what?'

Chief Superintendent Paxton's patience ran out. 'Look you two, I have no idea what you are driving at, but I would suggest you drop the subject. Understood?'

'Ye...Absolutely, sir.'

'Now, where were we before we got sidetracked? Oh yes. What to do with you two.'

'Well, if we were public servants and you wanted to get rid of us, you could always promote us,' said Sergeant Elliott, his respect for rank deserting him for a split second. 'Sorry sir, didn't wish to be flippant.'

Chief Paxton sat back in his chair and stretched before locking his hands behind his head. 'You know, Elliott, that may not be such a bad idea. I don't want to lose any more staff than I have already and I'd hate to lose two coppers with a bit of ingenuity. By the same token, to do anything but charge you with robbing a bank, and probably a dozen other charges we could lay, would mean turning a blind eye, and as you know, the police never turn a blind eye to anything. So, get the hell out of my sight and let me do some serious thinking.'

CHAPTER 28

*I*t was about ten days after the conference room and Paxton meetings that Inspector Webster received a telephone call from Ron Lange.

'Seems we have a slight problem, Simon.'

'Can you be a bit more explicit?'

'Mr Lee has contacted me. One of his preferential clients is being blackmailed and wants a job done on the blackmailer.'

'Okay, Ron. Give us a call after the hit's been made and we'll see what we can do about it. It's about time we had a decent murder case to solve, although I would have thought the last thing Mr Lee would want at the moment is a body, anybody's body. Sorry, Ron. I'll try to be a little more serious. Tell you what. Meet me at the Archibald Fountain in Hyde Park at two this arvo. Can you make it?'

'No problems.'

Webster replaced the receiver and turned to Elliott. 'Ron wants to see me about some minor case of blackmail going on with one of Mr Lee's clients. It all sounds a bit suss. Why would Mr Lee contact Ron and then Ron contact me if it wasn't something we were already involved with. God, here I was thinking we were getting away from the Taipan Club debacle and could get onto some real detective work, now we have a bit of stability in the place.'

Sergeant Elliott rolled up a piece of paper and had another three-point shot at the waste paper bin – and missed, again. 'The only common denominator, as far as we know, is Fisher and you can bet your booties he'll be involved somewhere. And you can count on no-one blackmailing Mr Lee as that would be one sure way to end up at the bottom of the harbour. Okay, we may think, or hope, he wouldn't do anything rash like that, but he does have some sort of a reputation to uphold, even if he is as placid as a pussy cat.'

'Well, I suppose there's only way to find out what's going on,' said Inspector Webster.

The day was hot, December hot with the sun beating down and no sign of the cooling afternoon sea breeze. Webster leaned against the brick edge of the fountain to be fanned by the air cooled by the spraying water, his dark blue suit now reduced to an open neck shirt and the coat slung casually over his shoulder. Ron, wearing a beige pair of slacks and a white short sleeve open neck shirt, approached Simon and smiled.

'Hi Simon. Sorry to bring you out in this heat. How about we go and find a seat under one of the trees?' The two men strolled slowly along the pathway lined with Morton Bay figs until they found an unoccupied garden bench.

'Okay, Ron, let's hear it. Someone's blackmailing someone and one of the someone's a client of the Taipan Club who's now seeking someone to assassinate the someone who's doing the blackmailing. Sounds all very simple to me, Ron. Look, I don't wish to be a party pooper or put a damper on things, but to be honest, I don't think I'm really interested.'

'Bet you a quid you will be.'

Simon looked bored and shook his head. 'All right, you're on. Now get on with it.'

'It's a bit of a long story, so bear with me. On the night Sue and I pulled off the Fisher sting, we saw Fisher have what we'll call a minor altercation with a female at the Club. The lady turned out to be Louisa Porter, wife of a politician up in Macquarie Street. On making discreet enquiries, the barman claimed Porter and Fisher had once been an item. Judging by the turn of events that night, that association is well and truly over and there now seems to be some animosity between the two. You with me?'

'So far, Ron, but there ain't no blackmail yet.'

'I'm coming to that. As you know, Fisher is no longer on the take from the Club and, as a consequence, his weekly income has been radically reduced. Unfortunately, Agnes, his wife, was in total ignorance of the scam Fisher was perpetrating. Not a happy lady with the pocket money Fisher was giving her when he was on the take, Agnes became even more unhappy when he lost that source of income and had her weekly allowance radically reduced. Now, being somewhat of a pragmatist, she decided to go into business herself. So where does she decide to get the cash to subsidise the social lifestyle to which she has become accustomed?'

'No, don't tell me.' Simon reached into his back pocket, withdrew his wallet and took out a pound note and handed it to Ron. 'Agnes is the blackmailer.'

'Yes. I don't know where or how she found out about Louisa and Nigel Fisher's little liaisons but, being corrupt as the Superintendent herself, she apparently decided the lovely Louisa may pay her to keep everything on the quiet, even though Louisa and

Fisher are no longer an item. Hence, we have a case of blackmail.'

Simon frowned in bewilderment. 'But how does Agnes know Louisa? Oh yes, of course, the society clique. She must have come across her at one of the social gatherings. So, Agnes Fisher is blackmailing the wife of a State politician because the polly's wife is, or was, shagging her husband,' said Simon, shaking his head in wonder.

Ron continued the saga. 'You see, Louisa is in the public spotlight to some extent. Her husband is a well-known politician and any scandal could be prejudicial, not just to him but to the Party, as well. There are some gambling places where it's quite kosher to be seen when you're in the public eye, like at the races. But an illegal casino in Darlinghurst is another thing. If that isn't bad enough in itself, for it to become common knowledge you were on the make for a one-night stand with a client of the casino would be cataclysmic for everyone concerned.'

'So where does Mr Lee come into it, apart from the fact it's happening on his patch?'

'Madam Porter has evidently approached Mr Lee to see if there is anything he can do to, how shall I put it, eliminate the problem. I have an idea Mr Lee is somewhat fond of Louisa because it's for sure Louisa has a soft spot for him. Anyway, he came to see me for a little chat. He's got enough problems with the Taipan Club and he's trying hard to keep it respectable, even if it is illegal,' Ron said as he got up to buy ice creams from a nearby ice cream vendor pushing a small kiosk trolley.

'Thanks,' said Simon as he peeled the paper off a vanilla paddle pop. 'We thought Mr Lee had a contract out on Superintendent Fisher, not his wife. Lee has denied the Mister Fisher contract, and I'd be very surprised if there's a contract on Misses Fisher. So, when did all this come about?'

'Don't know exactly. No doubt the little scene Sue and I

witnessed at the Club had something to do with it. No wonder Louisa crunched Fisher's nuts even though the poor bloke didn't appear to have a clue why she should be so narky.'

'Charming,' said Simon. 'And all because Agnes was blackmailing her. So, what now? We don't want to see Agnes done away with, neither does Mr Lee. It seems Agnes has hooked onto a fish that's just too big for her, and she doesn't know the danger she's in, and all because she wants to maintain her status in society. I tell you, Ron, what was that about the female of the species?'

Ron though for a moment as he struggled to keep his paddle pop from melting on his shirt. 'We have to come up with a ploy to make Agnes forget about blackmailing Louisa. For a start, we haven't any idea what evidence Agnes has that Louisa appears so willing to protect.' Ron finished the paddle pop and absently sucked on the empty stick. 'Simon, just a thought. How about a meeting with the girls? This appears to be girlie stuff and they have a far better intuition as to the whys and the wherefores of women's thinking. I know I'll never understand them.'

'Sounds like a good idea. I'll organise it and get back to you.' Ron started to rise from the bench when Simon put a restraining hand on his shoulder. 'Just one point,' said Simon, 'if we investigate the alleged blackmail, is it an official investigation, or is it one the police will turn a blind eye to?'

'Let's say it's a favour to Mr Lee. Even with him running a casino, I like the man. I think he's good value and I believe the police will benefit having him on their side. Apart from that, blackmail is an indictable offence and, although no-one has lodged a formal complaint, I think it would be a good idea to see what we can do, if for no other reason than to keep Agnes Fisher alive.

CHAPTER 29

The strong nor'easter had cooled the oppressive heat of the Sunday morning, the temperature now bearable enough to sit outside on the back lawn. Georgie and Simon had taken an early morning swim at Collaroy, just a five minute walk down the road. The surf was not worth writing home about, but that was not unusual for Collaroy, however the water was cool and refreshing after a hot, sleepless night. Georgie had erected a beach umbrella through a hole in a small round table and set up the director's chairs in preparation for what portended to be an interesting afternoon.

Noel and Sue had already arrived at the bungalow and, along with Simon and Georgie, sat chatting about mundane topics while they passed the time waiting for Ron's arrival. It wasn't long before they heard the side gate bang shut and, a couple of seconds later, Ron appear around the corner of the house. 'Hi Georgie, Sue. Good to see you again Noel, Simon,' said Ron before he sat down on one of the chairs. 'Before we start, best you put these in the Esky,' he said and handed Simon a six pack and a bottle of moselle. 'And before you ask, yes I'd love one of your cold ones. The bloody traffic over The Spit today, and I haven't air conditioning in the Beetle. It seems like everyone on the planet wants to get down to the beach all at the same time,' he said, his frustration and anger cooling with the aid of an ice cold beer. 'Geez, that tastes lovely. Now, has anyone mentioned the problem?'

'No, not really, just a heads up.' replied Simon. 'I thought it best to wait until you got here, and now you are, let's get on with it. The girls are itching to hear a bit of scandal. Ron, I think it best if you explain the situation and then we'll work out if there's anything we can do.'

Ron spent the next twenty minutes explaining the sad story of infidelity and extortion already related to Simon in Hyde Park. Strangely, no-one seemed as surprised as Simon had been when they learnt of the blackmailing of a politician's wife. When he had finished, Ron turned to Sue. 'Sue, you saw the incident between Fisher and Porter at the Club. Apart from the physical attack, what did you make of the episode?'

Sue looked at her glass of wine and decided she didn't need a refill, just yet. 'Well, it seemed pretty clear to me Fisher thought his friendship with Louisa, or whatever you like to call the relationship, was a lot better than what she thought it was. The animosity between the two was solely of her bidding. She had it in for Fisher, and I get the idea the poor bloke didn't know why, and probably still doesn't.'

'No wonder,' exclaimed Noel. 'Poor Louisa ends up being blackmailed by Agnes Fisher just because Agnes finds out her ever-loving husband was being dragged off to bed, not reluctantly, by the amazon with an inflated libido. And the idiot had to brag about it to all and sundry, not that that appears relevant.'

'Now, hang on a sec,' said Simon. 'Don't let's forget, we're hearing all this third hand. Let's go through it slowly and try to work out what's happened and the sequence of events. I doubt we will ever be able to come up with the rationale behind what's gone on, so let's try and keep it simple.'

'I'll agree to that,' replied Ron. 'It's easy to take everything at face value and come to some conclusion that may not necessarily fit the facts.'

'Okay, let's assume Noel's right about Louisa being blackmailed because Agnes finds out her devoted hubby may not be so devoted. Mr Fisher and Louisa Porter are having, or had, a tryst to put it more eloquently. Porter, Louisa I mean, doesn't want word of the affair to either get back to her husband, who is a State politician, or for the affair to become public knowledge. Let's look at the first reason first,' said Simon.

Georgie leant forward holding her empty wine glass with both hands. 'Porter, Mr Porter, that is, is reputedly going places with his political party and the higher he goes, the higher she goes, on the social ladder anyway. I've no doubt she doesn't want to jeopardize the marriage and the associated prestige, or her husband's career, all because of her easy virtue and overactive hormones.'

'Hell, I never thought the wife of any politician would consider her position prestigious,' Ron remarked. 'Anyway, if whatever Mrs Porter is up to did get back to Mr Porter, it would be more than likely everyone else on the planet would know, including his political party. It doesn't matter who you are, you can't keep any naughtiness secret forever in this town, irrespective of however scandalous or trivial it may be. And yes, I know such revelations haven't adversely affected the political standing of politicians, state or federal, who have been busted for the same thing. However, don't let's forget, there's always the chance someone in the party may take the moralistic high ground and try to crucify the bloke.'

'Sounds good to me,' said Ron as he tossed his empty beer can into the new metal garbage bin that had recently replaced the dilapidated plastic one. 'We still haven't any idea as to how Agnes Fisher found out about her husband's affair, nor do we know what evidence she is holding that will prove the affair did take place. Such proof must exist or Louisa wouldn't pay her off.'

'No, I can't agree to that. Agnes doesn't need evidence as all she has to do is ring the editor of the Daily Mirror, tell him who she is and what's going on and it will be all over the front pages. You can bet your life the paper won't take the time to verify the story, and who knows, Louisa may make page three,' said Simon as he took Georgie's glass and refilled it. 'But it seems as though things have got so bad for Louisa that she's now gone to Mr Lee to see if there's a way of having the problem removed. I think we all know Mr Lee isn't about to assassinate Agnes, or anyone else for that matter, even if he does want to help Louisa, which he no doubt does. Apart from running a very successful business that has attracted some very influential patrons, Mr Lee is proving to be an invaluable asset in his cooperation with police to set up a drug squad. So, no way in the world is Mr Lee going to throw away all that effort. And who knows, if he continues to keep his nose clean, one day he may even front the Licensing Board.'

Sue emptied her glass and placed it on the table in front of her. 'So really it boils down to finding a way to stop Agnes Fisher from blackmailing Louisa Porter.'

'Spot on, Sue. I suggested we get together for this little chat because you girls know what goes on in a girl's mind far better than us mere males. Apart from blowing Agnes away with a Magnum, I haven't a clue how to go about it,' replied Ron somewhat indifferently. 'Any ideas?'

'Simon, did I hear you say a while ago that Chief Paxton had asked Fisher if his wife played around?' Georgie asked.

'Yes, he did mention it to me after he had spoken to Fisher.

Fisher had told him he didn't think she did, but there were times when Agnes didn't come home at night, the excuse being she'd spent the night at a girl friend's place.'

'Holy hell. And of course, hubby believed her. How naïve can you get,' replied Sue with scorn. 'It all too easy. All we have to do is find out who Agnes is screwing and blackmail her to stop blackmailing Louisa.'

'Yeah, but just one second. Aren't we taking it just a little bit for granted that she is playing around?' asked Noel, sceptically.

'Noel, believe me, Agnes is playing around; I'll bet my booties on it,' replied Sue, with conviction.

'See, told you, Simon. Nothing beats women's logic,' said Ron, suitably bemused by the simplicity of such a scheme to unravel such a complex situation.

'Seems more like a daisy chain to me,' responded Noel. 'The further we go into this, the more people we will find being blackmailed for one reason or another.'

'Well, I for one would like to know how Agnes found out hubby was up to no good. I wonder if Louisa's husband, what's his name, Robert, that's it, Robert Porter, I wonder if he knows what's going on?' Simon said as he tossed another empty beer can into the growing pile of empties discarded into the garbage bin. He contemplated for a second, then reached for the Esky.

'That would be an interesting question,' remarked Ron with a thoughtful look on his face. 'Why don't you ask him?'

'And just how do we get to have a chat with a politician. The only time you ever see them is during an election. Once they're elected you never see or hear from them again unless, of course, they get a ministerial portfolio. And if they're at ministerial level,' said Simon getting a tad hot under the collar, 'they have this inflated opinion of themselves and will never give a straight answer. And if you ask why they don't give a straight answer, it's because they never deign to listen to anyone they regard as being their intellectual inferiors, which, of course, are us plebs, the very people who put them where they are in the first place. And as far as answering a "yes" or "no" question, they are completely incapable as they believe no question could warrant such a simplistic response,' said Simon with a tone of disgust.

'Well, pardon me. Sorry I suggested it,' Ron said defensively. 'I take it there are no politicians on your Christmas mailing list?'

'Gee, Ron, how perceptive, but I don't hold pollies in high regard. And you're probably right with your suggestion to go and ask Mr Porter if he's aware his wife's been shagging a police superintendent. If he does know, it won't come as any great surprise and if he doesn't know, well, he should. What do you girls think?'

Georgie, who needed no time to think about the question, was quick to respond. 'Robert Porter wouldn't know what day of the week it was, let alone if his wife was jumping into bed with someone. Men, including politicians, are so stupid when it comes to deception. They really think they're so smart with their extra marital goings on. Look at Mr Fisher. He wouldn't have a clue his wife not only knows about him but is making money out of it. And Porter, being a politician, wouldn't be able to lie straight in bed anyway.'

Sue poured herself another moselle and said, 'I agree with a lot of what you just said, Georgie, but I bet Mr Porter does know but won't say anything because it would be a case of the pot calling the kettle black.'

'You mean, you think the redoubtable Robert Porter, MP, is playing around on his wife?' asked Noel, becoming more perplexed as the conversation continued.

Sue shrugged, raised her eyebrows and nodded. 'Who knows for sure? We can sit here and speculate until the cows come home whether someone's jumping into someone else's bed. But don't forget, Porter is a politician, and that in itself opens up a can of worms. I agree with Ron. Let's go and ask Bob Porter what he knows. Maybe it would be a good idea to get everyone who's involved together for a real good punch up to see who's between the sheets with whom. That would include the Fishers, the Porters and we could bring in Mr Lee as the referee.'

Simon smirked at the idea. 'Sounds great. We just push them all into a steel cage and watch the feathers fly. No, let's be a little more subtle, at least for the moment. Noel and I will try and get to see Mr Porter, and Ron, can you have a quiet word with Mr Superintendent Fisher, if you can find him? He seems to have vanished off the planet over the last few days. Let's see if we can get sufficient info together to persuade Agnes Fisher to take her claws out of Louisa. If we can't, Louisa may make life pretty tough for Agnes, if not pretty short.'

ndrew and Noel sat under an umbrella of a footpath coffee shop in Macquarie Street. From where they sat, they could see the old building of the State Parliament on the other side of the street. They had just ordered the usual, one flat black and one cappuccino when a tall broad-shouldered gentleman, dressed in a dark brown suit and wearing a gaudy paisley tie, approached their table. Noel looked at the man and had a sudden thought flash across his mind; no, I don't want to trade my Holden for a Ford.

'Inspector Webster?'

'Yes. Mr Porter?'

'That's right. I believe you wanted a chat. I can only spare a few minutes, so if we can get straight into it.'

'Before we start. This is my sergeant, Sergeant Noel Elliott.' Mr Porter nodded to Noel and sat down at the table just as the two coffees arrived. 'Coffee, Mr Porter?'

'No thanks.'

'Mr Porter, we need to ask you some very personal questions regarding yourself and your wife. Naturally you are under no obligation to answer, but they may prove significant in a case of alleged blackmail currently under investigation.'

'Who's blackmailing who?'

'Never mind that at the moment. Mr Porter, are you aware that your wife, Louisa, is a patron of the Taipan Club in Forbes Street?'

'Yes, I know she goes there occasionally. Why?'

'Have you heard the name Nigel Fisher before?' Simon asked as he absently stirred his unsugared coffee.

'I think Louisa may have mentioned it. Look, can we stop beating around the bush and get to the point?'

Simon shrugged. 'By all means, Mr Porter. We've received a report claiming your wife has been on very friendly terms with a Mr Nigel Fisher.'

'Oh, cut the crap, Inspector. My wife has been, and probably still is, screwing Detective Superintendent Fisher and yes, of course I know about it.' Simon looked at Noel who was about to take a sip of his coffee; he missed and spilt half the cup over a neatly ironed white shirt and light blue tie.

'Bugger,' exclaimed Noel and tried to rectify the damage with a paper napkin.

'You knew about it?' asked Simon, amazed at the direction the discussion was now headed.

'Look, Inspector, let's not cloud the issue. Of course I knew. So did Agnes.'

'Well, it's obvious Agnes knew what hubby was up to. We weren't sure if you knew. But how did Agnes find out?'

'Good God, that's easy. I told her. Simon rested an elbow on the table, held his head and tightly screwed his eyes shut for a moment.

'I suppose you know there is now an allegation Agnes is blackmailing Louisa. Seems if Louisa doesn't pay up, Agnes will go public that the wife of a prominent parliamentarian is picking up men at an illegal casino and having her way with them. It's of little consequence whether your wife and Fisher are still at it or not. Either way, it augurs badly for the political career of an aspiring politician if it becomes common knowledge, wouldn't you say?'

'Agnes is bluffing. She would never do anything like that. As far as Louisa is concerned, I suppose it does sound a bit unrefined,' reflected Mr Porter. 'But let's face it, it's not as though she's committing a capital offence. And really, Inspector, whatever Louisa is up to, it isn't life threatening, is it?'

'Strange you should use those words, Mr Porter. We've had word your wife has made an approach to a third party in an attempt to have the problem eliminated, if you get my drift,' said Simon as he finished his coffee.

'I'm sorry, but I think I'm losing the plot here. Are you trying to tell me Louisa is looking for someone to do a job on Agnes?'

'Seems so,' replied Simon, simply. 'Does it really surprise you to think Louisa would go to so much trouble and expense to keep your reputation in tact?'

The question Simon had asked required nothing more than a "yes" or "no" answer but, being put to a politician, Simon was not too surprised when he received a question in response. 'Just what are you two gentlemen trying to achieve?' Simon could see that Mr Porter was getting a trifle angry.

'Mr Porter, we're trying to obtain sufficient information to present to Agnes Fisher that will convince her that it is in her best interest to cease blackmailing your wife. Louisa has your best interest at heart and she is paying the blackmail to protect your career.'

Mr Porter frowned and shook his head. 'Eminently altruistic. Let's keep everybody happy, the Party included. But before we go any further, you say you want information that may persuade Agnes to back off. Well gentlemen, I may be able to help you there. Agnes is a nice lady trying to stay afloat at a social level way beyond her economic means. When I found out what Louisa was up to, I told Agnes, certainly not thinking she would stoop so low as to blackmail Louisa.'

'How did you find out about Louisa?' Noel interrupted.

'Well, it wasn't hard to work out something was up as I do keep an ear close to the ground. Louisa would say she was going to the Club; sometimes she did, sometimes she didn't. I know a few people who spend some time there, and irrespective of what you may think, they're not all criminals. Anyway, let's just say I heard it on the grapevine. Does that answer your question, Inspector?'

'Yes, admirably, thank you, sir. And how did you get to know Agnes?' Simon asked.

'I met Agnes at a restaurant in Double Bay. It was some social function although I can't recall what it was in aid of. As it turned out, we found we had something in common, which, of course, we did as both our spouses were jumping into bed with each other. It didn't surprise her as she had expected something was going on. Anyway, they say what's good for the goose so Agnes and I became good friends. It started off on a plutonic basis, I suppose it still is, but with a little adultery thrown in. Hell, it's not like we didn't have the opportunity, what with Louisa and Nigel going at it hammer and tongs. I still believe we have a good friendship and would be very surprised if Agnes would wish to bring my career down.'

'You mean you and Agnes...' Simon didn't get to finish the question.

'Yes,' replied Mr Porter.

Simon looked at Noel and said, 'It looks like Sue was right on the button about Agnes, but I would never have guessed who she was having it off with. So, Mr Porter,' Simon continued, turning to the politician, 'I would say you have a very loyal wife who's trying to protect your career, in spite of her infidelity. And irrespective of your feelings for Agnes, it certainly appears she's not providing you with a great deal of support, what with her threat to go public.'

'Yes, I can see that now. Maybe I'm a bit of a bastard, but it's not like I'm the only politician to have an interest in women. At least I'm involved with only one woman, even if that woman is blackmailing my wife. Come to think of it, she's probably paying the blackmail with my money,' said Mr Porter in a vain attempt to display some virtuous attribute. 'Hell, I could name a few politicians on both sides of the House who would make the most of any opportunity presented. And that includes both men and women. Good God, Inspector, it's not as though I'm shagging the Parliamentary Whip or the honourable member for wherever, is it?'

Somehow the conversation was over. Mr Porter shrugged and looked at his watch. Both Simon and Noel looked at each other, a look of bewilderment on their faces, both struck dumb by the politician's revelations. It was Mr Porter who broke the impasse. 'I'm sorry, gentlemen, I think I may have surprised you.'

'To say the least, Mr Porter. I must admit, I didn't quite expect our conversation to be so forthright and I honestly can't think of any further questions at this moment. If it comes to that, I'm having trouble getting my head around what you've just told us. I think it's probably a good idea if the Sergeant and I go away to some quiet spot and do a bit of thinking. You realise we are trying to protect all involved in this sordid little story. Hopefully, after we've determined who's in whose bed when the music stops, we can sort it out without blackmail or assassination.'

'Thank you, Inspector Webster. I appreciate your sensitivity in dealing with this case,' said Mr Porter as he got up from his chair and took a card from his coat pocket. 'If you do have any more questions, please give me a ring. The number is a private telephone that will get you straight through to my office.' With that, Robert Porter, MP, walked away along Macquarie Street towards Hyde Park.

CHAPTER 31

*I*t was a hot Sunday morning and the sixty foot cruiser was moored at the Rushcutters Bay marina. Already aboard the "Chez Anne" was the permanent skipper, Charlie Chambers, also known as "Chic", Adam Vance, a young deckhand of about twenty, and a young married couple, dressed in white, employed to keep the guests well watered and fed. By eleven o'clock all those invited for a pleasurable day on the harbour were aboard. Charlie, having edged the cruiser from its birth at the marina, now slowly navigated through the host of motor yachts, cruisers and yachts anchored in the bay.

The eleven guests were seated in the large carpeted main saloon taking advantage of the air conditioning while the young married couple plied the guests with drinks and canapés. The Fishers, Agnes and Nigel, sat together on a lounge running the entire port side of the saloon, together with the Porters, Robert and Louisa, Noel and Simon. Sue and Georgie sat on two lounge chairs located on the starboard side. Mr Lee, displaying some surprise at making a reacquaintance with the lovely Sue from Adelaide and, following an enlightening discussion with

Sue, Noel and Ron, had reclined into a bean bag located at the starboard aft end of the saloon, near the main door giving access to the deck outside. Chief Paxton, wearing shorts, a Hawaiian shirt and sneakers reclined in a similar bean bag to the port side of the door and in front of the lounge. Ron sat on a small stool between Sue and Georgie. There was a well stocked bar at the forward end of the saloon with a companion way on the forward starboard side giving access to the deck below.

It was Simon who had put forward the idea to all concerned that an all-in get together may resolve some of the differences and antagonism plainly evident, to varying degrees, within the group. With the gathering now waiting expectantly for someone to take charge of the situation, all eyes finally came to rest on Simon who concluded he was the unelected leader and up to him to commence proceedings.

After drawing attention by using the old spoon and glass trick, Simon commenced. 'Ladies and gentlemen, I realise this little get together may be an inconvenience for some of you. However, by the time we get back to Rushcutters Bay this afternoon, I hope some of you may have changed both your thinking and attitude towards those with whom you may now regard with some antipathy.

'Chief Superintendent Paxton, thanks for coming along. Most of what you will probably hear today may not concern you, but as we are dealing with fraud, corruption, conspiracy to murder, and probably a host of other offences, we thought it might save a lot of time if you were all present. Apart from that, a nice day on the harbour hearing a soap opera unfold will, no doubt, be uplifting. In view of the cordiality inspired by the venue, and the generosity provided by our host, may I suggest, Chief Superintendent, we dispense with ranks with your name being "Chief" for the day?'

'Yes, that's fine.'

'I know the venue is somewhat unusual, but thanks to a suggestion from Mr Lee, who just happens to own the "Chez Anne", I was delighted to accept his kind offer as I believed it provided us all with a neutral playing field. Apart from the neutrality of the venue, I also considered it somewhat of a difficult place from which to retreat should any of you feel so inclined.

'Initially, I thought it appropriate to summarise the situation as I see it. However, I came to the conclusion that you are probably all aware of what's going on and my summation may be totally incorrect. As a consequence, each one of you is going to tell your own sordid little tale, and please don't think you can put one over us by claiming you don't know what the story is. Everyone here has a bit of knowledge of the events, some more than others. I appreciate that relating your own story may be difficult as the truth often hurts. However, as I mentioned to the Chief, whatever may have started out as one individual's trivial indiscretion has turned into a series of malicious events, including blackmail and conspiracy to murder. If you feel your story is disturbing, take comfort in the fact that the next story will probably be worse. Let's face it, we're all in the same boat, if you'll excuse the pun.' No-one laughed.

'And who's going to get the ball rolling? You don't expect anyone to actually volunteer to be the first to bare their soul?' asked Nigel, a hint of annoyance in his voice.

Sue surveyed the scene and came to the conclusion, not surprisingly, that few, if any, of the people in the saloon were at ease. She leant over and whispered in Ron's ear, 'I think we're starting about three drinks short, no-one's relaxed yet. And what does Simon hope to achieve here today? This place has all the ingredients for one hell of a punch-up, even if it's not in a steel cage.'

'I don't know really, but we have two couples jumping into

bed with the other's spouse. I'm putting my money on Agnes and Robert becoming an item. Louisa has already dumped Nigel, so that leaves Nigel and Louisa at loose ends. But then again, I don't watch that TV show, what is it, The Days of the Bold?'

'Since you raised the issue, Nigel, looks like you can go first; after all, rank does have its privileges,' said Simon.

'Hell, where do I start?' Nigel asked himself.

'Try at the beginning when you discovered Chief Rose was helping himself to the slush fund,' replied the Chief unexpectedly. It seemed the Chief was more interested in proceedings than Simon thought.

'Alright, I'm dead anyway. When Rosey started borrowing cash from the police slush fund it wasn't hard to work out what he was up to. I played along with his little scheme, not that he ever had any idea I knew what he was doing. I suppose I was aiding and abetting as I was well aware he was pulling a swindle. You see, Rose would submit vouchers for payment to informants without all the necessary documentation that's needed. Apart from the lack of paperwork, none of the informants ever existed; they were all bogus.

'Anyway, I found out he would take the money to Canterbury races on a Wednesday and back a sure thing. I haven't a clue who gave him the tips, but it must have come from someone close to a stable because he rarely lost. This gave him the cash to pay back the slush fund and give him a bank to go gambling, which he did at the Taipan Club. I knew we could shut down the Club whenever we liked but I saw the opportunity to make a bit on the side. I went to see Mr Lee and we came to an arrangement. It was an insurance policy; he pays the premium and we lay off taking any action. I didn't gamble myself but found the Club a great spot to have a beer.'

'Great spot for a beer or a great spot for your womanising?' interrupted Agnes with a sneer.

The look Nigel gave Agnes was not pleasant. 'For both, but you wouldn't understand, so why bother?' came the hostile response. After a long pause and some deep breathing aimed at reducing his anger level, Nigel continued. 'I found the cash Mr Lee was paying me, when added to my police pay, was sufficient to keep Agnes relatively quiet. It also helped me pay for my place of refuge at Potts Point.'

'What do you mean "refuge at Potts Point"', Agnes interrupted again, a look of bewilderment on her face. 'You mean to say you'd pick up a woman at the Taipan Club and take her back to some sleazy hotel up at The Cross?'

'Oh, shut up, you stupid old cow. I've been renting a flat over there for years just to get away from you and your incessant demands for more money, which I don't have,' came Nigel's angry response.

'Well, listen here, buddy boy. Whether you know it or not, I do have a social life and certain obligations, all of which require oodles of money. If you can't, or won't give it to me, I'll find it elsewhere.' With that, Agnes adopted a childish pout and sat back on the lounge.

'Look, do you want me to continue with my little tale, or do you want a domestic thrown in?' asked Nigel irritably.

Simon made a pronouncement. 'Agnes, you'll get your turn, as will the rest of you. I suggest there be no more interruptions during each revelation. We can have a cat fight after everyone's had their fair go. In the meantime, I think it's a good idea if we all just shut up and have another drink to calm down,' Simon beckoned to the young married couple to keep the drinks coming. 'Now, Nigel.'

'Okay.' To cut a long story short, if I got lucky at the Club, I'd take the girl back to Potts Point for the night. Agnes never seemed to care if I stayed out; she probably thought it was work. I met Louisa and we had something more than a one night stand. This went on for a while until she apparently had had enough, although I did think it was very abrupt, the end of the relationship, I mean. A few weeks ago, I started to chat up Sue, over there,' he said nodding to Sue. 'I didn't have a clue who she was or who the bloke she was with was.'

'Bet you can't say that again in half an hour,' taunted Agnes, downing a double scotch and incurring a look of rebuke from Simon.

'After the bloke left, who I now know was Ron, I thought Sue was fair game. I don't know if it was the couple of beers I had earlier that clouded my judgment, but it never occurred to me that it might be a set-up. I should be really pissed off with both you and Ron, Sue, but strangely enough, it's okay. I don't really give a damn.'

'And you became the subject of a blackmail scam demanding you confess your sins to the Chief,' said Simon, finishing off the story for the benefit of the others.

'Yes', Nigel flippantly replied. 'Sure did.'

'Does anyone else, apart from Agnes, have any questions?' asked Simon.

"Yes, I do,' replied Mr Lee. 'Nigel, right from the start of our little agreement, I had another insurance policy, and that was the ability to blackmail you for the extortion of funds from the Taipan Club. In effect, all the money I paid you for insurance against the Club being shut down was money down the drain. But I acknowledge that was my fault and very stupid. And yes, the thought of having you thrown over The Gap did cross my mind, but I guess we all feel like we'd like to do that to someone or other at times.'

'Okay, so I made a mistake. I needed money, and lots of it. If you were married to Agnes, you'd soon find out how much money you didn't have and you'd end up trying anything to get more.' Apparently neither Agnes, nor Nigel had ever stopped to reason why he was prepared to go to such lengths to keep her happy.

'Has anyone anything else to say, or wish to join in on this conversation now?' asked Simon, fully prepared for the outburst Agnes would, no doubt, launch. He wasn't wrong.

'Bloody hell, yes,' said a very angry Agnes, the whisky having done nothing to sooth her temper. She bounced off the lounge and stood in front of Nigel, her arms akimbo, her head and shoulders forward, a look of cold hostility in her eyes. And then she let fly. 'Why, you pompous bastard, I knew you and Louisa were screwing your little hearts out right from the beginning. And you know how I found out? Well, I'll tell you, you so-called detective bigwig. Every night you and Louisa were shacked up in your little love nest, Robert Porter and I were shagging ourselves stupid. Besides, I really enjoyed the intrigue of sneaking off for an illicit affair behind your back. And you want to know something else? I started blackmailing Louisa, threatening if she didn't pay me, I would reveal that the wife of a big shot political figure in State Parliament is having an extramarital romp with a superintendent of police after having picked him up in some grotty, illegal gambling casino.'

Noel looked at Sue, pulled a face and raised his eyebrows. Bugger me, he thought, all hell is going to break loose soon and Simon was right; you can't get off this tub. Just at that moment the comely young lady and handsome young man, both dressed in white shirts and shorts, entered the saloon carrying hors d'oeuvres and drinks of beer and wine. Noel was not the only one to think the couple's entrance was timed impeccably to prevent a blood bath.

'Excuse me, young man, can I have a double scotch and soda?' asked a very angry Agnes.

'By all means, madam.'

Robert Porter looked at Agnes with a serious look on his face. 'Agnes, I'd like to think you were bluffing Louisa, and you weren't out to destroy my career, not deliberately anyway. Is that right?'

'Look, Bobby boy, my husband can't afford me. You and Louisa have bags of money to throw around and I needed more. Louisa just happened along at a very opportune time and she couldn't help setting herself up to be blackmailed. Would I go so far as to ruin your career? Guess we'll never know now,' Agnes took her whisky from the young man in white and threw the contents down her throat in one gulp. 'Better get me another,' she said, handing the glass back to the surprised young man.

As Agnes vented her spleen on the unjust cards fate had dealt her, husband Nigel listened on with increasing indignation. With the attention drawn to the young man in white, Nigel Fisher, exasperated to the extreme, couldn't control himself any further.

'What the bloody hell do you mean "can't afford you", you stupid woman. If you didn't try to lead a life way beyond our means we could live very comfortably, thank you. And who wants to be part of the snob pack strutting around in the belief the rest of society is composed of nothing but plebeians. Bloody social hypocrites. And as for your little affair with a politician, have you no conscience? Good grief, woman, if you're going to have a bit on the side, at least pick someone with some moral integrity. God, a politician, the ignominy of it all. Obviously, you have no scruples and an absolutely deplorable taste in men.'

Agnes looked thoroughly shocked, and for a moment dumbfounded, by Nigel's outburst. Eventually, after her mind became a little clearer, she again let fly. 'You, you bloody simpleton. What about yourself? It's quite all right for you to finance a love nest and drag any poor unsuspecting female away for a night to satisfy your own lecherous lust. Hell's bells, for the time and expense it takes you to chat up a bird at the Club, you may as well go next door and rent a girl for five minutes.' The glass of whisky was snatched from the tray held by the young man in white and disposed of in a similar manner to the previous drink.

CHAPTER 32

*E*veryone in the saloon sat riveted to the Fisher's verbal brawl unfolding in front of them. Even Charlie, after anchoring the "Chez Anne" in Athol Bay, just off Taronga Zoo, couldn't help but find things to do in the saloon, like polish the ship's ornate brass bell that hung behind the bar. Sue and Georgie listened intently, wondering how the exchange would end. Unfortunately for Sue, her listening was about to be interrupted. 'Hey, Georgie, where's the loo, I'm busting?'

Georgie looked around and said, 'I haven't a clue, but when you find it, let me know.' Sue got up and tactfully whispered in Louisa's ear who pointed to the companion way then indicated subsequent directions with a hand. A few minutes later Sue returned and gave Georgie a whimsical look. Just at that moment, the tension within the saloon was broken by the pert young lady in white as she announced that lunch, consisting of a smorgasbord, was available on the afterdeck.

Considering the mood of the pre-lunch discussions, lunch itself was a marvelous success, free from anger, bitterness and the enraged spouse. To everyone's surprise, even Agnes seemed to be chatting amicably with Nigel. As Georgie waited her turn to indulge in the platter of prawns on offer, she turned to Sue. 'Hey, Sue, you've something to tell me?'

Sue frowned. 'Correct me if I'm wrong, but I don't recall Louisa having left the saloon since coming onboard. If I'm right, how did she know where the loo was, unless of course, she's been onboard before?'

'You mean...'

Sue raised her eyebrows. 'Louisa and Mr Lee?'

Georgie shook her head. 'Look, I don't want to know. The whole thing is just becoming too convoluted for my liking. As soon as lunch is over, let's go down to one of the cabins and change for some sun baking.'

'Great idea,' replied Sue. 'At this stage, I really couldn't give a fig as to what happens now. Just at the moment I have better things to think about; where did you say the lobster was?'

Several of the people onboard, including the Fishers and the Porters, took the lunch time break as an opportunity to have a look over the "Chez Anne", sixty feet of opulence and extravagance. The highlight of the inspection was what could be called the stateroom, a palatially decorated cabin with a king size bed. It was while surveying the plush creature comforts of the cabin that Robert Porter noticed a pair of onyx and diamond earrings in a glass dish located on a bedside table, a pair remarkably like those he had given Louisa as a birthday present a few months previously. Robert Porter, visibly shaken by the possible ramifications of this discovery, quickly withdrew from the stateroom and sought solitude on the open deck while Louisa, totally oblivious as to the cause of her husband's rapid withdrawal, left in pursuit leaving the Fishers alone in the cabin.

'And what's wrong with those two?' asked Nigel.

'Don't know,' replied Agnes. 'I get the idea he recognised the earrings beside the bed because he stared at them for a moment then turned tail. Say, I wouldn't mind owning this boat. You drag your women off to your pokey little flat at Potts Point and I'll drag my lovers down here,' she said running her hand over the luxurious quilted bed.

'I get the idea Mr Lee rarely uses this place. He doesn't strike me as being the type,' Nigel said as he opened a cupboard not expecting to see anything of significance. He quickly shut the door, his face turning pale.

'Anything of interest in there?' enquired Agnes

'No, not a thing,' Nigel replied. Nothing that would interest you anyway, Nigel thought as he remembered the way Louisa had looked in the sheer negligee he had bought her when their relationship had been on more intimate terms. His head spinning, Nigel and Agnes made their way back to the saloon where Simon had herded the rest of the guests together, leaving the nice looking couple in white to clear away the lunch things.

The idle chat immediately ceased and the mood took on an air of oppressive apprehension. 'One hell of a way to spend a Sunday afternoon,' remarked the Chief to Ron as they took up their seats in the saloon.

'Oh, I don't know. I think it's been quite entertaining, considering. Beats the hell out of watching the idiot box,' replied Ron, sitting himself on the stool between Georgie and Sue.

'Okay, who haven't we heard from?' asked Simon, looking around the group. 'Ah yes, Louisa. How about you tell your story?'

'You don't really want to hear it, do you?' Louisa asked. 'Yes, I suppose you do, but before I start.' Louisa got up from her seat on the lounge and proceeded to the bar where she opened a fridge cabinet. She withdrew a small bottle of rum and poured a decent size nip into a glass before adding a smidgen of Coke. After swallowing the contents of the glass, she paused for a moment then took a deep breath. Refortified, Louisa returned to the lounge, sat and crossed her well endowed shapely legs. Noel gave Simon a knowing glance; Louisa's been here before today. So just how friendly are Louisa and Mr Lee?

Well, as you know, I'm married to a State politician who is doing very well and is on the way up in the Party. Any politician's wife will tell you that it's not easy being married to someone who's supposed to work a full twenty four seven. If it's not the constituents, it's Parliament. If it's not Parliament, it's the Party. It's just one damn thing after another. And don't think I don't know what goes on at those Party conventions, Robert. The biggest decision delegates have to make is what type of beer to drink or who they'll shag after the meeting. You seem to have all the fun and only drag me along when it's politically correct for you to be seen with the little old lady.

'Anyway, I thought it was about time I had a little bit of fun too. I had heard some gossip about The Taipan Club which sounded rather exciting, so I decided to have a look. Needless to say, it turned out to be quite a trendy place and not at all what I expected. After a couple of visits, I was introduced to the owner, Mr Lee. I didn't know him before I started going there, but he seemed a nice bloke and he took the time to look after me. He showed me the different games and taught me the finer points of gambling, not that I ever spend much at the tables. As it was, I found you could be a bigger winner at the Club without spending a penny. It didn't take Nigel long to make himself known to me, and I found him suitable for serving my specific purposes, and that was to satisfy my female urges. As I said,

Robert was rarely home, and when he was, he was usually too tired to perform, not that Nigel was anything to write home about.

'Everything was rosy for a while until one night this lady, using the term very loosely, came up to me in the Club and introduced herself as Agnes Fisher. Naturally I knew straight away she was Nigel's wife. What I didn't know was the reason for her to want to speak to me. She cleared that up within two minutes; pay up or she would expose Robert, the prominent politician, as being the husband of a slut, who picked up strange men in illegal casinos. And those are her words, not mine.'

Somewhat surprised by the descriptive language used by Agnes, Nigel finally took umbrage and turned to her. 'So, now you think I'm strange?' he interjected.

Agnes frowned, closed her eyes and shook her head. 'Oh, Nigel, give it away.'

'Look, just shut up and let me get on with it,' Louisa said in annoyance. 'Okay, my private life with Robert could be a lot better, but that doesn't alter the fact that I'm very fond of the man and couldn't let Agnes destroy him, so I started paying her. Bloody ironic, isn't it, she's blackmailing me for screwing around on my husband while my husband is screwing around on me, and with her. In fact, it wasn't until I found out a little more about Mrs Fisher and the fact she was screwing my husband that I realised I didn't have to pay her a nickel. After all, we were all in the same boat and I could have been blackmailing her for the same reason she was blackmailing me. But then again, I would never lower myself to blackmail anyone.

'I also found out about her social aspiration of becoming a member of Sydney's "A List". If it was revealed her husband, a superintendent of police, was indiscriminately ploughing his way through the female population, and she herself was jumping into bed with a politician, she would become the laughing stock of the socialites. That, of course, isn't to say some of those on the "A List" aren't up to the same thing, and just as morally bankrupt, it's just seems they're a bit more discreet.

'As I had absolutely no idea what was going on in Agnes's pea sized brain, I couldn't take the chance that she might not be bluffing, and go public to the detriment of Robert's career. As I couldn't see how to get out of the mess I was in, I approached Mr Lee and asked for his advice. We discussed the matter at some length but came to no agreement. He suggested that if I felt the same way in ten days time, he would see what he could do. In view of the way things have turned out, I have no great desire to pay Mr Lee some incredible amount of money to have the little old would be if she could be eliminated. By the same token, I refuse to pay Agnes any more money seeing I could get just as bitchy and blackmail her if I wanted to, but I don't. So, I'm just going to ignore Mrs Fisher and get on with my life, which looks like it's without Robert.' With her story completed, Louisa picked up someone's glass of wine and finished it off before asking the handsome young man in white for a rum and Coke.

It was abundantly clear to Agnes that Louisa's story was nowhere near complete. 'And who the hell are you to call me a "would be if she could be", you, you, Jezebel. You're nothing without Robert, and while he's in politics, you'll go along for the free ride.'

Agnes's outburst didn't seem to faze Louisa one iota. She calmly turned to Mr Lee and asked, 'Mr Lee, I have no burning desire to blackmail Agnes, but this little irritation I have will just not go away. So, further to our previous discussion, how much did you say it would cost?'

Mr Lee, untouched by scandal up to this point, thought for a moment before responding. 'Louisa, you know when we spoke of this earlier, we didn't get as far as costs. Before we go any further, I should warn you a contract can prove quite expensive, depending on the subject, of course, and any special requirements you may have.'

'A ball park figure?' asked Louisa.

'Anywhere from three to five for a basic job, including tax.'

'Hundred?'

'No. Thousand, and that's just for the basics without extras.'

'You're kidding me? Five thousand pounds to eliminate someone who's already a pain in the bum and a blight on society?' After a moment to recover from the shock of such an exorbitant price, and a further moment to reconsider, Louisa said, 'I suppose it might be worth it. I don't suppose you have liquidation sales? No, I didn't think so. Okay, what about the extras?'

'Well,' said Mr Lee as he pulled a notebook from his short's pocket and flicked through the pages. At last he found the page he was looking for. 'Ah yes, here we are. Now, to eliminate the wife of a police superintendent, an extra thousand because of his occupation and rank. Oh, and as I said, these figures are inclusive of all taxes, by the way. Any special requirements, such as method of elimination, bullet, poison, over a cliff and the like, and the disposal of the cadaver, etcetera, is open to negotiation. Payment can be made with a fifty percent deposit on making the booking, the balance to be paid within seven days of the elimination. We do have a lay-by arrangement should you find it difficult to come up with the cash.'

'And how do I know if the job has been successfully carried out?' asked Louisa, entranced with the ease of having someone done away with.

'Photos. We have an independent photographer who will cover the elimination, either in still or video photography, depending on the method of elimination used.'

While this bipartisan conversation was being conducted, the

remaining guests present in the saloon remained silent, probably horrified as to the nature of the conversation to which they
were privy to. Simon, a police detective with many years experience, had never come across a situation where a known gangster was calmly in discussion with a client negotiating the costs
involved in an assassination, with the proposed victim sitting
less than six feet away.

The raging anger that had been flaring so brightly within
Agnes moments earlier had now dwindled to a gloomy flicker
as she listened intently to the debate on how much it was going
to cost to have her eliminated. They keep saying "eliminated"
she thought. Why can't they say murdered, or bumped off or
dispatched, anything but eliminated which sounds so final.

Fortunately for Agnes, the Chief interceded on her behalf.
'Mr Lee and Louisa, you are both very close to committing an
indictable offence; conspiracy to murder. Should you enter into
an agreement relating to the death of Agnes Fisher, or if she is
the subject of a physical attack, be it lethal or otherwise, you
may very well find yourselves under arrest. The fact that you
have openly discussed the matter in front of nine witnesses, one
would think that both of you would make every effort to ensure
nothing untoward happens to Agnes.

'The problem you have created for yourselves is that should
Agnes fall in front of a train, or under a bus, the police will be
on your doorstep to ensure you had no involvement in the
matter. By the same token, if any of the nine witnesses to the
conversation should harbour covert malevolent inclinations
towards Agnes, it provides that person with a wonderful opportunity to do away with Agnes, knowing full well the suspicion
will immediately fall upon you, Mr Lee and you, Louisa.'

By now, Agnes was a troubled woman, very close to intoxi-
cation and really, at that moment, she couldn't give a stuff how
intoxicated she became. In fact, on returning from a brief visit

to the lower deck, she had asked the handsome young man in white for another double scotch while Louisa, now wishing she had started some serious drinking sooner, asked the young man to leave her a bottle of rum and a can of Coke.

'Before we move on, there are a few questions I would like to ask my wife,' said Robert Porter as he got up from the lounge and made his way to stand in front of the bar. 'Louisa, I know of your relationship with Mr Fisher, just as you are now aware of my relationship with Agnes. What I didn't know of was, or is, your relationship with our redoubtable Mr Lee. I would like to know just what the nature of your relationship with Mr Lee is, or is Agnes's description of you as being a whore correct?'

'Hey, hang on. You mean you turned me down, a superinten-dent of police, for a gangster?' asked Nigel, flabbergasted at even the thought of it. 'Louisa, you must be out of your mind. And you're not even discreet about it, leaving your negligee in his cabin.'

'Totally agree,' chimed in Robert Porter. 'If you're going to spend the night with your stud, at least don't leave your jewellery lying around for all and sundry to see it.'

'And when's the last time you ever bought me anything, let alone a sexy negligee? Fine to buy one for the girlfriend; bugger the old lady, you bastard,' said Agnes with a hostility Nigel had never seen.

'Oh shut up, you, you charlatan,' said Nigel as his anger started to get the better of him. 'And while you're casting asper-sions on people, Agnes, you, the wife of a superintendent of police, prefer a bloody politician to have it off with. Just how degrading is that?'

Not to be outdone in the out-flowing of profanities, it was the taciturn Mr Lee who unwound himself out of his bean bag, stood up and said, 'Just hang on, the lot of you. Let's get one thing straight. I might be on the wrong side of the law, but a gangster, I'm not. I consider myself a businessman, and a very successful one at that, as you may have noticed,' and with a wave of the arm, indicated to the "Chez Anne". As far as my relationship with Louisa goes, that's between Louisa and myself, so you, Robert and you Nigel, can both bugger off because neither of you know how to treat a lady.' Chivalry wasn't quite dead, just very close to it.

CHAPTER 33

*W*ith the turmoil going on in the saloon, Chic Chambers decided it was time to up anchor and head for a new location and a change of scenery. Knowing the harbour as he did, Charlie nosed the cruiser past Bradley's Head and across the harbour towards Watson's Bay and Camp Cove, another area protected from the blustery nor' easterly wind. Whether it was the cat fight in the saloon dying a natural death, the induced effect of copious quantities of alcohol, the fact that the cruiser was now heading off across the harbour, or a combination of all three, there was a noticeable decline in hostilities within the saloon. Apart from lunch time when everyone had taken to the afterdeck or availed themselves of the opportunity to have a look around the "Chez Anne", it was the first time people seemed to be mobile, some stretching their legs with an idle stroll around the saloon, others venturing out onto the deck. Overall, a feeling of relaxed informality had supplanted the earlier hostility to the extent that some of the antagonists were now involved in courteous chit chat.

Around the sides of the afterdeck was a white vinyl lounge

where both Noel and Sue now reclined, Sue in an electric blue bikini, Noel in a pair of black Speedo budgie smugglers. Georgie, wearing an elegant black one piece swimsuit lay on her back upon a white beach towel spread across the deck.

'I don't think I could have endured another session after lunch if this morning's debacle was any indication of things to come,' said Sue.

'I'll go along with that. I'm emotionally drained just listening to them,' replied Georgie, as she raised herself onto her elbows to accept the glass of gin and tonic offered by the pretty young lady in white.

Meanwhile, it was Simon who approached Mr Lee who was standing against the port rail, his back to the harbour, a can of beer in his hand. 'Mr Lee, mind if we have a word?'

'No, not at all, but please, call me Graham as I feel I have known you for years. And how about you grab yourself a beer to keep things on an even keel?' suggested Mr Lee amicably.

Having grabbed a can off a tray held by the young man in white, Simon stood next to Graham Lee and leant against the railing. 'Your conversation with Louisa, was that for real? Would you have really entered into an agreement with her for a contract on Agnes?'

'Simon, I think I'd better show you this,' he said and withdrew a notebook from his pocket. 'You recognise this little book?'

'Yes, it's the one you referred to during your conversation with Louisa. It gave me, and probably everyone else, the impression it contained a list of contract prices.'

Graham Lee smiled. 'It does, but your impression was only fifty per cent right,' he said and handed the book to Simon. With great dexterity, he managed to flip the pages while holding a beer, the look on his face softening with the hint of a smirk now vaguely detectable.

'Come on Simon, you disappoint me. You know everything there is to know about me. I have to play tough at times; or at least look like I'm playing tough. But if you go through my file again, you won't find any mention of physical violence by me or by anyone on my behalf. I run a casino because it's what people want; they provide the demand and I'm brave enough to satisfy that demand. If it wasn't me, it would be someone else, and that someone else would probably be a real gangster. Until the Government sanctions legal casinos, there will be a niche for the Taipan Club. So until then, I'm just providing an up-market place where professional people can go with some sort of discretion and anonymity assured.'

'Phew,' exclaimed Simon. 'You had me worried there for a while. And you're right, I should have known better so please accept my humble apologies, although there is one thing. Does Louisa believe the discussion was real?'

Mr Lee looked at Simon and smiled. 'Let's go and have another beer,' he said, leaving the question unanswered.

It wasn't long before Ron and Simon joined Georgie, Sue and Noel on the afterdeck, leaving the Chief and Mr Lee in conversation with the Fishers and the Porters in the saloon. Georgie, still sunbaking on the deck, propped herself on her elbows and looked at Simon. 'Now we're alone out here, Simon, what do you think's going to happen?'

'God knows. They're all getting stuck into the grog so I reckon it'll be a case of kill or cure. The way I see it, Nigel's deeply repentant for the situation with Agnes. He even gave the Chief that impression when he spoke to him some weeks ago. We haven't seen very much of him at Day Street lately, especially since he volunteered to go undercover in this new Drug

Squad. He's very lucky in one way as he could have gone for a row with all the offences he's committed. The downside is that if the mob ever finds out who he is, he'll end up on the bottom of the harbour wearing concrete booties.'

'And do you think Agnes will ever get back with him?' Sue asked.

Simon shrugged. 'Who knows? Agnes is guilty of being exactly as Louisa described her; a "would be if she could be". Whether Agnes ever takes the time to realise it is a moot point. As for the Porters, I'm sure Louisa does have a soft spot for Robert, in her own sort of way, although I have my doubts her feelings, whatever they are, could be reciprocated. Robert is an aspiring politician who might just end up premier of the State, one day. Somehow I don't think there's a place for Louisa in his life, or for any female for that matter, irrespective of any mutual feelings they may share. I'm sure Louisa would like more out of a marriage than tagging along after a politician where she'd probably end up like a puppet on a string. But that's their problem, and they'll sort it out for themselves. Who knows? Who cares? Oh look, Nigel, over there, Lady Jane Beach.

CHAPTER 34

The backyard lawn of the Collaroy bungalow was neatly mown, the yard tidy. Around a garden table with a blue, yellow and green sun umbrella stuck through a hole in the middle, sat five people, all clearly in good cheer and becoming cheerier.

'Ron, pass me a light beer, please,' asked Sue, who normally didn't drink beer, but it was a hot, thirsty day.

'Coming over,' called Ron as he shook the water off the can he had extracted from the Esky, and lobed it gently to Sue. She pulled the ring-pull top and took a long drink, savouring the cold, bitter, refreshing taste of the amber fluid. Ron rocked back on his chair, a thoughtful look on his face. 'Simon, everything seems to have worked out for everyone, one way or the other. I know you all did this job as a favour to me, and it's really appreciated. I hope there is some way I can repay you for your handling of a pretty sensitive situation. So, thanks everybody, it has been fun.

'Now there are a couple points someone may be able to

clarify for me, including the personal details of the Porters and Fishers? I hear Nigel, or should I say, Superintendent Fisher, has moved on to greener pastures.'

'Yes, he has,' replied Simon, 'although whether the pastures are greener is a debatable point. Once the manpower establishment of the Drug Squad was finalised, Nigel just disappeared and hasn't been seen around Day Street for yonks now. There's a rumour going around he's been seconded to the DEA in Washington for a couple of months before taking up the position offered by Chief Superintendent Paxton.

'From what I hear, he gave Agnes an ultimatum; curb the spending and come back down to earth, or pack your bags and get out. I don't know if he was bluffing but, by all accounts, it worked and Agnes has evidently lowered her aspirations to sensible and affordable heights.'

'You mean to say the police hierarchy has turned a blind eye to Fisher's little transgressions?' asked Georgie. 'From the sound of things, your illustrious boss was a curse on constabulary morality in more ways than one.'

Simon smiled and tossed his empty can into the metal garbage bin with a "clunk". 'Yes, I know, he's a sleaze and a con man. He would probably have made a better living out of being a baddie, but I think he would eventually have got his fingers burnt, irrespective of which side he was on. He probably chose the only alternative available to him by going undercover, but I reckon his insurance premiums just took a hike. I feel a bit sorry for Agnes, but then she may have been the catalyst that started Nigel off on his mid-life crisis. It's clear she was a major consideration in his decision to go undercover, not that anyone forced him into it.'

'Oh, I wouldn't say that,' said Noel. 'Paxton did give him a choice; stay in the Force and go undercover or go to jail. I suspect Nigel may have considered the longevity of both options; a convicted police officer's lot in Long Bay, or the underworld finding an undercover cop in the midst. Neither option can guarantee a long life expectancy.'

'Yes," said Simon. 'But I think I now know why Paxton wanted Fisher to confess to his crimes. Sure, Paxton could have crucified Fisher, but he probably thought if Fisher had enough moral courage to confess, then the police hierarchy could turn a blind eye. There aren't too many volunteers for undercover work, which is quite understandable.'

'Has anyone heard how the Porters are doing?' asked Georgie, as she poured herself a moselle.

'Yes, and they're not,' replied Ron.

'Not what?'

Ron smiled. 'Sorry Georgie, I mean they're not doing anything, at least, not together. Seems they both have their expectations in life and neither can fulfill those expectations with the partner they had chosen. Louisa didn't mind playing second fiddle to Robert, up to a point. But the one thing she couldn't tolerate was all the crap that went on with the Party politics and the bullshit expounded by mental pygmies on subjects they know nothing about and that no-one gives a damn about in any case.

'No, Louisa was fond of Robert but she couldn't hack the politics and the lifestyle demanded. I think Robert could see the writing on the wall when Louisa started her own independent lifestyle, going to places like the Taipan Club, being able to be herself without having to be a polly's dress accessory when needed. The bit you girls will be interested in is that Louisa and Mr Lee are, according to all reports and my own observations, what you'd call an item. She now works at the Club and is living with Mr Lee. It seems Robert is the only one left out in the cold, but I think he would prefer it that way. He can now focus all his energy on politics as he certainly couldn't on Louisa.'

'Simon, there is one question I've been meaning to ask as it's driving me nuts,' said Noel. 'While we were out on the boat, Louisa asked Mr Lee for a price on doing away with Agnes. Mr Lee referred to a book he carried from which he quoted some prices. Surely that book contains some very incriminating evidence against Mr Lee and we never confiscated it. Why not?'

'Ah, yes, the book. At the time, that was driving me nuts too, Noel,' replied Simon. 'I asked Mr Lee about that while we were onboard the "Chez Anne". He was quite happy to show it to me and it did contain various price lists. However, the prices we imagined it to contain were, in reality, the prices of beer and wines and the details of various distributors with whom Mr Lee was dealing. He faked it, and did a very good job at it too.'

'Did Louisa know it was faked?' asked Georgie.

Simon smirked and shrugged. 'Now, that is a very good question,' he replied and dug into the Esky for another beer. 'I suppose it doesn't make much difference one way or the other. What was more important is whether Agnes believed it and from the look on her face at the time, I reckon she really did believe they were actually counting the cost of having her bumped off.'

Georgie poured herself another glass of wine and frowned. 'And all this happened because we wanted Chief Inspector Rose cut down to size. Did we achieve our aim?' she asked Simon.

Simon pursed his lips and thought for a moment then said, 'The police hierarchy had Rose in their sights before we ever decided to do anything about him. He was well aware that I knew what he was really like, regardless of the reputation he nurtured, hence his animosity and fear that one day I would expose him. As a consequence, he would have preferred to see me out of the Force altogether and he was hoping that by making my life difficult, I'd chuck it in.

'Apart from my falling out with Rosey, Noel and I were completely unaware Paxton and Sergeant Mathieson were working on Rose and his corruption. However, it seems Rosey did the only thing he could possibly do to save his reputation and end his career on a positive note and that was to drop dead. By dying before the investigation was completed, he received a police funeral with full honours. For all the trouble we went to by robbing a bank just to make him look stupid turned out to be an utter waste of time. Mind you, the repercussions of that robbery have been nothing short of earth shattering, with the unexpected involvement of senior police, politicians, gangsters, loose women, and blokes who think they're God's gift to women.'

'Woooa. Just stop right there,' said Ron. 'So, it was you who robbed the bank. I knew it. It couldn't have been anybody else. Chief Paxton knows you did it, too, doesn't he?'

'Even the Commissioner knows,' replied Simon. Chief Paxton has made some pretty wild accusations and they're probably all correct. He does see our side of things and knows the reasons why we did it, which is nice for us. He also confirmed our thinking regarding the proofs of the crime, and admitted it would be a hard case to prosecute. Things would've turned out differently if we had taken the cash, and I'm sure Paxton would've been forced to take some action against us. Mind you, it wouldn't look good having an investigation into the conduct of one chief inspector followed immediately by another investigation of a chief inspector. And I doubt he would have promoted me to Rosey's position of chief inspector if he knew he could gain a conviction against me for bank robbery, would he? Anyway, as far as the bank job goes, it seems both the

Chief Superintendent and the Commissioner have turned a blind eye.'

'And thank God for that,' exclaimed Georgie. 'I can't wait for Simon to get on with a good murder case. Just how do you expect me to come up with a better idea of doing away with a little old lady who doesn't like spiders if you're not working on real murders?'

ABOUT THE AUTHOR

John Henderson was born in Singleton in the state of New South Wales, Australia. The family moved to the town of Yass soon afterwards where he spent his younger days before a move to Sydney. John went to Manly Boys' High School, represented the district in cricket and spent a lot of time surfing. He joined the Army in 1968 and toured South Vietnam in 1969-70.

Following his discharge from the Army and a brief stint in the Commonwealth Public Service, John chose to write crime satire. With his dry, cynical sense of humour, The Simon Webster Fiasco series represents an amusing and skeptical view of life and bureaucratic nonsense, as viewed by the author.

John now lives in Canberra with his wife, Jill, and cat, Fergus.

 twitter.com/JohnHenderson07